By the sam

Ellen's G

My Enemy M

I Think He Was George

Shamila

Ravishment

Aliza, My Love

The Hanging Tree

The Hanging Tree

Published by The Conrad Press in the United Kingdom 2021

Tel: +44(0)1227 472 874
www.theconradpress.com
info@theconradpress.com

ISBN 978-1-913567-81-1

Printed and bound in Great Britain by Clays Ltd, Elcograf S.p.A

Typesetting and Cover Design by The Book Typesetters,
www.thebooktypesetters.com

The Conrad Press logo was designed by Maria Priestley.

The Hanging Tree

A 17th-century Whodunnit

The second diary of Lady Jane Tremayne

JAMES WALKER

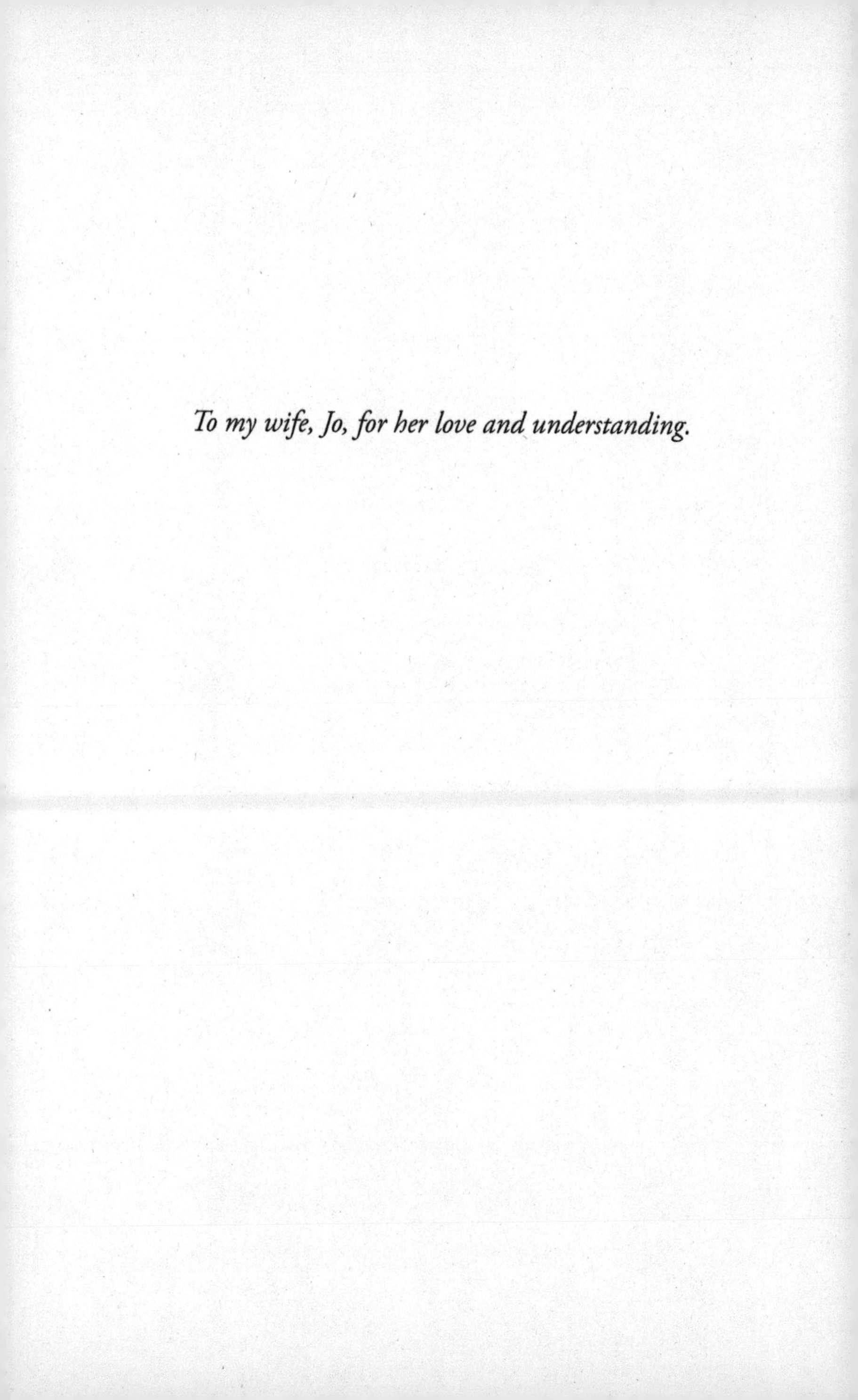

To my wife, Jo, for her love and understanding.

1

May 31st 1654, Altringham Manor, South Devon

I had not long woken from a deep, restorative sleep. I felt a pressing desire to relieve my bladder but I was reluctant at first to leave the warmth of my bed. Six weeks had now passed since I had given birth to a son, Lucas, and apart from some nagging discomfort I was grateful for having made a full recovery. Fortunately, my labour had not been an overly arduous one, but I was increasingly concerned that Lucas was a sickly child and might not be long for this world.

I had given birth once before to a daughter by my first husband, the late Sir Paul Tremayne, killed at Worcester three years previously. Sadly, she had succumbed to disease whilst still an infant, and it pained me greatly to contemplate the possibility that I might lose another child before it had barely begun to live. I was also increasingly anxious about the fate of Thomas Sumner, Lucas's father, to whom I had been secretly wed less than a year by means of a spousal contract. Even at this moment, he could be lingering in some dank prison cell awaiting execution, and all the while ignorant of the fact that I had given him a son.

It was one thing for my sympathies to lie with the Royalist cause and for me to detest the so-called Commonwealth, which Oliver Cromwell had now established. It was surely natural enough, too, to fall in love and for that to result all too quickly in the arrival of a babe. Yet, it was quite another to secretly wed a renegade, knowing perfectly well that hiding him from the forces of the law was in itself a hangable offence.

However lonely I might have felt in my bed at night, and however much I might have longed for a child, I sometimes wondered if I had acted too hastily in marrying him, only to now repent at leisure.

It frustrated me, too, that as a consequence of having to keep my marriage a secret, it was also necessary to keep the birth of my son equally so. Of course, it had been quite impossible to keep either secret from my immediate household, whilst I had also drawn my closest family members and friends into my confidence in the certainty that neither they or their household members would betray it.

What had proved harder, though, was having to broaden that select group still further when I had given birth. The midwife, who had attended upon me, had had to be sworn to secrecy, with the encouragement of a particularly generous payment for her services. Then the vicar of the parish of the nearest village, Tipton St Johns, had also had to be told the truth for the purposes of giving Lucas baptism; a service he had in the event been willing to perform in the privacy of the Hall rather than at the church font.

As a true royalist, he had assured me that my secret was safe with him, but that had still left the delicate matter of what entry to make in the registry of births. After some discussion it had therefore been agreed that a space should be left for the insertion of the father's name in happier times when hopefully the nation's true King had been restored to his throne.

Thomas, meanwhile, was perfectly handsome, and I believed there was no malice or violence in him, but the boredom that went hand in hand with having to remain incognito on my estate had encouraged him to drink too much strong beer. When in his cups, which had occurred with increasing frequency, I'd discovered he could be both sullen and short tempered.

Then, when spring had barely arrived, and I was all of seven months pregnant, he had departed in order to participate in a plot to assassinate Cromwell, and I had heard nothing of him since. To add to my fears, within a fortnight of my giving birth, news had reached me via my younger sister, Caroline, who had visited me from her home in Exeter, that the plot had been foiled and that three of the ringleaders had been arrested.

'Do you know their names?' I had asked, instantly fearful that Thomas was one of them.

'No, I'm sorry. Do you believe one might be your husband?'

Of course I did, and for many nights after receiving this unwelcome news my state of anxiety, exacerbated by not having long given birth, had made me struggle to sleep. Finally, only two nights previously, sheer exhaustion had plunged me into a deep, apparently dreamless slumber, and I was pleased to have slept as well again for a second successive night.

Now, as I rose from my bed and pulled back the curtains, I received confirmation of what I had suspected, namely that it was drizzling steadily. It had been a disappointingly wet spring and the sight of yet more rain was somewhat dispiriting. However, it was not enough to diminish my resolve to go riding again for the first time since giving birth. My firm intention was to pay a visit to my best friend, Olivia Courtney, at Fetford Hall, which is only about two miles away, and I was damned if I would let a little rain deter me. Anyway, looking westwards, I could tell that the rain clouds were beginning to break-up, and concluded that by the time I was dressed and ready to leave the sun might well be out.

I therefore summoned my pretty, eighteen-year-old maid, Mary, and bade her hurry to the stables to ask the stable lad, Toby, to saddle my mare, Hera.

'Then make haste to return and help me dress,' I added.

I would not set out on my journey, however, without first paying Lucas a visit and spent at least half an hour in his company before doing so. I had followed the social convention, which required women of my class to engage the services of a wet nurse, considering myself fortunate that my steward, Harry Parson's wife, Melissa, had a six-month-old daughter, and had willingly agreed to breast feed Lucas in return for remuneration of a shilling a week.

The cottage that Harry and Melissa, and their family of three children, occupied, was also no more than three hundred yards from the Manor House, so I had no qualms in allowing Lucas to spend his nights in Melissa's care. When I was not fretting over Thomas's fate, it was an arrangement that gave me every expectation of being able to enjoy a good night's rest. All the same, the more sickly Lucas became, the more I worried that I should have ignored convention and suckled him myself.

By the time I set out on my ride, I was feeling very anxious. Melissa had looked exceedingly tired and had confessed to Lucas having kept her awake more than half the night. He was grisly even now and hot to touch, making me suspicious that he was suffering from a fever. It was enough to make me consider calling out the aloof Dr Gladwell, who resided in Ottery St Mary, some three miles away, and I resolved that I would do so if he was no better when I returned. There would be a fee to pay, of course, but I was determined to do everything in my power to keep my son alive.

The thought that he might die before his father had even set eyes on him, brought me close to tears, so I was grateful that my ride helped to raise my spirits somewhat. I was pleased, too, that the sun had begun to shine and I was able to enjoy its warmth along with the familiar beauty of the countryside through which I passed.

The sight of Fetford Hall, built in the Jacobean style, some forty years previously, with an imposing westwards view, was one I always found uplifting, especially as I knew it was a place where I could be assured of a fond welcome. Indeed, in the years which had elapsed since I had first come to Altringham Manor as a young bride, Fetford Hall had become like a second home to me as my friendship with Olivia Courtney had blossomed and I had come to know her family well.

It grieved me that Olivia had lost the man to whom she was betrothed at the Battle of Langport, nearly nine years previously, and now seemed destined to end her days as an old maid. A pretty redhead, with freckles and a winning smile, in happier times she might well have attracted another suitor. However, too many royalist families had been broken by the long years of civil war, culminating in the terrible defeat at Worcester; their menfolk either killed or forced into exile.

For all the heartache it had now brought me, I still thought myself fortunate to have been able to rush into a headlong romance with Thomas Sumner and bear him a child when no such opportunity had presented itself to Olivia. All the same, I knew her to be far more cautious by nature than I am. Further, she'd confessed to me on more than one occasion that she'd decided to devote herself to her love of music and riding; two things in which we had a common interest.

I also rather envied her the support of a close, loving family, namely her mother Constance, still healthy and active, for all that she was nearly sixty, and her younger brother, James. He was stocky, handsome, and only the previous year had taken the pretty Becky Trowton as his bride. Her arrival could easily have created tensions, but fortunately she had proved herself to be a sweet-natured person and Olivia told me she welcomed the fact that she had now found herself a sister.

At first, I had thought Becky rather too garrulous and self-indulgent. However, after she had been raped in the very grounds of the Hall by the villainous Master Tailor, John Turnbull, within weeks of her marriage, the valiant manner in which she had coped with such a dreadful experience, had won both my sympathy and respect. It had led to us forging a firm friendship, and not long before I had given birth, she had announced her first pregnancy.

2

A Tragedy

Upon my arrival at Fetford Hall, I had barely handed Hera over to the care of the stable lad when Olivia came to greet me. I could immediately tell that something was amiss as her usual smile was absent. Instead she looked so troubled that I was immediately concerned that someone might be dangerously ill.

We immediately exchanged kisses to the cheek and Olivia's first words were ones of welcome and delight that I felt sufficiently recovered from Lucas's birth to be able to mount a horse and pay them a visit. Nonetheless, I remained convinced that all was not well.

'Forgive me, Olivia, but you do not seem yourself. Is anything wrong?'

She gave me a knowing look as we proceeded to make our way inside. 'Everyone is in robust health I assure you. But, oh, Jane, I'm afraid there has been a tragedy, which I find most upsetting. A young woman has hanged herself in a wood, no more than half a mile from here, and it was I that found her. I was following a way that leads through the wood and caught a glimpse of the red dress she was wearing.

'Oh dear, how awful. And when was this?'

'Just yesterday morning. It was such a shock that I am still quite put out by it. I fear that the sight of her will continue to give me nightmares. I dread to think how she must have suffered before she died. And I do wonder what could have driven her to do such a thing?'

By now Constance had appeared, bestowing her usual warm smile of greeting and offering a cheek, which I was happy to kiss. I caught a familiar whiff of lavender as I did so and thought that despite Olivia's assurances, she was looking rather tired.

'So how is Lucas?' Constance was quick to ask, an entirely predictable question that I wished I had been better prepared for. I hesitated slightly, trying unsuccessfully to get a grip on my emotions. 'I fear he's unwell,' I mumbled. 'I've a mind to call a doctor if he's not better by tomorrow morning.'

Constance gave me a consoling hug, whereupon James and Becky also appeared, side by side, and all conversation was of Lucas's health, along with some other more inconsequential matters. My thoughts, though were never far from Olivia's shocking revelation, so once we all sat down together to eat a midday meal, consisting principally of a delicious herring pie, I couldn't resist asking Olivia if she'd any idea who the unfortunate woman was who'd apparently chosen to kill herself.

'I haven't the least notion who she was. I certainly don't believe I'd ever set eyes on her before so I can't believe that she lived locally.

'And why do you think she killed herself? Did she leave any note on her person?'

'No, she left none that I could see. When I fetched James and he cut her down we could find nothing to even offer some clue as to her identify so who she is remains a mystery. However, there was a disturbed pile of stones and twigs beneath her feet. I think she must have stood upon them, placed the noose around her neck, and then kicked the pile away.'

'And you say she was wearing a red dress. Was she also wearing any jewellery?'

'No, none that I can recall. What I can say is that she was a pretty young thing and that both the dress and the shoes she was wearing were of good quality. She had pale skin, too, and delicate hands.'

'So, no farmer's daughter then,' James quipped.

'No, I wouldn't have thought so.'

'And no sign of how she came to be there, I suppose,' I asked rhetorically. 'You'd think someone would have seen her if she merely walked there from some distance away, carrying a rope.'

'Perhaps they did, but she could have concealed the rope under her dress,' Olivia suggested.

'Yes, that's possible. Even so, it seems strange to me that she should choose to hang herself in such a way and leave barely a clue as to her identity.'

'What are you suggesting then?' Olivia asked.

'I'm not really suggesting anything, but isn't it at least conceivable that someone else played a part in her demise. I mean she could have been strung-up, couldn't she?'

'Murdered then,' James exclaimed.

'Yes, indeed, although in that event I'd say the manner of her death was more akin to an execution.'

'But who would possibly want to commit such a dreadful deed?' Becky asked.

'Someone she betrayed, perhaps, or at least thought she had,' I suggested.

'But all this is just pure speculation,' Constance exclaimed. 'Chances are, she was just some poor waif of a girl who had lost her way in life and was determined to do away with herself.'

'A melancholic, you mean?' I asked.

'Yes, quite so.'

'Well, if she had family, they must be desperate to know her whereabouts,' Becky said.

'In which case they may soon come looking for her,' James added.

'But if she hails from say Honiton or Exeter, and slipped away without even leaving any clue as to which direction she was heading in, how would they know where to look for her?' I asserted. 'She could be long buried before they even think to come anywhere near here. Anyhow, I assume the coroner's been notified?'

'Yes, he has, and he's due to arrive tomorrow. No doubt he'll assemble a jury on the village green,' James told me.

'And where's the body been taken?'

'It's been lain out in the church for the present although if the verdict's one of suicide she will forfeit any right to a Christian burial, of course.'

I pondered what I had been told for a few moments, whilst taking a sip or two from my glass of the fine claret that James had generously insisted we should enjoy with our meal. There was still yet another question on my mind.

'Has anyone thought to summon a doctor?'

'…No,' Olivia confessed. 'The poor girl was clearly stone dead.'

'Did you touch the body?'

'Certainly not.'

'After I cut her down,' James added. 'I also had one of our servants, Ned Stockwell, help me put the corpse over the back of my horse. I'd say it was barely cold so I'd be pretty certain she hadn't been dead all that long when Olivia found her, if that's what you're wondering about?'

'Yes, I was, but also whether there were any marks on the body. I mean such as bruising to indicate that she could have been involved in some sort of struggle, or marks around the wrist or legs to suggest she was tied up. And then it might be helpful to know if she was with child or had ever given birth?'

'I can tell you, she was as thin as a rake.'

'Even so, she could still have been in the early stages of pregnancy. The knowledge that she had conceived, and out of wedlock, too, might have been what drove her to kill herself, if indeed she did die by her own hand.'

It was not even a year since I had entertained the coroner, John Carpenter, following John Turnbull's foul murder of mistress Hodge. I had formed a positive impression of the coroner's character, but his task on that occasion had been a relative straightforward one as there had been no reason to doubt the cause of death. What had now occurred would surely present him with a more difficult deliberation unless he chose to look no further than the barest facts and direct his jury accordingly.

The mysterious young woman, whoever she was, meant nothing to me save that my natural curiosity was aroused along with a growing conviction that she had not committed suicide. As such, any finding that she had in fact done so would allow her murderer to escape any possibility of being brought to justice, whilst the woman's corpse would be denied a Christian burial and merely thrown into a pauper's grave in unconsecrated ground. This was a prospect that I found hard to countenance, and before the meal had even ended, I had made up her mind to visit the church and examine the corpse myself.

I encouraged Olivia to come for a ride with me without giving the least hint of my intentions but we had no sooner ridden away from the Hall when I revealed what I had in mind. Olivia looked at me in horror at the very idea.

'Really, Jane, what are you thinking of? This is really none of your business, you know, and I assure you that I have no wish to set eyes on that poor girl again. I tell you, the sight of her hanging from the branch of the tree, was quite terrible. I fear it will give me nightmares for some time to come.'

'Do not distress yourself on that account, Olivia. You don't even have to enter the church with me. Just wait outside and I'll return in no time at all, I promise you.'

'You may well find the body has been locked away in the vestry.'

'In which case I'll be back even sooner.'

'And what if you're able to discover something of importance. What will you do then?'

'I'll certainly return tomorrow in order to speak to the coroner.'

While Olivia remained with the horses just outside the church's gate on what had fortunately become a dry and pleasantly warm afternoon, I made my way inside the building. I did not do so without a measure of trepidation, but I had looked on the dead often enough to feel able to steel myself for what awaited me. I also preferred not to dwell at all on the fact that it would not be enough to merely look upon the face of the dead woman. I needed to examine her body, too.

In the event, I had barely closed the door of the church behind me when I realised that someone else was already present.

'Good afternoon, Lady Tremayne, what brings you here?'

It was none less than the vicar of the church, Stephen Havelock, looking down his somewhat long nose at me. Tall and angular, with a trim, black beard, he was still a little short of his thirtieth birthday and far too full of himself for my tastes. Nor did his support for the Directory of Public Worship, which Parliament had introduced in preference to the Book of Common Prayer, endear him to me, either.

'Forgive me, vicar,' I said with a forced smile, 'but I understand that the body of the young woman found in nearby woods has been laid out in your vestry?'

'Yes, what of it?'

'I was wondering if I might be able to... see her body?'

'Why on earth should you wish to do that... unless you think you know her?'

'It's possible that I might, vicar.' That was not in fact the case at all, but his question had unwittingly thrown me a lifeline, of which I was happy to seize hold.

'Very well then. The body's been placed in a coffin in the vestry. If you care to follow me, I'll show you.'

Even as we entered the coffin's presence, I was aware of an unpleasantly pungent smell, and as the vicar proceeded to lift the lid of the coffin this became even stronger. I shuddered and couldn't help but wrinkle up my nose. Still, I stepped forward without hesitation, and was immediately struck by how attractive a face the dead girl had possessed along with curly, auburn hair. The merest glance also confirmed that the red dress she was wearing was well made.

'Well, do you know her?' the vicar asked sharply. He was clearly as disgusted by the smell of death as I was and in a hurry to close the lid of the coffin.

'Unfortunately I don't think I do, but vicar would you allow me to look more closely at her body. You see, I'm wondering if she might have been pregnant…'

'There's no sign of that, I can assure you, and what's it to you even if she was? The coroner will be here tomorrow; let him examine the body if he's a mind to.'

I realised that arguing with the vicar would get me nowhere and I was also conscious of Olivia waiting for me outside. I therefore merely thanked him for his time and quickly withdrew.

'You saw the body then?' Olivia asked me.

'Yes, I did. The vicar was in the church and let me take a look but he would have no truck with me examining her corpse.'

'That's hardly surprising.'

'No, although it was still frustrating, all the same. And who's to say what the coroner might do when he arrives tomorrow… I must come back, I know I must.'

Olivia gave me an exasperated glance. 'You'll likely be accused of interfering in matters that don't concern you. Really, Jane, have you learnt nothing from what occurred last year?'

'What I've learnt, Olivia, is that if I hadn't been so persistent, that devil Turnbull might still be at large, raping and murdering innocent members of our sex. All I want is five minutes of the coroner's time. It shouldn't take longer to convince him that an examination of the corpse would be worthwhile.'

3
Suicide?

Upon my return to Altringham Manor in the late afternoon, I went straight to see Lucas and was much encouraged to find him sleeping peacefully. Melissa also assured me that he had not long taken milk from her breast and had been far more settled than of late. Nor, when I touched his brow did he feel so hot, so, with a feeling of relief, I saw no need to call out Dr Gladwell. Yet, when I visited again in the morning it was only to discover that Melissa had experienced another troubled night and that Lucas still seemed quite poorly.

To make matters worse, my ride to Fetford Hall and back had tired me far more than I had been expecting, which made me sigh a little at the prospect of getting back on my side-saddle again quite so soon. I wondered, too, if rather than go back I should travel instead to Ottery St Mary in order to seek out Dr Gladwell. I was uncertain what to do for the best, but as I hesitated Lucas at last began to fall asleep. Once again, I touched his brow, and thought he did not seem overly hot, so after some soul searching concluded that any visit to the Doctor could again be put off.

I had not long set off on my journey, however, when my conscience began to prick me into thinking that I'd made the wrong decision. I thought, too, that Olivia's admonishment had been better founded than I had been willing to admit at the time. The death of some waif of a girl who was a total stranger to me, whether by her own hand or that of another, was really not my concern, and I should have known better than to seek to interfere.

The difficulty was that I knew that I could be both stubborn and selfish and that once my curiosity was aroused I found it hard to rest until that had been satisfied. In the end, I came close to turning my horse round and heading instead towards Ottery St Mary until my natural curiosity and selfishness won out. I also assuaged my conscience with the reflection that doctorsq were not only expensive but also very often unable to provide any curative remedies.

As I approached my destination it grew both wet and windy and I felt anxious about the possibility of developing a chill. It had been sunny when I had set out and I had paid no attention to the possibility that the weather might change, as a consequence neglecting to don my riding cloak, although my broad-brimmed hat still offered me some protection against the elements. It was also by now mid-morning and I worried, too, that if I went straight to the Hall I might be too late to speak to the coroner before he began his deliberations. Accordingly, I decided to head for Harpford village green in the hope of catching sight of him there. Failing that, I resolved to go in search of him at the church.

John Carpenter was a tall, robust man, growing more stout with the passing years, and as soon as I rode into the village I was pleased to see him standing on the green, talking to some of the men of the village, whom I presumed would be acting as his jury. He was quick to recognise me and raised a hand in welcome, which I returned in kind.

'Good day to you, Lady Tremayne,' he called out to me, his ruddy complexioned face breaking into a smile. 'What brings you to Harpford this day?'

'The hope, Sir, that I might speak with you before you convene your jury.'

'By all means. Am I to take it you have some information of importance concerning the death that has brought me here?'

By now I was in the process of dismounting from my horse, grateful that the rain had abated 'I merely wished to urge on you the desirability of examining the deceased's body before reaching any conclusions as to the cause of death. That is,' I added hastily, 'if you've not already determined anyway that such an examination would be wise?'

He gave me an enigmatic smile, which I found rather irritating, not knowing whether behind it he was really laughing at me. 'And why is that of interest to you, may I ask?'

'It was my good friend, Lady Courtney, who first discovered the body. When she told me that the poor woman carried nothing on her person to identify her, and had not even scribbled out some missive in explanation of her intentions, I was troubled that she might in fact have been murdered. I also think that an examination of the body might reveal signs of bruising, and equally well whether or not she was pregnant, or for that matter had ever given birth.'

'Well, as it happens, my dear Lady, it's been my intention to take a look at the body. If I'm to determine whether or not she was pregnant, however, I might need the services of a doctor, and I'd been hoping to conclude my investigations and invite the jury to consider its verdict before sunset today. You'll agree, I imagine, that the knowledge that she was carrying a child, assuming that it was conceived out of wedlock, might well have been a motive for suicide?'

'Yes, I would. All the same, I struggle to understand why she would presumably walk miles from who knows where, carrying a rope on her person, and then proceed to hang herself with it without leaving behind anything that can either identify her, or offer any explanation for such an extreme course of action?'

'It is a strange case, I grant you, but then those so possessed by melancholia that they wish to do away with themselves, cannot be expected to act rationally. I'm also not prepared to delay matters simply to explore the possibility she was with child, but as I say I'm prepared to examine the body and you're welcome to come with me if you so wish.'

Shortly thereafter the coroner set off in the direction of the church on foot while I remounted Hera. I was quickly able to tether her next to the Lychgate so I and the coroner strolled into the church side by side, closely followed by his clerk, a nervous looking young man with only the beginnings of a beard. We had barely entered when the vicar, John Havelock, appeared, looking quite startled by my presence.

'Good morning to you, vicar,' the coroner said, introducing himself before turning to me. 'I expect you know Lady Tremayne. She's anxious that I should examine the deceased's corpse for signs of any bruising or the possibility that she may have given birth.'

'So I am already aware,' the vicar said tartly.

'Oh really?'

'I am sorry,' I hastened to explain. 'I should have mentioned to you that I came to the church yesterday and asked the vicar if I might examine the corpse.'

'I told her ladyship that she had no right to examine it.'

'And indeed you were correct to do so, but I have that authority, and I'm prepared to allow Lady Tremayne to be present.'

'Very well, as you wish.'

The vicar then led us into the vestry where I thought the smell of death was now even more pungent than the previous day, but then, despite the morning rain, it was somewhat warmer. The task that we were about to perform was also hardly one that I welcomed. Nonetheless, I was determined to have the stomach for it, so remained as composed as I could as the corpse was once more exposed to view.

Fortunately, the fact that both the woman's dress and the shift she wore underneath had been buttoned up at the front, made it relatively easy to expose bare flesh without having to remove the corpse from its coffin. I wondered how prurient an experience this was for male eyes but then concentrated instead on the abdomen. There was no swelling to suggest she was carrying a child, but it was apparent from the stretch marks I could make out that the girl had certainly given birth at least once.

'See here' I declared,' and here,' pointing as I did so.

'So, no virgin then, and perhaps even a married woman,' the coroner responded.

'And look here, too,' I added, scanning my eyes over the woman's breasts and shoulders. 'There's a bruise there on her left shoulder. She could have been punched, don't you think?'

'It's possible. Let's take a look at her arms.'

As the sleeves of the dress came down to the wrists this was easier said than done but after some manhandling of the corpse I was able to see that there was significant bruising to her left arm, both above and below the elbows.

'She has surely been roughly handled by someone,' I declared.

'You cannot be certain of that,' the coroner said. 'She could simply have tripped and fallen awkwardly.'

'In which case you'd expect to see bruising on her legs, wouldn't you?'

We then duly examined the corpse's legs, revealing one bruise on her right leg.

'It might well have happened in a separate incident,' I said.

'Whatever, it's hard to say that this examination proves anything for certain.'

'But the bruising to both her left shoulder and left arm are consistent with her having been punched and then grabbed hold of in the roughest of ways by someone far stronger than herself, you must admit.'

The coroner shrugged. 'Or of her having taken a bad tumble, perhaps as she was making her way through the wood, her mind intent on nothing but self-destruction, and not giving the least thought to her own safety.'

'That I might believe, if there was also bruising to her left leg, but there is none.'

'She could have fallen against a tree or tumbled down a bank...' It was a response that caused me to tut in sheer frustration. 'Dear Lady, I do understand the force of your argument, I merely assert that there are other possibilities. I will be frank with you that I am inclined to advise the jury to reach an open verdict.'

'By which you mean what, exactly?'

'Simply that there is too little evidence to be certain of the cause of death. Yes, her body was found hanging from a tree, but there's nothing to identify who she was, and too little evidence to determine whether she died by her own hand or that of another. All that we can say with any confidence is that she has given birth at least once and that from the cut of her dress and her general appearance she was no pauper. Yes, I'll grant you that the bruising to the body suggests that she might have been strung up and for that reason alone I'm not prepared to recommend any finding of suicide. An open verdict will also allow her to be given a Christian burial, don't forget.'

'And for the sake of her soul, whoever she was, that would be welcome, of course. But might it not make sense to defer any finding until more evidence is gathered. I mean, might there not be witnesses who saw her in the vicinity of the wood, perhaps in the company of others? Think, too, that she may have a family who are searching desperately for her even as we speak.'

'Her body needs to be buried and soon.'

'It could be embalmed, could it not?'

'But at who's expense? Would you be willing to cover it?'

'I might. Look, at least defer the burial for twenty-four hours and speak to the Constable. He could make enquiries in the locality and ask if anyone remembers seeing the girl, either alone or in the company of others.'

'No, that's not possible, I need to be back in Exeter by midday tomorrow, but I tell you what I will agree to. The

Constable still has the whole afternoon to make such enquiries as I'm prepared to defer the start of the inquest until five o'clock. I doubt we'll need more than an hour to complete the hearing, which will still afford me time to be most of the way back to Exeter in daylight.'

'So be it then. I know I saw the constable as I rode into the village. I take it you're willing to seek him out and make the necessary request?'

'I am, though you must appreciate that he'll be preoccupied at present with assembling a jury. I'm assuming that won't delay him long but it must still take precedence over anything else I might ask of him.'

I was grateful to the coroner for his co-operation and said so. It was a relief to find anyone in a position of authority who was willing to be so accommodating, and in the event within an hour the Constable was able to set about the task of seeking out anyone who might have seen the girl on the day of her death, either alone, or more crucially, with others. I'd been tempted to go with him but restrained myself, deciding that it was not my place to interfere in his business and that he was perfectly capable of performing such a task by himself.

Instead, I met with Olivia who had come to the village with the intention of giving evidence at the inquest, and once I had introduced her to the coroner and explained what was happening, she invited us both back to Fetford Hall. As had been the case on the occasion of our first meeting the previous year, I found myself enjoying the coroner's company. Though his loyalties might lie with Cromwell, I still found him both charming and solicitous, and I could judge from the interaction between us that he thought me desirable. Yet, had he known that I was secretly married to a notorious renegade by whom I had borne a child, I could not imagine that he would have been anywhere near so well disposed towards me.

A game pie was lubricated by the contents of fine bottle of Bordeaux wine from the cellars, which helped to loosen tongues somewhat. However, discretion caused all of us who were present to avoid any political discussion until James simply could not resist talking sarcastically of Cromwell being not so much our Lord Protector as a King in all but name.

I tensed, worried that such language would offend the coroner, but he merely smiled equably.

'I do not believe he has any wish to reign as a King; it would be against all his principles. I expect, too, that he'll soon create a new parliament.'

'I'll believe that when it happens,' James responded gruffly, whereupon Constance looked to move the conversation onto less contentious ground, enquiring of myself and Olivia if we would like to perform a duet together on the harpsichord for the enjoyment of all present once our meal was eaten. 'Or perhaps you might prefer to sing, Jane. You know what a fine voice you have.'

'Yes, do sing for us,' James said encouragingly.

I was a little uncertain, conscious of how out of practice I had become of late but when the coroner declared that he would also be delighted to hear me sing, I relented.

'Why not sing *Why so pale and wan, fond lover?* Olivia suggested, referring to a song by the richly talented William

Lawes, who had been tragically killed during the civil war. 'You know it's one of your favourites.'

I nodded in agreement and performed the song so well that the coroner was clearly impressed.

'My, you have a beautiful voice. As fine, if I may so, as any I've heard.'

'I'm delighted that you should think so.'

I then sang another song by Lawes, *Gather ye rosebuds while ye may*, which seemed to send the coroner into an ecstasy of delight until he noticed the hour from a clock standing in the corner of the room.

'Oh dear, is that the time? I'm afraid I must return to the village and prepare for the inquest. I'll need you to be present by five o'clock in order to give evidence, Lady Courtney. And no doubt you'll wish to discover if the Constable's enquiries have proved fruitful, Lady Tremayne.'

4

An open verdict

It was so nearly five o'clock when Deputy Constable Smith returned to the village, that I'd become anxious that the coroner would have to commence the inquest proceedings without him, especially as he'd made it clear that he wouldn't delay a minute longer. The Deputy Constable was a short, rotund individual, who clearly enjoyed his beer, and, on what had become a warm afternoon, was obviously sweating profusely; his face being exceedingly red and his double chin visibly wobbling from his exertions.

'Well, have you discovered anything?' the coroner asked him.

'Only this, Sir. Three people I spoke to, told me that on the day afore the woman's body was discovered, they saw a coach being pulled by two horses, one of which had a black coat and t'other brown. They also told me that the coach was being ridden by a man in a dark coat with a hat pulled well down so it was hard to make out his face. The coach's curtains also made it impossible to see inside.'

'And did they see this in the vicinity of the wood?'

'No more than a quarter of a mile from it, sir. They also all said that they saw it in the early evening.'

'Did you ask them if there was anything particularly distinctive about the coach itself?

'Well, yes Sir, I did, but they couldn't think of anything. I then asked 'em if they'd ever seen the coach afore and they all said they hadn't.'

I felt an inner conviction that the dead woman had been travelling on this mysterious coach and decided to speak out.

'I think this should be investigated further,' I asserted. 'It strikes me as too much of a coincidence that a coach of all things should have been seen so near the wood. I warrant that the woman was travelling on board and probably against her will.'

'That's no more than supposition, I'm afraid,' the coroner retorted. 'I need to convene this inquest this afternoon so that the woman's body can be given burial. Even if I did adjourn, I see little prospect of being able to find this mysterious coach. After all, it could have come from anywhere…'

I turned to the Deputy Constable. 'Did you ask what direction the coach was travelling in?'

'As I recall, m'lady, one man told me that it was travelling from the west.'

'Then the chances are it came from Exeter,' I declared.

The coroner shook his head. 'You can't be sure of that. I'll grant you it might have come from the direction of Exeter, but no more than that.'

'But wherever it came from, what was it doing in these parts? It's some miles to the London road and I know of no one living in this area who owns a coach, even supposing they have the means to do so.'

'I'm sorry, Lady Tremayne, the presence of this coach in the vicinity of the woods is by itself insufficient evidence to satisfy me that I should delay matters any longer. Mind you,

I'm still happy to recommend an open verdict to the jury, and I'll concede that what the Deputy Constable has discovered strengthens the case for such a finding. The door will then at least be left ajar for further investigation. Now I really must get on.'

The jury were duly assembled on the village green and then invited to enter the church in order to examine the corpse. Once they had returned they heard Olivia's account of how she had discovered the body as well as Constable Smith's evidence of the mysterious coach. Following this the coroner reported to them that an examination of the deceased's body had confirmed that she had died of asphyxiation, had previously given birth, and had bruising to both her left shoulder and arm.

'This is an unusual matter,' he continued. 'The cause of death is clear but I would counsel you that it is extremely difficult to be certain that this was done by her own hand. To begin with, there was absolutely nothing on her person to identify her, and nor did she leave behind her any letter explaining why she should have wished to kill herself. Furthermore, no one has yet come forward to claim her body and no one who's seen the corpse has recognised her. I therefore have to conclude that she was a stranger to these parts and could have travelled some distance to reach the wood, which is in quite an isolated location. It's conceivable that she was indeed brought to the wood in the coach that was sighted in the near vicinity the day before her body was found. Otherwise, I have to conclude that she came to the wood on foot from who knows where, presumably concealing the rope on her person. She'd then have tied it around the branch of a tree, as well as building the pile of stones and twigs on which she proceeded to stand with the noose round her neck, before finally kicking away the pile in order to hang herself.'

'Remember, too,' he went on, 'she was wearing a distinctive red dress, so if she did indeed simply make her way on foot to the place of her death you'd think that someone working in the fields would recall seeing her. Yet no one who the good Constable has spoken to today has any such recollection. I therefore have to counsel you that it is quite possible she was strung-up with the express intention of making her murder look like a suicide, though what the motive could possibly have been for such a foul deed I cannot begin to speculate upon. In any event, the best advice I can offer you is that you should deliver an open verdict, remembering as you make your deliberations that a finding of suicide would deny the deceased a Christian burial. Should you feel that you need time to consider the matter then I'm sure you'll be welcome to use the church.'

The jury then chose to take up the coroner's offer and it was to be another half an hour before they came back outside again, indicating that they were able to deliver their verdict.

Looking at the faces of the twelve men, three or four of whom I had developed a passing acquaintanceship with over the years, I felt anxious that they might be about to ignore the coroner's clear advice and instead deliver a verdict of suicide. However, in the event, and much to my relief, they accepted it and duly entered an open verdict. It was obvious that there had been some debate between the jury members on the merits of doing so, but all that now mattered was that good sense appeared to have prevailed.

Unfortunately, despite the verdict I had been hoping for, I could see little or no prospect of the authorities choosing to investigate the matter. That might change if by any chance a relative or friend came looking for the deceased, but I fancied, even then only if they could provide some compelling evidence that she'd indeed been a victim of foul play.

'I'm still convinced that she was murdered. It simply isn't credible to me that she'd have walked miles to her death, carrying a rope on her person with which to kill herself, and leave nothing to identify her let alone explain her actions,' I asserted to Olivia when we next rode together two days after the inquest had taken place. The weather had become even warmer than of late and we had decided to head for the coast with the intention of riding our horses along the beach so long as the tide was in our favour.

'If you're right, I'd liken it to an execution. Still, there's nothing we can do about the matter, is there?'

'Perhaps not, unless it was possible to trace the ownership of the coach. I'm convinced she was on board and I think there's every chance that it came from either Exeter or somewhere near to the city.'

'But it was just a plain, black coach with nothing to distinguish it from any other.'

'Except that one of its horses had a black coat and few men in the county possess the wealth to be able to own a coach. If it was in fact unmarked then I'd wager its owner is likely to be a rich merchant.'

'Maybe so, but you're not seriously looking to become embroiled in another investigation, surely? I still say that the events of last year don't appear to have taught you anything.'

'Alright, but I still say if I'd not pursued matters as I did, a murderer and rapist would very likely still be at large today posing a serious threat to all womankind in the county.'

'Even so, you could have been killed.'

'I don't believe so and anyway I only did what was right. I've a mind to visit my sister, Caroline, soon, and when I do, I think I'll ask the city's gatekeepers if they've any recollection of seeing a coach of the right description leaving or entering the city the day before the woman's body was found.'

'And what if any of them do?'

'Then it should not be too difficult to trace the owner. Exeter's but a small city, after all. I also imagine that my attorney, Gilbert Overbury, or for that matter his clerk, might be of assistance. I fancy that Gilbert knows every man of any importance in the city and his clerk's good at sniffing out information.'

'You'd have to pay for his services, mind. Can you really afford that?'

'Perhaps not, but if the fee was a modest one, I might still be tempted.'

5

Thomas returns

Two days later I became unwell. I feared that something I had eaten had badly disagreed with me as I had been violently sick not long after my midday meal and was still feeling quite wretched. I was fretful, too, about Lucas who was continuing to sleep poorly as well as struggling to take milk from Melissa's breast. It increasingly pained me to have placed such an burden on her, and I was coming close to regretting not having put him to my own breast, however unthinkable it might be for a woman of my status in life. At the same time there remained the vexed question of whether or not to call out Dr Gladwell. I was coming round to the idea that there was really no alternative, but still hesitated to do so, wondering what good it would actually achieve.

Outside, I could see that it was a pleasantly dry day, with high, broken clouds and a good deal of sunshine, but I did not feel up to going outside. Instead, I endeavoured to concentrate on some needlework, which I had already been putting off for far too long, until tiredness overcame me and then I sat up with a start, realising that I had fallen asleep for a few moments at least. A sound then made me glance out of the window and I gasped in surprise, before scurrying towards the front door.

I opened it just in time to see Thomas dismounting from his horse and the stable lad, Toby, now a gangly thirteen-year-old, come running forward to take the animal's reins. I immediately noticed that Thomas had regrown his beard and also allowed his hair to grow long once more in the cavalier style. Above all, though, he still appeared to be the same vigorous, handsome man I had so readily fallen in love with.

'Thomas, my love,' I cried out. 'I've been so worried. Thank God, you've come home. You have a son, Lucas. The name we agreed…'

In a moment we were in each other's arms and Thomas brought his lips to mine in a fervent embrace. 'My darling Jane. How I've longed for this. You look as beautiful as ever.'

'My, Thomas, you flatter me. I've not been feeling well and must look as pale as death.'

'No, a little tired perhaps, but still beautiful, I assure you. And our son; is he well?'

'Let me take you to him. He's with Harry's wife, Melissa. As you'll recall she was willing to be his wet nurse.'

Holding hands, we made our way directly towards the cottage, barely walking more than a few yards before I decided that I could not hide my concern for Lucas's health.

'I must be honest with you that he's a sickly child. I worry that he might not be long for this world, though the thought of losing another babe drives me to despair.'

'Have you called a doctor to him?'

'No, not yet, although I've come very close to doing so, I can tell you. Frankly, I often doubt that their so-called remedies are of any benefit. There's also the little matter of their fees…'

At that Thomas merely grunted and upon reaching the cottage, banged loudly on its door.

'Thomas, if the babe's asleep…' The warning came too late to prevent the sound of an infant's cry. 'You must have woken him.'

As I feared might be the case, we found Lucas in a distressed state, and when Thomas insisted in taking him in his arms, the babe's cries grew even more raucous.

'There's nothing much wrong with his lungs,' Thomas quipped before gratefully handing him back to Melissa.

'And I think he has your looks,' I said. 'I can see it around the eyes and mouth.'

Thomas was less than convinced. 'I don't see how you can tell? He's still too young. What's his birth date, exactly?'

'The 18th April. He came at seven o'clock in the morning.'

'And your labour was not too long, I trust?'

'No more than eight hours, thank God.'

He looked at me tenderly. 'I was fearful, you know, that I might return to find you… dead, and the babe also…'

I smiled at him. 'Your concern does you credit, my love. For my part, I have feared for your life ever since I heard that the plot against Cromwell's life had failed. I thought you were bound to be arrested and put on trial and then more than likely sentenced to death.'

'I'm fortunate that I was not amongst the ringleaders of the plot and was able to make my escape. Many brave men have been less fortunate. Some might be transported to the West Indies, if they're lucky.'

Leaving Lucas to Melissa's care, we returned to the Manor House to take our ease.

'I'm afraid, we must be prepared for soldiers coming in search of me again as they did last year,' Thomas said.

'Have you actually been followed, do you think?' I asked in some alarm.

'Not to my knowledge, but I fear that Cromwell has his spies everywhere and I imagine my involvement in the plot will have been known about, or at least suspected. Cromwell's men would also expect me to return to the part of the country where I was born and where I can count on being amongst friends with the same sympathies. I think it can therefore only be a matter of time before they're at our door.'

'Then you must resume your former disguise, though God knows you're plainly enough dressed these days, anyway. Just shave off your beard once more and let me cut your hair. If Cromwell's men do then come searching once more, all you need do is play the tenant farmer as you did before.'

Thomas began to pace up and down. 'Except that I'll soon begin to feel like a caged beast once more and no doubt seek consolation in the consumption of too much hard liquor. Damn Cromwell and all his works!'

'But we will still have each other and now we have a son too.'

'If he lives!'

'Pray God he will but even if he does not, there's no reason why I should not still bear you more children.'

Even as I said these words I could see a lascivious look in Thomas's eyes. He was dusty and smelly, too, from having spent hours in the saddle and I dreaded to think how long it might be since he'd last changed any of his clothes. I decided to insist that he take a bath for all that this would involve

Mary and my housekeeper and cook, Alice, in a good deal of hard labour.

At least I possessed a copper bathtub and knew he was not too averse to bathing occasionally. If I also refused to sleep with him unless he did so, I was confident that this would act as an incentive and in the warmth of summer the experience should be pleasurable enough for him. Once we were alone together I could even contemplate joining him, and then it struck me forcefully that I might very soon be pregnant again.

Three days later I set out for Exeter, accompanied by Olivia. We had decided that we would go shopping together as well as visit my younger sister, Caroline. It would also be an opportunity to see my nephew, Michael, to whom Caroline had given birth the previous July and was apparently still thriving.

Such a visit was only made possible by Caroline's husband, John Thorpe, having relented upon the assertion he'd made the previous year that I would no longer be welcome under his roof as a consequence of my marriage to Thomas. I'd never confessed his actual name, even to Caroline, but had made the difficult decision to admit to her that I was pregnant by a man I had married in secret, and then sworn her to secrecy. John, however, being a doctor as well as being a stout Puritan, had become suspicious when I'd suffered a bout of morning sickness in his presence. It had led to him plying Caroline with questions and the truth had emerged. Worse, he had even guessed that Thomas was my husband and it was this which had turned him so against me.

Ever since I'd had to live with the fear that he might seek to expose Thomas, for all that I knew Caroline had begged him not to do so, both for her sake and mine. The news that he was willing to entertain my presence in his house had therefore come as something of a pleasant surprise, and when I had visited her following Lucas's birth, Caroline had made it clear that it had taken a good deal of persuasion on her part. Knowing what an intransigent individual he could be I was pleased she still had such influence over him. It ran contrary to my fear that she was in fact completely under his thumb and that their marriage was no longer a happy one.

Nevertheless, my sister's news had still come with the rider that only short visits during daylight hours would be tolerated when he was likely to be absent from the house on his rounds, so it remained clear that he was only willing to countenance the occasional visit on sufferance. Still, it was better than nothing, and I was willing to be grateful for small mercies.

At the same time the fate of the mysterious young woman, whose body Olivia had had the misfortune to discover, still troubled me, much as I imagined the image of such a death haunted Olivia, for all she might prefer not to admit it. I therefore remained determined to question the city's gatekeepers and most especially the keeper of the city's East Gate, through which I surmised that any coach heading in the direction of Harpford was most likely to have travelled. It was also naturally enough the gate through which Olivia and I would enter the city, so I thought it would be easy enough to make the necessary enquiry without unduly delaying our other plans.

I thought the East Gate to be by far the most impressive that the city possessed as it was almost a castle keep in its own right, standing three storeys tall with twin towers flanking the actual gateway, and topped by substantial looking battlements. I was also pleased to be able to find the gatekeeper in his room on the building's ground floor where he appeared to have fallen asleep in his chair. He looked worn out by old age with heavily lined features, thinning white hair and an equally white beard.

'Pardon me,' I said while at the same time nudging him awake by placing a hand on his left shoulder. He woke up with a start, coughing and spluttering as he did so. 'I'm sorry to wake you but I need to ask you something…' And then I hesitated. A week and more had now passed since Olivia had found the body and I thought the likelihood of the gatekeeper having any recollection of a coach passing through the gate was highly remote. In all probability, he'd have been sound asleep in his chair.

By now he'd risen to his feet and was looking at me curiously so I pressed on. 'I need you to cast your mind back eight days. I'm wondering if you might have any recollection of a black coach having passed through your gate on its way out of the city? It would have been unmarked with but a single coachman wearing a cloak, its curtains closed and pulled by two horses, one with a brown coat, the other black. At a guess it might well have left around midday, perhaps a little later.'

At first he looked at me blankly, as if to confirm my expectation that he would recall nothing. 'I dunno about that, ma'am,' he said, scratching his head. 'Ye'll understand, a lot traffic passes through these gates even on a single day. I canna be expected to remember that far back…'

'No, I don't suppose you can. I quite understand. It's just, well, I wondered if you might have any recollection of a coach of that description coming and going from time to time?'

'Um, I don't know about any closed up curtains but I do know a coach passes through these gates quite regularly that be black and be pulled by two horses.

'is one of these brown and the other black?'

'That I canna say.'

'And would you happen by any chance to know who owns the coach?'

The gatekeeper shook his head. 'I've not the least idea, ma'am.'

'Oh well, never mind. I'm still grateful for your assistance.' And with that I took a penny from my purse and handed it to him.

'Thank ye, ma'am.' He grinned at me, revealing several missing teeth. 'I've had a thought. It be eight days ago when I wasn't feeling at all well. My son, Daniel, 'e be thirteen now and a good lad, stood in for me. 'Appen 'e might remember the coach.'

I gave him a surprised look, thinking him too old to have a son of that age, but then it occurred to me that the boy might well have been the progeny of a second marriage after his father had been left a widower.

'And where might I find him?' I asked.

'E'll be working. Only two days ago 'e started 'is apprenticeship as a wheelwright.'

'Nearby, I trust?

'Aye, just in Bedford Street, ma'am.'

He proceeded to give me more detailed directions and I decided to make time to pay Daniel a visit. Olivia, however, was less than enthusiastic.

'I don't think this is a good idea,' she complained. 'Be careful that you do not embroil us in matters that are not in the least our concern. It was bad enough what that wretch Turnbull put us through last year because you would not leave well alone. If that poor girl really was murdered, God knows what devilry she was involved in.'

'I merely wish to get at the truth. She still deserves justice, doesn't she?'

'From beyond the grave, I somehow doubt it.'

'Well, it's hardly out of our way and it need delay us by no more than another five minutes or so. I pray you, be patient with me, Olivia.'

'When am I ever not patient with you?'

We smiled at each other and were soon able to locate the wheelwright's premises whereupon I proceeded to seek out Daniel. He was a thin and lanky with short, greasy hair and a ready smile, which suggested an amenable personality.

'Ma'am, certainly I do recall the coach ye speak of,' he told me. 'I saw it leave, I'm sure I did. T'was the black horse that most brings it to mind and what's more I saw it come back, too.'

'Was this the same day?'

'No, ma'am, it was the following day, in the morning. My pa was still poorly, ye see. He was better by the afternoon, as I recall.'

'Do you remember by any chance if it had curtains at its windows making it impossible to see inside.'

'I can't say about that when it left. Yet I do remember that when it came back I had a sight of a man sitting inside the coach. Ye see 'e had his face to the window.'

'Would you recognise him again, do you think?'

'I might do, ma'am. T'was the face of a man who expects to be obeyed, I reckon, so I took 'im to be the owner of the coach.'

'And how old would you say he was?'

'In his thirties, I expect, and 'e was wearing a beard but it was neatly trimmed, and, oh yes, 'e 'ad a hat on, too.'

I gave him a grateful look, telling him how obliged to him I was for his trouble. Then I produced another penny from my pocket and handed it to him.

'Thank'e, ma'am,' he said with a smile that reminded me of his father. I was left feeling pleased with myself for what I had now discovered, which showed on my face as I emerged into the bright sunshine and walked over to where Olivia was waiting for me.

'My, you look like a cat who got the cream,' she declared

'Do I, indeed. Well, perhaps I have, for what the lad has now told me means that a coach answering to the description given by the good people of Harpford left Exeter on the day the girl probably died and returned the following day. But there's more, too, because when the coach returned, its curtains weren't closed, and there was a man looking out of it who the lad thinks he might recognise if he were to see him again. I tell you, Olivia, between him and his driver, they could well have strung the girl up. Mind you, what I can't begin to understand as yet is what possible motive they'd have had for doing so.'

'I knew it, I just knew it!' Olivia said in exasperation, 'you're encouraged enough to want to continue with this… this…'

'…Investigation. Yes, perhaps I am. And you'll help me, Olivia, I know you will, for all your tutting at me with disapproval.'

'So what are you planning to do next?'

'Discover who owns the coach, of course. Mind you, I can't see how we can do that ourselves. We'll need assistance and I think I know who'll give it to us. I know it'll delay us a little longer, but I think we should visit the attorney, Master Overbury, who was of such assistance to us last year. His chambers are nearby, after all.'

'And how do you think he can be of any assistance this time?'

'First, because he's surely well acquainted with the wealthy in this city and only a man or woman of significant means can afford to own a coach and two horses. Second, because as a lawyer I imagine he will engage the services of those who are capable of establishing the whereabouts of others.'

'What, do you mean spies?'

'In a manner of speaking, yes, I suppose I do.'

'But their services won't come free of charge, will they?'

'No, that's true enough, but it still has to be worth an enquiry. If the cost is too high, I accept that I may be halted in my tracks, frustrating though that would be.'

The question of cost also reminded me that the next loan repayment was shortly due to the moneylenders who'd enabled me to meet the fine imposed on my estate as a consequence of my late husband's involvement in the Civil War. It was bad enough that I had been left a widow, worse that I had had a severe financial burden placed upon me that I could only discharge thanks to the practice of usury. What also worried me was that sooner or later my estate would suffer such a poor harvest that my income would be insufficient to enable me to discharge the debt. Then I might even have to sell my beloved mare, Hera, and God knows what else besides, or face penury.

Deciding to put such pessimistic notions to one side, Olivia and I quickly made our way to Master Overbury's chambers, and once again leaving Olivia in charge of the horses, I went inside. In contrast to the whiff of sewage and horse dung that I was prepared to tolerate in the streets, the smell of best polish which greeted me was altogether pleasanter.

Much as I recalled from my previous visits, the scene inside the clerk's room was also one of what I could best describe as organised chaos, with documents of all descriptions cluttering both the large desk that faced me as I entered, and every conceivable nook and cranny besides. Only the floor was relatively free of documents, and even there I could still make out the odd pile or two lurking surreptitiously at the clerk's feet.

'M'lady,' the clerk said, rising quickly to his feet and offering me an obsequious smile. His hair was still as greasy as I recalled although perhaps a shade greyer while his complexion was, if anything, even redder, no doubt caused, I reflected, by too great a liking for strong liquor.'How can we be of service to you?'

'Is your Master here?'

'I'm afraid he's in court, m'lady. He said he might return at about one o'clock. Can I take a message or would you care to call back?'

'I might well be able to return later in the day before travelling home, say at around half past four.'

My Master will certainly be here by then, m'lady.'

'But then again perhaps you can assist me in his absence. You see, I'm trying to establish someone's whereabouts and I wonder if this is a service that you're able to provide. Failing that perhaps you know of someone who does? What I know about this person is that they're probably male and in their thirties with a trim beard and an authoritative manner, as well as being the owner of an unmarked black coach pulled by two horses, one of which has a black coat. I also have good reason to believe that the person in question lives here in the city as their coach has been seen passing through the East Gate on a number of occasions.'

'Then m'lady, they should not be difficult to identify. Indeed, my Master might well know, or know of, such an individual, personally.'

'Just what I thought, but if by chance he does not…'

'Then m'lady, from time to time I have successfully established the whereabouts of certain individuals on my Master's instructions..' He now lowered his voice. 'It usually involves discrete enquiries at taverns and the like and of various persons of my acquaintance.'

'I see. In that case tell your Master that I'll definitely be returning later today and wish to give him instructions on the matter we've been discussing.'

'I'll be pleased to do so, m'lady.'

6

A month had passed since our visit to Exeter, it was now high summer, and I was busy sewing. I had never been the most skilled of needlewomen, but necessity dictated that clothes require mending from time to time. It was also not a task I felt I could simply delegate to servants, given that I had no more than Mary and Alice, both of whom were kept busy with other essential tasks.

Then I paused , deciding instead to stare out of the window for a few moments while taking in the familiar view of open countryside presently basking in the heat of a warm summer's day. Thomas had risen early and gone fishing, declaring that he would be out all day. Whilst I missed his company I was pleased he had discovered an activity that kept him amused and also meant he was less inclined to lounge about, drinking strong liquor until he became thoroughly inebriated. God knows, though, I could imagine nothing more tedious than standing, or perhaps sitting on a riverbank, waiting for a fish to take the bait, but then each to their own, I supposed.

'M'lady, a letter has come for you.'

I was startled out of my reverie and turning my head gave Mary just the hint of a smile. 'Thank you, Mary.'

Taking the letter from her, I quickly broke the seal and then glanced at the letter's contents. I was pleased to see that it was written by Master Overbury and was just what I had been hoping for.

....It accords me pleasure to report to you that certain enquiries having been made, I am satisfied that a coach with horses, answering to the description you provided, is in the ownership of a certain Hugh Graveney. I have every reason to believe that he is a man of considerable wealth through his trade from the Indies and the ownership of a number of merchant ships. I would also add that I have heard suggestions that not all of his wealth has been honestly acquired. I refer to the possibility that he may not be above smuggling certain merchandise into the country and even that he may enjoy profit from acts of piracy on the high seas. I must, however, be plain that I am aware of no evidence that would substantiate such suggestions.

I myself have had occasion to meet with Sir Hugh and have not been enamoured by his personality. I think him cold and arrogant. Such men may well be successful but can, I think, make enemies along the way; thus the suggestions I have mentioned above. I would judge his age to be approaching forty and he wears a trim beard so may well answer to the description you gave me of the man seen looking out of his coach. I also know him to be a married man with children and he is in possession of a large town house in South Street. I imagine, too, that he possesses a country estate, and its whereabouts could be established, I expect, should you wish further enquiries to be made on your behalf.

I must also advise you that I believe that his wealth, how so ever acquired, has given him influence in high places, even as far as London, and as such his sympathies must be seen to lie entirely with the Lord Protector. Further, I have one other piece of information to impart to you that may be of relevance to your concerns. It has been said to me by a fellow lawyer, who has had dealings with him, that Graveney is the owner of one of the city's bawdy houses, which is to be found in Smythen Street. Either he will enjoy a direct profit from its goings on, or he'll exact a high rent for the use of his property for such purposes.

I enclose my account for your kind attention and remain your most obedient servant.

I read the letter a second time and then a third, gradually absorbing its implications as best I could. I felt a rising desire to discuss its contents with someone else and my first thought was naturally of Thomas. He'd told me very exactly where he intended casting his rod along the banks of the river Otter so finding him ought not to be at all difficult and involve me in no more than a fifteen minute walk. On the other hand, there was Olivia, whom I had not seen in more than a week, and had planned paying a visit to that very afternoon, having informed Thomas that this was my intention. Of course, I could speak to both of them on the subject, if I chose, so it was, perhaps, more a question of which of them I spoke to first.

I was not sure, either, who would be less sympathetic to my growing desire to investigate matters further. The chances were that both of them would counsel caution, and perhaps wisely so, but whereas Thomas could even seek to forbid me from taking any further action, Olivia had no such power over me. Not that I was obliged to bow to Thomas's will, of course, and such authority as he possessed was limited by the secret nature of our marriage and the fact that he remained effectively in hiding.

In the end, having continued sewing for another quarter of an hour in order to complete the immediate task in hand, I went to the stables to ask the stable lad, Toby, to saddle-up Hera, and from there then made my way to see Lucas. His health still gave me cause for concern but I was beginning to feel that he was stronger than I had initially feared and might, after all, survive what I knew to be the especially dangerous first few months of his existence. Certainly, he had of late given Melissa less sleepless nights and was definitely beginning to gain in weight.

I found him asleep, and being reluctant to wake him, did not stay long. I decided I would visit again as soon as I returned from my visit to Fetford Hall, which in the event I reached not long after midday. Olivia and her family had already sat down to enjoy their main meal of the day, an eel pie, given that it was a Friday, and James encouraged me to join them.

'Becky's also given us some exciting news yesterday, haven't you, my dear,' Constance declared eagerly.

'My, you're not…'

'Yes, I'm with child.'

'Well, that is good news. My congratulations to you both.'

After nearly a year of marriage I had been beginning to wonder if Becky might be infertile. I knew that allowances had to be made for her having been raped by that fiend, Turnbull, and that the experience had been a thoroughly traumatising one for her. At least her pregnancy confirmed that normal marital relations had been restored and I could but hope that Becky would be safely delivered of a healthy child. My one fear was that for all her pretty looks she was slight of build and might therefore struggle to give birth successfully. Pregnancy is without doubt a mixed blessing and I could only give thanks for my own good fortune in having survived two births in good health.

Lucas's health was also asked after and I was pleased to report that this seemed to be improving. Everyone present had been made aware, too, of Thomas's return but there was an understanding between us that his name was best not mentioned. It was not that any of the servants were thought to be untrustworthy but I had been insistent that in such dangerous times it was best to be extremely cautious, especially as the last thing I wanted was to implicate any of my dear friends in my decision to marry and harbour a known renegade. At the first opportunity I then began to share with them all the information that I'd received from Master Overbury and to ask their opinion on what, if anything, I should do next.

'I'm still convinced that the young woman was murdered and it now looks to me as if this Hugh Graveney may well have had something to do with this,' I declared. 'Master Overbury has also not spoken well of his character and suggested that he has made enemies. What's more it seems that he owns a bawdy house in the city, and I've been wondering if the deceased could even have been a whore. I can't, though, imagine what she could have done to cause him to execute her…'

'She could have betrayed him in some way,' James suggested. 'And when he discovered this, he saw her as nothing better than a traitor who deserved execution,'

'But why not just kill her and then dispose of the body? Olivia asked

'Yes, but don't forget that the death was meant to look like suicide,' I asserted. 'The coroner's jury could easily have come to such a verdict and that would have been the end of the matter. As it is, I would now like to establish the deceased's identity and the obvious starting point for that has to be the bawdy house which Hugh Graveney owns.'

I could see Olivia looking at me sceptically, clearly thinking that this was a terrible idea but to my relief she said nothing. After all, we'd already had this conversation and I felt more determined than ever to try to get to the bottom of this mystery. Instead, it was Constance who spoke up.

'Are you sure that's wise, my dear?'

'Probably not,' I confessed, looking Olivia in the eye even as I spoke. 'But the poor woman, whoever she was, deserves justice.'

'Ah,' James said with a grin. 'But for all you know she was neither poor nor deserving.'

'You're surely not suggesting that it was right to string her up?'

'No, forgive me, I was jesting. But have you considered that she might after all have killed herself? The presence of the coach could just have been a coincidence.'

'No, I don't believe that for a moment.'

'But it has to be possible.'

'Many things are possible but that doesn't make them true. If it wasn't the coach that brought her to the wood, how did she get there, and what's more without anyone coming forward to say they'd seen her?'

'You can't be certain she didn't just walk. She might have been careful to keep out of sight, and even if some people did see her they might have forgotten, or live in remote hamlets.

'Well, whether she killed herself or not, I think it's still worth trying to find out who she was. She may have left behind a family, that's desperate for news of her, and she had certainly given birth so there may well be a child yearning for its mother.'

'Then search for her if you must,' Constance declared, 'but do not be surprised if it leads you into dangerous waters. If she was killed, her murderer will not take kindly to your prying.'

'Exactly my sentiment, mother,' Olivia added. 'But Jane is stubborn and won't listen.'

'I will tread carefully, I swear I will.' Again I caught Olivia's eye and knew what she was thinking. *Who said anything about I? Where you lead I tend to follow.*

'But think, Jane, you are a wife again and a mother too,' Constance asserted, making me alarmed that she might actually mention Thomas by name. 'Your first duty is surely to them.'

'I will never be neglectful of my duty, I do assure you. I wish only to establish the poor dead woman's identity and, if I can, get closer to establishing what really happened to her. I see nothing wrong with that, truly I don't.'

Later when Olivia and I were alone, walking side by side in the Hall's rose garden, now enjoying its summer bloom, Olivia asked me the inevitable question.

'So when do you mean to return to Exeter to pursue this quest of yours?'

'As soon as possible. Are you happy to come with me?'

'Content might be the better word, if only in what I fear is the forlorn hope that I might keep us both out of harm's way.'

'No harm should come from making a few innocent enquiries…'

'Come Jane, hardly innocent. I still fear that you will stir a hornet's nest.'

'In which case I will turn to the forces of the law to take matters further.'

'That was an uphill struggle a year ago, as I recall. At first, the likes of Magistrate Crabb would have nothing to do with your suspicions.'

'I made the mistake of accusing the wrong man. I will endeavour not to fall into that trap again.'

The two of us strolled on for a short distance in silence, appreciating the warmth of a pleasant summer's afternoon as well as both the colour and aroma of the roses we passed.

'You know, Olivia,' I said suddenly. 'The more I think about the woman who died the more I think that she must have been more than a common prostitute.'

'Perhaps more a courtesan, then?'

'Yes, and by her looks and the delicacy of her skin, a well-kept one. Indeed, I'm wondering if she could even have been Hugh Graveney's mistress?'

'But I struggle to imagine any circumstances in which a man would coldly execute his own mistress. I accept he might murder her in a fit of rage but that's a different matter altogether.'

'Who would have believed that a King would execute two of his own Queens until King Henry, the eighth, did so.

Remember, too, that they were both found guilty of adultery.'

'So, you think that could have been the motive for this woman's execution; if indeed that was what it was?'

'I merely think it's a possibility, and that a man of sufficient vanity might be capable of seeing any act of betrayal as worthy of death.'

I decided that the time had come to return home. I agreed a day when Olivia and I would ride into Exeter together, and was about to mount Hera when Olivia had one more question for me.

'Will you be honest with Thomas about your plans? I can imagine him being less than pleased.'

'I don't know, I might. Anyhow, he knows he cannot stop me even if he might not approve. We have an understanding that I am my own woman and free to make my own decisions.'

'That might change, I fancy.'

'...But not so long as our marriage remains a guarded secret and he remains in hiding...'

'He could come to resent that situation, don't you think?'

'I don't see why, though, I grant you, he's like a caged beast at times.'

7
Poor Jessica

Five days later, having arrived in Exeter, and left our horses at a livery stables, Olivia and I made our way on foot to Smythen Street where I was confident we would have no difficulty in identifying the bawdy house.

'As needs must, we'll have to ask, but I imagine they'll be some sort of lewd sign above the premises' front door, or some painted whore standing outside it,' I declared.

I was still smarting somewhat from the arguments I'd had with Thomas when I'd told him of my intention to visit the bawdy house out of a desire to try and identify the dead woman. I had been quite taken aback by how annoyed he'd become, demanding that I do no such thing.

'As your husband I command that you leave this matter well alone.'

'But I merely wish to establish the poor dead girl's identity…'

'I don't believe that. You'll try to take the matter much further than that, I know you will, and that could be dangerous. You really shouldn't meddle in matters that are none of your business. The dead woman, whoever she was, has nothing whatsoever to do with either of us, and neither her identity or her fate, sad though it was, need be of any interest to you.'

'You can't stop me visiting my sister in Exeter, or going shopping there, and what I might also choose to do whilst I'm there need be no concern of yours.'

'But I do have every right to be concerned with the possible consequences of your… your recklessness, and as your husband I have the right to expect that you will obey me.'

We had both stared at each other, his face a picture of exasperation, while I ruminated on whether to stand my ground or pretend acquiescence. In the end I decided on the former.

'I won't let you stop me doing what I think is right. What's more you can't make a prisoner of me even if you might wish to. I am still mistress of this Hall and its estate and every person living here looks to me not you.'

'So, you defy me then?' he shouted

'Yes, on this occasion, I do.'

'On your head be it then if this ends badly.'

With that he had stalked off and our normal state of relaxed intimacy had remained strained ever since. Worse, he had on one occasion drunk so much wine that it had caused him to become thoroughly inebriated, and once in that state he had again tried to order me to obey his wishes. It had led to an even fiercer argument between us and I had been badly shaken when he had even raised a fist to me. However, promptly realising that he'd gone too far, he had backed off, finally managing a somewhat befuddled apology, which I had accepted.

Now as Olivia and I made our way along the street, bringing the nosegays of flowers that we wore around our necks to our nostrils to help disguise the stench emanating from an open sewer that ran down it, the image of Thomas raising his fist to me was still seared on my brain. It made me fearful that one day he might go further and actually strike me and I could only pray that such a day would never come. Certainly, whilst I could recall arguments with my late husband, Paul, he had never behaved in a threatening manner towards me. All the same, he'd not possessed Thomas's fondness for wine and strong beer and I did not recall ever having seen him the worse for drink.

'Here, this must be it,' Olivia said, interrupting my reverie.

Following her pointed finger, I saw just ahead of us a sign above a door upon which was depicted the painted image of a young, bare-headed woman with long tresses and a crudely seductive smile on her face. The prospect of seeking to enter such a place made me uncomfortable but I had not come this far to back-off, so steeling my resolve I strode up to the door and knocked loudly, twice. It was almost instantly opened by a woman of middle years wearing a Lincoln Green dress, whom I fancied would once have been beautiful. Advancing years had however begun to fatten her figure and also to wrinkle her face, while her expression was stern to the point of being faintly menacing

'Yes, what ye want?' she asked gruffly in a heavy Devon accent.

I hesitated but only for a moment, having already practised in my mind how best to explain myself.

'I am Lady Jane… Tremayne of Altringham Manor. At the end of May an unknown young woman, in her twenties I would judge, was found hanged from the branch of a tree in woods near the village of Harpford. She was wearing a red dress and petticoat but nothing else, not even a ring on her finger, that offers any clue as to her identity…'

'So, what's that t'do with anyone 'ere?'

'It's just… well, I've reason to believe that she came from this city. She was pretty, some might even say beautiful, with curly auburn hair and fair skin, a well-shaped nose… Oh yes, she'd given birth, perhaps just the once…'

I was watching the woman carefully as I gave this description, and thought I noticed the slightest change in her stern expression, betraying a hint of recognition. 'Mean's nothing t'me,' was, however, her almost immediate response.

'Are you sure of that? It might have been a few years ago now…'

'I still dunno see why 'e think we might know 'er 'ere?'

Again I hesitated. I'd been reluctant to mention a certain name, sensing that to do so might be counter-productive but now decided that it was worth the risk.

'I'm thinking that she might be known to the owner of this property. I'm told his name's Hugh Graveney.'

The woman looked immediately startled and without a further word simply stepped back and slammed the door shut.

'Wait… please,' I appealed to her.

'Go away. I've no more t'say t'thee. Go away, d'ye hear!'

'We're onto something here,' I said to Olivia as we walked slowly away. 'She recognised my description of the dead woman, I'm sure she did. And why slam the door in my face the moment I mention Hugh Graveney's name?'

'I think she's frightened of him.'

'And with good reason, too, given what he might well be capable of.'

'Yet suspicion alone proves nothing.'

I grunted, feeling decidedly frustrated. There was a part of me that was willing to contemplate finding a way into the bawdy house and then either bribing or intimidating the woman we'd just spoken to into revealing all she knew. Nevertheless, my more sensible self was already concluding that such an option was likely to be unrealistic, if not downright dangerous.

'We'd best go and visit my sister now,' I said grumpily and the two of us proceeded to retreat the way we had just come.

'Xcuse me.' I turned to see a young woman walking hurriedly towards us. Her head was covered by a maroon-coloured shawl but otherwise there was nothing modest about her appearance as her dress was crimson red and her face rouged. It was obvious where she must have come from. 'I over'eard yer conversation and can be o'help to thee but only if ye're willing to pay. I'll take a shilling.'

I eyed the whore quizzically. As she came closer I could tell she was beginning to lose her looks and wondered what the future might hold in store for her. Too many of her kind were liable to end up in the gutter begging for pennies. I decided that it was worth my while reaching inside the pocket of my dress, which held the coins I invariably carried on my person, and extracting the necessary item of silver.

'Here it is then. If you can tell me anything that might help me identify the woman who died, this shilling is yours. You have my word on it.'

The whore's face broke into a grin, revealing two blackened teeth. 'I can do better than that… I can give ye 'er name…'

'Can you indeed.'

'I think we should walk on, mind. No point in drawing attention to ourselves, is there.' At that the woman glanced behind her before giving me a nervous look. 'I know Betsy, that's the woman you just spoke to, wouldn't take kindly to me talking to thee.'

'Is she frightened of Hugh Graveney?' I asked. 'It was when I mentioned his name that she slammed the door in my face,'

'Aye, I think she's right scared o' him. He's the owner, after all, and could shut us down whenever he chose. He doesn't want the world to know 'is business either. Betsy's warned me to never reveal his name to anyone but you knew it anyway.' She then quickened her pace until we were well out of sight of the bawdy house whereupon she glanced behind her a second time. 'If she was gonna come after us, I'd 'ave seen 'er by now...'

'So what were you about to say concerning a name?' I asked.

'That I think the woman ye spoke of is Jessica Martins. I'd say she was a beauty and 'er 'air was right curly.'

'She worked with you, then?' Jane asked.

'Fer a while. We got t'know each other. She'd a way with men. That and her looks got 'er noticed by no less than Master Graveney, though when he first came a visiting he chose to use the name o' John Carter. 'E took 'er as 'is mistress and then 'e set 'er up in 'er own place. T'was 'ere in the city. It must be eight months ago now.'

'You visited her?' Olivia asked.

'I did, several times. But when I went there, it must be three weeks ago now, no one answered, and I've called again since but still no one's been there. I've been worried about 'er, I can tell 'e. T'think she hanged 'erself, it's awful...' She began to sniffle.

'I don't believe she hanged herself,' I said quietly.

'What, ye think she were murdered?'

'I'd liken it more to an execution.'

'Oh poor, poor Jessica!'

'I'm sorry to be the bearer of such grim news. But tell me, did you ever meet this Hugh Graveney?'

'Aye, I rubbed shoulders with 'im, ye might say, when 'e come a wenching fer Jessica. Then once, when I visited her in the place 'e set er up in, 'e was there. I 'ad t'leave afore she and me 'ad said two words t'one another. 'E didn't take kindly t'me coming, ye see. Jessica said 'e 'ad a fierce temper. I think she grew t'be a mighty scared o'im, fer all she boasted she could wrap any man round 'er little finger.'

'Do you think he ever hit her?'

'E might well 'ave done. She never said but I saw a nasty bruise on 'er face once. She said she'd walked into a door but I didn't really believe 'er.'

'Did she ever tell you anything about him? I mean, aside from your bawdy house, where his wealth came from?'

'No, all I ever learnt from her was his real name and that he was the owner. I don't believe she knew more than that.'

'And she never spoke of any quarrels between them?'

'No, not that I recall.'

'And what did this man look like?'

'I'd say 'e was in his thirties. 'E were quite tall, too, and stockily built with a neck like a bull's.'

'Did he wear a beard?'

'Oh aye, 'e did that. It were trim, mind. And I recall 'e 'ad fierce eyes. The day 'e practically threw me out, I thought 'e might 'ave taken a fist t'me if I hadn't done as 'e ordered.'

'And was there anything else you remember about him; for instance, his voice?'

'Um, not really. 'E was well-dressed, I'd say that, and 'is accent was that of a man born and bred in these parts...'

'Well, I am most grateful to you for what you've told us.'. And with that I handed over not only the shilling but another two pennies as well.'

'That's kind o'thee, I must say.'

'Are you willing to give me your name? You see it's possible that I might need to contact you again.'

The woman looked nervous. 'I'm not sure, I don't want to put myself in any danger...'

'I don't see why you should be. You've made no accusations against anyone,' Olivia stressed.

'I've still talked to thee about Hugh Graveney.'

'And when did she warn you never to speak of him to anyone?' I asked.

'Oh, it must 'ave been six months ago now, not long after I first visited Jessica.'

'Will you at least give me your Christian name?'

'...Oh, very well, I'm Janet, if 'e must know.'

'Thank you, Janet. I've just one more question for you. Can you tell me exactly where it was that Jessica lived?'

'It be in Paul Street....Number 19. Now, I'd better be getting back.'

I smiled at her. 'Of course you must. And thank you again. What you have been able to tell me has been invaluable, really it has.'

'If it's that Hugh Graveney who's killed Jessica then I hope 'e rots in hell.'

'I hope to see him executed for his crime, first.'

'Aye, if 'e made poor Jessica swing then it's only right 'e should pay the same price.'

Janet then turned and retreated the way she'd come, leaving me with a strong feeling of vindication. 'I knew it was right to pursue this and now we are really beginning to get somewhere, are we not?'

Olivia felt unable to share my enthusiasm. 'We could find ourselves trying to grapple with an individual just, or perhaps even more dangerous than Turnbull.'

'We must proceed with care, I grant you. From what we've just been told, it's also plain that he put the fear of God into Betsy.'

'So what do you intend to do next?'

'I'd like to return to Master Overbury and seek his advice. I need to settle his account don't forget, and I'm wondering if we might even be justified in putting a case to one of the Justices that there's enough evidence here to justify an arrest. Graveney needs to be questioned and testimonies taken from both Janet and Betsy. I know time is getting on and I still want to see my sister but this is important. As needs must we can come back another day.'

8
Insufficient evidence

It took us no more than ten minutes to make our way to Master Overbury's chambers. I expected that at this time of day he would still be at court, but I was ready to ask his clerk if it would be convenient for us to return later in the day once we had paid my sister a visit.

I reflected that in the past year the building we were about to enter had become familiar territory to me for the most unexpected of reasons. I had never imagined myself becoming an investigator of rapes, murder, and now what amounted to an execution, but I was prepared to travel wherever fate chose to take me. Had I also been born a man I could also imagine myself being drawn to pursue a career in the noble profession of the law, and found myself envying Master Overbury the sense of purpose such a life must afford him.

As luck would have it, his clerk announced that he was in fact in chambers, and upon hearing my voice he emerged from his inner sanctum in order to greet both myself and Olivia. Tall and angular, he was a man with a commanding presence and a deeply resonant voice to match.

'It's a pleasure to meet you both again, dear ladies,' he declared, sweeping us a bow. 'I assume you're here to settle my account, Lady Jane. I trust my report was to your satisfaction?'

'Indeed it was, good sir. The information it contained has enabled me to visit the bawdy house here in Exeter and establish the identity of the poor woman I believe was executed. What's more, I've every reason to believe she was the mistress of Hugh Graveney, the owner of the coach that was seen in the vicinity of the wood the day before her body was discovered.'

'My, my, Lady Jane, you have been busy.'

'I would welcome your advice if you could spare me a few minutes of your valuable time?'

'Of course, Lady Jane, if you and Lady Olivia would both care to enter my inner sanctum. Please excuse the amount of documentation you'll find scattered everywhere. I am in the middle of preparing for an important trial next week.'

On previous visits I had marvelled at what I could best describe as the organised chaos that presented itself to me when I entered Master Overbury's inner sanctum. Now, on this occasion, the piles were so many and so high, I could scarce believe that it was possible for him to make sense of any of it. Undeterred, however, I came quickly to the point.

'I require your opinion on whether it's worthwhile petitioning the Justices, or as needs must the Sheriff, to authorise Hugh Graveney's arrest?'

Overbury lounged back in his chair and smiled sagely at me. I was conscious that he found me sexually attractive and the feeling was mutual. However, I also appreciated that the smile was mostly induced by the fact that only the previous year in the same room I had sought his advice on precisely the same question in respect to having the wretched Turnbull arrested.

'As you know, Lady Jane, I am ever at your service, but I fear you may be getting a little ahead of yourself in imagining that you yet have sufficient evidence against him…'

'How so? I now know that it was his coach that was seen near the wood where that poor girl died only the day before her body was discovered…'

'Which, with all due respect, could be pure coincidence. You still have no evidence that she was on board the coach…'

'Save that is it credible she'd have walked sixteen miles from Exeter wearing nothing but a red dress without anyone seeing her?'

'Forgive me but have you questioned every person living between Exeter and the wood where her body was found?'

'No, of course not.'

'In which case you cannot say whether she was seen or not. Further, whether she was on board the coach or not, you also cannot say with any certainty where she might have set off from.'

'I now know that her home was in Exeter where Graveney set her up as his mistress…'

'Yes, but it doesn't automatically follow that she travelled from there to the wood. I grant you, it's perfectly possible, but you don't have any witness evidence to prove it, do you?'

'No, not as such.'

'Forgive me, Lady Jane, I am playing devil's advocate with you, but I need to test the merits of your case.'

'Of course you do, Master Overbury, I fully appreciate that.'

'There is also a more fundamental issue that concerns me.'

'Oh what is that?'

'Whether you can even be certain that the woman who was found hanged is the same person who has been identified to you?'

'But surely, she must be. The whore, Janet, who spoke to us this morning, recognised her immediately from my description and told me that she has not been able to find her at home since the body was discovered. Surely, everything fits together perfectly?'

'Did you ask this Janet whether the deceased possessed a red dress?'

I looked round at Olivia before shaking my head, cursing under my breath as I did so. 'But all women of her profession have them.'

Overbury smiled gently. 'Of course, it's but a minor detail. Far more importantly, the body might well have to be exhumed for the purposes of a positive identification. It's fortunate that it's not been in the ground too long.'

'But how is Graveney to explain the disappearance of his mistress?'

'A good question, I grant you, but that supposes that we can take matters to the point where he'll be required to do so.'

'Forgive me,' Olivia interjected, 'I would just like to point out that the East gatekeeper's son saw the coach leave the city and then return the following day, and what's more saw a man sitting in it who answers to Graveney's description.'

Overbury shrugged. 'It would help us far more if he'd remembered seeing the woman. As it is, you'd expect Graveney to be travelling in his own coach so by itself this proves nothing. I've another concern, too, namely that we have no witnesses to the actual death and nothing to tell us why she was killed, if indeed she was...'

'And that's exactly why Graveney needs to be questioned,' I insisted.

'I'm sorry, Lady Jane, but the evidence you've laid before me is entirely circumstantial and Hugh Graveney's a wealthy man with influence in high places. Before any case could be made it would certainly be essential that this Janet, you speak of, was willing to put her mark to a sworn testimony. Do you think she'd do that?'

'I would hope so but she's in fear of the bawdy housekeeper, who in turn evidently lives in fear of Hugh Graveney. At the very mention of his name she took fright and closed the door on me. We were fortunate that Janet overheard our conversation and came after us, but she made it clear that at Graveney's instigation her keeper had told her months ago never to reveal his name to anyone.'

'So, she's placed herself in some danger by speaking to you at all.'

'Yes, I think she has. Even so, I believe she might still be willing to provide what you require. Would you then be willing to petition for me as you did before?'

'I am ever willing to act on your instructions, Lady Jane. There would be my usual fee to meet, of course, and you should understand that even with her sworn testimony my advice must remain that any petition would still be likely to fall on deaf ears.

'So, what more can I do to make a case against this Hugh Graveney?'

'That's a difficult question, I grant you. Discovering a motive for such an evil crime, would certainly be of great assistance. After all, in my experience men do not usually murder their mistresses. Their wives on the other hand…' There was a hint of humour in Overbury's voice but he immediately grew serious once more. 'Then again, find someone who is privy to his affairs and has some knowledge of the actual crime. He clearly had the coach driver as an accomplice in its commission, quite possibly another man as well. They indeed are likely to have strung her up at his command.'

'I'm afraid, all far easier said than done. Still, I've a mind to visit the dead woman's home here in the city. I think I'll make enquiries with her neighbours to discover what they might have seen or heard.'

'A logical starting point, I grant you, Lady Jane, but I would urge you to be cautious.'

'I'm touched by your concern for my welfare, Master Overbury, but have no fear, I have every intention of displaying all due caution. In any event, I'll also give thought to your kind advice and should I wish you to proceed will require your clerk to approach the whore, Janet, for the necessary sworn testimony. Of course, I appreciate that without that nothing at all can be achieved.'

'Try not to be disappointed by his advice,' Olivia said as we walked away from Overbury's chambers.

'I'm not, I assure you. It was really only what I expected, and God knows I cannot afford to waste money on ventures that are likely to end in failure. Thomas would also be less than enamoured, of that I can be sure. I'm loath, too, to place Janet in jeopardy. Perhaps I should just be satisfied with what we have achieved. At least we now know the dead woman's name and have some idea of who she was, but as to why she died and in such a fashion…'

My voice trailed away and Olivia shuddered in recollection of the grim sight of the woman's body hanging from the branch of the tree. 'Shall we go to your sister's now?' she asked.

'Yes, we must or there'll be no point in going at all. With luck John will be out on his rounds.'

Unfortunately, however, that did not prove to be the case and I had no sooner entered my sister's well-appointed town house than I was confronted by my brother-in-law. Despite myself, I stepped back a little, and he did the same, both of us avoiding eye contact with one another, and equally discomfited by each other's presence.

'Good day to you, John,' I managed to which he first responded with a grunt. 'I'm on my way out,' he added. 'I expect, sister-in-law, that you'll be gone before I return.'

'Yes, John, I've no intention of outstaying my welcome.'

'Good.'

He was then confronted by Olivia to whom he managed to be only passingly civil, saying merely, 'Lady Olivia,' and nodding to her before walking out of the door.

'Why does he have to be so insufferable,' she said, quite loudly enough for him to hear her as the door had barely closed behind him.

'You know why, Olivia. He hates us and can barely bring himself to tolerate our presence. He also feels that I am beholden to him. After all, if it were not for Caroline's entreaties, he would have exposed my marriage to Thomas with God knows what dire consequences.'

'Caroline should never have told him in the first place.'

'He dragged it out of her. It was not her fault…'

At that moment Caroline appeared at the top of the stairs, holding her now one year old son, Michael, in her arms. I was pleased to see that both mother and son were looking healthy although I was struck by how stout my younger sister was becoming. By comparison I thought myself still slight of build, my own pregnancies notwithstanding.

'Welcome, dear sister, and to you, Lady Olivia. I apologise for my husband's rudeness. There is much sickness about and he has been working long hours. It always makes him ill-tempered.'

I was inclined to the view that my brother-in-law had been born with a sour temperament but chose to make no comment 'You're looking well, Caroline, and Michael, too,' I said instead.

'And your son, Lucas? I trust he's better than when we last met?'

'Somewhat, yes. Certainly, he is giving his wet nurse fewer sleepless nights.'

That Caroline had chosen to breast feed Michael whilst I had not been willing to entertain doing the same with Lucas, was a matter that I found somewhat ironical given that I suspected my own financial circumstances were far more parlous. However, John had been insistent that no good mother should expect another woman to feed her baby and I knew that Caroline never failed to obey him.

Indeed, I worried that she was completely cowed by him and even believed, having once seen bruises on her arms, that he was not above inflicting physical punishment if she ever dared to cross him. Such a reflection all too quickly brought to mind the aggression that Thomas had shown towards me. I almost shuddered, in fact, at the thought that both my sister and I might have trapped ourselves in cruel unions from which only death would bring release.

By now Michael was beginning to take his first hesitant steps in life and the next ten minutes were spent doting upon him until Caroline suddenly announced that she had some good news. 'I am once more with child.'

'Congratulations, Caroline. When is the child expected?' I asked.

'According to my reckoning it should be born by the end of January. John is naturally delighted'

The more talk there was of babies and the pleasures of motherhood, the more I was conscious of Olivia becoming subdued. It was a tragedy, I thought, that she now faced the prospect of ending her life as an old maid, dependent on the charity of her brother James and Becky. It was still open to her to be a doting aunt to their children, and indeed an equally doting Godmother to Lucas and other children that I might bear, but this could never be the same as giving birth to children of her own.

As quickly as I could I therefore sought to move the conversation on to other matters and in particular began to tell Caroline what I had discovered about the identity of the woman Olivia had found hanging from the branch of the tree. The moment I then mentioned Hugh Graveney's name

Caroline raised her eyebrows.

'He and his wife and children are all John's patients.'

'Really.'

'Yes, he visits frequently. One of their daughters is a sickly child and the wife, Sophia's her name, is also frequently ill. John is well paid for his services. We've even been to their house for dinner on a couple of occasions.'

'You'd consider them friends then?'

'No, I wouldn't quite go that far, but certainly we are well acquainted with them.'

'And what is your opinion of Hugh Graveney?' Olivia asked.

'He's charming enough and a hospitable host…' Caroline hesitated.

'Do I detect a 'but'?' I asked.

'Like many men, he's got a wandering eye as well as a high opinion of himself, boasting of his wealth and power both here and in the Indies. I fancy there's a cruel streak in him, too, but then that's not uncommon either.'

'And his wife?'

'She's very much in his shadow. They're two opposites in fact, for she's quiet and retiring. I think she was once a real beauty, mind, but child bearing and ill health have robbed her of much of her looks.'

'It wouldn't surprise you then if I told you that the woman found hanged was Hugh Graveney's mistress.'

'No, not in the least… Oh my God, you don't suspect him of being responsible for her death, do you?'

'Yes, I do. There's probably not enough evidence to have him arrested, but the very fact that his coach was seen near the wood the day before Olivia discovered the body, makes me think that he was most likely to have killed her, or at least had her killed by one or more of his henchmen.'

'I take it he has many servants?' Olivia asked.

'Oh yes, we were well served at dinner. His house is one of the largest in the city and newly built. You can't mistake it, if you pass along Northgate Street.'

'And I imagine he might well own a house outside the city?'

'Yes, from what he's boasted of in my presence, I know he owns several fishermen's cottages in Topsham and there was talk of our being invited to his country home. I'm trying to remember where he said it was... Oh yes, somewhere near Honiton.'

'You're sure of that?' I asked, a little more sharply than I intended.

Caroline gave me a cross look. 'Well not totally so, but wait a moment, I recall him saying that it was useful to have a house to the east of the city close to the London Road as he had business interests that take him to London from time to time.'

'Thank you, Caroline, that's been most helpful.'

'You're not going to seek further evidence against Graveney, I hope?'

'I don't know. I expect Olivia here would agree with you that it might be unwise. It just frustrates me that any man should be able to get away with murder. Even the dead deserve justice.'

9

Another search

By the time Olivia and I returned to Altringham Manor it was after eight o'clock in the evening so Olivia had accepted my invitation to stay the night rather than ride on to Fetford Hall at such a late hour. Both of us were feeling weary from what had been a long day and Olivia was complaining of being saddle sore. For my part, I had a nagging sense of anxiety over Lucas's welfare, which I knew would only be assuaged once I was able to hold him in my arms. I also simply could not decide whether it was best to leave well alone, or return to Exeter in the near future in the hope of being able to discover more about the sad fate of Jessica Martins.

Short of being able to personally cross-examine Hugh Graveney, I wasn't even certain of where to begin any further enquiries. However, by the time I came to dismount from Hera I had made up my mind that the only logical step I could take would be to visit the house where Jessica had lived as Graveney's mistress. I knew I couldn't expect to find anything more there than a house left empty and bolted, but I had a mind to speak to neighbours in case they could recall seeing or hearing anything that might be of significance.

Toby, the stable lad, came forward as he always did to take the horses to the barn that had become a makeshift stables since the previous autumn. It was then that the murderer and rapist, Turnbull, in an act of arson, had torched the stable block, which remained a blackened ruin. I immediately thought that Toby looked anxious.

'Is something wrong?' I asked him even as I was in the act of dismounting.

'M'lady, soldiers 'ave been 'ere…'

I tensed in fear. 'They haven't…'

'No, m'lady, but the Master's remained in hiding.'

'He's at the old woodman's cottage then, in the woods?'

'Aye, m'lady.'

I turned to Olivia. 'I must go to him, I shouldn't be long although I must see Lucas as well. Have Alice prepare a meal for us.'

'Beggin yer pardon, m'lady, 'e should know, they asked questions o' all o'us. No one betrayed the Master, mind.'

'I should think not, indeed, but thank you for telling me that, Toby. Tell me, did they question the Master?'

'I don't think so, m'lady. I think 'e 'id 'imself away in the wood where they could n'find 'im.'

I made my way to the cottage, counting my blessings that yet again we had enjoyed a narrow escape. After all, three times soldiers had come searching the previous year, on one of which Thomas had only managed to elude capture by going up onto the roof and crouching behind a chimney pot.

After the failed plot to assassinate Cromwell it was always likely that they would come again. However, dressed as he was in the plain attire of a servant, with his hair cut short and clean-shaven, I wondered why Thomas had chosen to hide when he could just as easily have played a game of pretence.

'I know it stood me in good stead when they came searching for me the last time, but I decided not to try my luck that way again in case they started asking too many questions,' he explained to me once I had thrown myself into his arms out of sheer relief at his deliverance from danger.

'Pray God they never come again. The stable lad, Toby, told me that everyone was questioned.'

'So I understand. I think it's as well I decided to hide.'

'Their loyalty is to be commended. I will personally thank each and every one of them.'

But the soldiers surely searched the wood, didn't they? How did you elude capture this time?'

'I went beyond it, across the field to that copse.... What's it's name?

'I don't believe it has one, though I know where you mean.'

Anyhow, had they come that far, I would at least have had a view of them approaching. I had a mind to try and shin up a tree if I had to.'

'Will you come back to the house? Olivia's staying the night.' As I spoke these words I detected a flash of annoyance cross his face.

'No, I think it's safer if I stay here, at least for a couple of nights, perhaps longer. I've been thinking that they could deliberately return at dawn in the hope of catching us unawares.'

'That could still be a risk to you, even here?'

'True, but there's still less risk, I think, and I doubt I'll sleep well. I can be up and ready for trouble even if they should come at dawn. So, how was your visit to Exeter?'

I proceeded to explain as succinctly as I could, expressing my frustration at Overbury's advice that the evidence against

Graveney was too circumstantial to make it at all likely that any petition for a warrant of arrest would be successful. I also made brief mention of Caroline's acquaintanceship with him.

'Call it a woman's intuition, if you like, but I sense he's the kind of arrogant man who thinks himself above the law and is capable of reeking vengeance on anyone who crosses him, even his own mistress.'

'You should be content with what you've discovered and pursue this matter no further. You'll incur my further wrath if you do. Whatever the man's character, from what you say about his owning a house near Honiton, his coach may have had every reason to be on the road where it was seen.'

I shook my head. 'No, I don't think so. Surely it ought to have been on the London Road if that was its destination.'

'Well, you've discovered the woman's name and background. Be satisfied with that. She was no more than a courtesan, after all.'

'Yes, I suppose you're right…But now, I must visit Lucas. You could come with me? And Alice will be preparing supper. At least join me and Olivia for that.'

Thomas was willing to agree to both my suggestions although without the enthusiasm I would have wished for. It had already become apparent to me that he was uncomfortable in the presence of babies and although he was never discourteous to Olivia they seemed to lack any rapport. I wondered, too, if he thought Olivia a bad influence upon me, for all that I believed I had the stronger, or at least the more wilful personality.

As soon as I then set eyes on Lucas, I was troubled and even more so when I gently put a hand to his brow for he was exceedingly hot.

'I think 'e may have a fever, m'lady,' Melissa said. 'It's come upon him in the last few hours.'

'Is he too tightly swaddled, do you think? When did you last change him?'

Melissa looked at me a little sheepishly. 'This morning, m'lady...'

'And you've left him lying in his crib all day?' No wonder he's so hot!'

'I fed him around midday, m'lady, as I always do...'

'Well change him now and don't swaddle him any longer either, at least for a few hours. It's still a warm evening, after all.' Melissa stared at me in alarm at such an order. 'Getting some air to his body can do him no harm, I think. I'll return in the morning and see how he is then. And when you swaddle him again, do so lightly, is that understood. I want him to have some freedom to move his limbs.'

Melissa dropped me a curtsey. 'Of course, m'lady.' And then, albeit a little hesitantly, she also paid Thomas the same courtesy. 'Master.' He responded with a nod of the head.

'I must keep a more careful eye on how Melissa is caring for our son,' I declared to him once we'd departed. 'She would never be deliberately neglectful, I'm sure, but she's got children of her own to care for.'

'Well, it's all women's business to me,' Thomas said. 'But if you've doubts about her, it's all the more reason not to go gadding about in Exeter.'

'I haven't been doing any such thing! First and foremost, I went to Exeter to see my sister and nephew.'

'Come, come, Jane, it was for more than that as you know full well.'

'The end result was still the same and I've told Caroline I'll go back in a month's time. You surely can't object to that?'

He raised a hand as a sign of peace. 'No, of course I don't.'

10

The trail grows warmer

Some four weeks later, on what was turning into rather a blustery and damp August day, I had returned to Exeter as I said I would, with Olivia for company, and we had just left our horses at the livery stables. So far as Thomas was concerned, indeed, for that matter, so far as Olivia was concerned, our purpose in doing so was solely to shop and to visit my sister, Caroline. In the weeks that had passed since our last visit I had given all my concentration to the welfare of both Lucas and Thomas, whilst putting to one side much, if any thought as to the fate of Jessica Martins.

Fortunately, Lucas's fever had quickly abated and with every passing week he had grown a little stronger. Thomas, meanwhile, had remained as restless as ever, and now spent an increasing amount of time fishing. My attempts to restrain him from drinking more than was good for him had also largely fallen on deaf ears although at least there had been no repetition of his threatening behaviour towards me. However, had I been honest with him about my true intentions, I suspected that matters might well have taken a very different course.

'Why are we going this way?' Olivia asked me. 'I thought we were going to visit your sister before going shopping.'

'We're going to visit the house where Graveney set up his mistress.'

'Oh, are we indeed?'

'I hope you're not angry with me?'

'No, nor really surprised either. Have you told Thomas that this was what you were planning?'

'I saw no reason to. Anyhow, I'm not confident that we'll discover anything of value, in which case I promise you I'll let matters lie as they are.'

'Well, I imagine that the house will either be empty or he'll have found a new tenant for it...'

'Or perhaps even a new mistress,' I suggested with a twinkle in my eye.

'You're not thinking that's why he had Jessica Martin done away with, are you?'

'No, I can't imagine he'd have gone to such lengths just because he'd grown bored with her, or found her tiresome. It had to be something far more serious than that.'

'So, are you just going to knock on the front door?'

'I see no reason why not. If anyone answers I'll say I'm looking for... for a Bessy Jenkins...and, of course, they'll say they know of no such person, at which point I'll apologise for troubling them and we'll walk away.'

'So, you'll have achieved precisely nothing.'

'No, not exactly. We'll know that the house has become occupied again, or at any rate that it's not just been totally neglected, and the appearance of whoever answers my knock might just tell us something useful as well...'

'You mean if it's a woman and she's dressed like a whore!'

'Yes, it could be that, but look, that's only a starting point, for I mean to knock on the doors of some of the neighbouring houses as well. If anyone answers, I shall ask them what, if anything, they remember of Jessica, and of any comings and goings. They may remember nothing of any note but it still has to be worthwhile asking the question.'

Number Nineteen, Paul Street, turned out to be a narrow fronted, three storey dwelling at the end of a row of similarly sized properties. It looked to be well-maintained with clean plasterwork, solid looking oak beams, a tiled roof, and lead-paned windows, behind which were closed curtains. This suggested to me that we would find no one at home and this was confirmed when two firm taps on the door produced no response, not even the sound of some movement within.

'Time to try next door,' I said, which involved us in taking no more than a few steps to the door of a property that looked far more run down with shutters rather than windows, peeling plasterwork, and a thatched roof.

At first there seemed to be no response to my firm tap and I considered tapping again when I thought I heard some movement.

'Who is it?' It was a woman's voice and sounded old.

I hesitated, wondering what I could say '...Can you help me? It's about Jessica Martins.'

I half-expected the woman to deny all knowledge of the name. Instead, the door slowly opened and I found myself looking at the kindly face of a woman, whom I imagined must be in her sixties, and who smiled at me somewhat anxiously.

'I'm mighty worried about Jessica. I 'aven't seen 'er in more than two months. Do ye know what's 'appened to 'er?'

I took a long breath. 'I've sad news for you. I'm afraid she's dead.'

The old woman put her hand to her mouth in shock. 'Oh, that be so sad. She was a sweet girl. How d'she die?'

'I've every reason to believe she was murdered.'

'Oh, that be awful. Poor, poor girl.'

'I wonder if we might speak to you in private?' I asked. 'You see, we're trying to find out who might have been responsible for her death, and as her neighbour it's occurred to me that you might be able to give us some helpful information.'

'Aye, ye may, but my 'ome's very simple, mind, and I can see yer fine ladies.'

'Thank you, that's quite alright. Allow me to introduce myself, I'm Lady Jane Tremayne and this is my friend, Lady Olivia Courtney.'

The room we stepped into was dark and possessed no more than two chairs, which the old lady offered us both. Olivia, however, insisted on remaining standing.

'So, would I be right in thinking that you got to know Jessica quite well?' I asked as the old woman took her seat.

'I dunno about that but she was a friendly girl, always 'appy to pass the time o'day.'

'And did she have many visitors, do you know? I'm thinking in particular of any men who might have come to her door. I see you've got a good view of the street from where you're sitting.'

'Aye, she did that, pretty young thing that she was. And I know what she was, course I do. She was just a fancy whore with her made up face and her red dress, but I did'nt 'old that agin 'er. Life's 'ard and she told me once she was an orphan. So it was either that or starve.'

‘Was there one man in particular who came to her door? He’d be in his late thirties with a trim beard, I think, and dressed like a gentleman. His name is Hugh Graveney.’

‘I dunno about any name but a gent came often to ’er door, who looked like ye say. ’E used to come even afore Jessica arrived so I reckon ’e’s the owner and kept ’er there as ’is woman. She weren’t the first, neither. There was another girl, about a year ago now. She not be as pretty as Jessica but still ’ad a ’igh opinion of ’erself. Reckon ’e tired of ’er. I wouldn’t be surprised if she ain’t back in the bawdy house, or begging in the gutter.’

‘And was he Jessica’s only male visitor, so far as you’re aware?’

The old woman sighed and brought her hands together as if in prayer. ‘No, ’e wasn’t. There was a young lad who used to come to her. I doubt ’e be older than ’er, so in ’is twenties. Good looking, too, without any beard…’

‘And well dressed?’

‘Aye, well enough, I’d say. Certainly, I took him to be a gentleman, too. After a while he came more often…’

‘What, as often as Hugh Graveney?’

‘That be ’ard to say for sure, but yes I think ’e did…’

‘And did their paths ever cross, I mean the two men’s?’

‘Not that I know of, but I can tell ’e, I did ’ear some shouting on more than one occasion. I think it was the older man, the one you call Graveney. ’E looks the sort of man to me who’s got a fierce temper if anyone crosses ’im.’

‘So, you’re telling me he lost his temper with Jessica?’

‘Aye, I am. I’m sure ’e even struck ’er once. I ’eard a blow and then ’er screaming out in pain.’

'Can you remember how long ago that was?'

'Let me think. I 'aven't seen Jessica since May and I think it was around then. As it 'appens, I may not 'ave seen 'er at all after that.'

'You don't remember her leaving the house with Graveney? He might even have brought a coach for her. It would have been at the very end of May.'

The old woman shook her head. 'Nay.'

'And what about the young man; have you ever seen him again?' Olivia asked. Again the old woman shook her head.

'Well, I much appreciate what you've been able to tell me and I've just one more question for you,' I said. 'Did Jessica ever speak to you about her situation and any difficulties she might be facing?'

The old woman stared out of the window for a few moments before responding. 'Not as I recall. As I say, she was friendly and we'd pass the time o' day. I think it was when she told me 'er name that she also told me she was an orphan and that both 'er parents died when she was still young, but that's all, I'm afraid.'

'No, no, you've been most helpful, really you have.'

11

And warmer still

Bidding the old lady a good day, Olivia and I returned to the street whereupon I placed a hand on Olivia's wrist.

'I think the young man, the old woman has just told us about could be the key to why Jessica was murdered.'

'You're thinking that Graveney took revenge upon her?'

'It has to be a possibility, yes, and if he still lives we need to find him.'

'But how? We haven't even a name.'

'We need to see inside Number Nineteen!'

Olivia looked aghast. 'We can't go breaking into it and what would it gain us even if it were possible?'

'Perhaps nothing at all, I grant you, especially if it's been emptied of all Jessica's possessions. On the other hand… We should have asked the old woman if she remembers seeing anything of Graveney since Jessica's death…'

'Whether she does or not, he'd look to cover his tracks quickly enough, surely?'

'You'd think so. I agree. All the same, I'd still like to see inside, just to be certain. Look, there's an alleyway here. We might be able to gain access from the back.'

'And be seen by many prying eyes, I don't doubt.'

I glanced up and down the street. There were only a few passersby. 'It's quiet enough. Come.'

The alleyway was narrow and dark and we quickly came upon a tall, wooden gate that clearly afforded access to a yard at the back of Graveney's house. I then turned the gate's handle but it failed to open.

'It was never likely to be left unlocked,' Olivia said.

'No, wait, I think all that's preventing me from opening it is a bolt. I might be able…'

On tip toe I then managed to reach over the top of the gate and feel for the bolt, which I drew back.

'We're in luck,' I said with a grin.

'But not yet inside the house. That could still be a lot harder to achieve.'

As was to be expected, I found that the back door to the house was firmly locked and the lead-paned window next to it was small. I examined it closely.

'If I could but break the glass pane nearest the window's handle, reach inside and turn it, the window should open.'

'But would you be able to climb through it, seeing how tiny it is?'

'Not in any dignified manner, I grant you. But with your help I think I might just be able squeeze through. My dress will hamper me, of course.'

'More than that, you could ruin it. And besides, how do you propose to break the glass? Shattering it is also bound to attract someone's attention.' Olivia looked about her nervously. Fortunately, the yard was in a secluded position and not much overlooked save by one window to our left. 'What if they run for a Constable to arrest us?'

'If it were to come to that, I'd be prepared to bluff it out. For all any Constable would know, this could be my home, and I'd say I'd lost my key. Anyhow, I need an object with which to break the window.' My eye fell upon a rusting piece of metal that looked as if it was a discarded poker, once used for the fire. 'I think this would do the job, very well.'

'No Jane. In God's name, this is madness. I know you're impulsive but…'

Apparently oblivious to Olivia's appeal, I simply picked up the poker and prepared to thrust it at the window whereupon Olivia tried to restrain me by placing a hand on my right arm. 'Please, Jane,' she hissed. 'Listen to me!'

I shook my head. 'I mean to get at the truth of what happened to Jessica…'

'Break that window and you will put Graveney on his guard. Think of that.'

'I doubt it. If you leave a property empty you always run the risk of a break-in. He'll think some vagabond has been in search of valuables, nothing more.'

'And what if they're there and we fail to take them?'

'We were disturbed and fled with nothing. He does not know us, don't forget.'

'He or one of his men might have chosen this hour to return…'

'I'll take that risk.' And with that I aimed the poker at the pane nearest to the window's handle and thrust it forward. The glass instantly shattered and Olivia gasped at the noise of it doing so.

'Christ, Jane, what have you done?'

'Courage, Olivia, I need to knock out more of the glass so I can safely get my hand around the handle.'

'Wait! Is that someone coming?'

We both tensed in fear. I had at least closed the gate behind us but had left it unbolted, reckoning that to do otherwise might impede a hasty departure should that be required. The sound of footsteps came closer, but then faded away as the individual, whoever they were, continued on their way along the alleyway. As quietly as I could I then proceeded with the task in hand until I felt able to safely turn the handle and the window swung open.

'You need to help me get inside, Olivia, and then keep watch.'

The window had opened wide enough and was also sufficiently low to the ground for me to be able to clamber through it. All the same, if I had not had Olivia holding onto me from behind, I might have easily landed head first on the parlour's stone floor. As it was, I was able to break my fall with my hands before landing in an undignified heap.

'I'm alright,' I reassured Olivia. 'I'm just going to see if I can open the back door.'

Although this had been locked, its key was hanging conveniently by a hook on the wall next to it so I was quickly able to let Olivia in.

'I thought you wanted me to keep watch?'

'Now I've been able to let you inside, I've changed my mind. We can be that much quicker if two of us search.'

'But search for what, exactly?'

'Letters, I hope.'

'She was most likely unable to either read or write.'

'Perhaps, but remember she was more than just a common whore. I don't suppose she was stupid, either. 'I'll go straight upstairs to the bedrooms. You search down here.'

I ran up the stairs only to feel slightly nauseous when I reached the landing. I dismissed this, however, as no more than an effect of the tension to which I had exposed myself, not to mention the shock and exertion of practically falling through a narrow window. Taking some deep breaths, I steadied my nerves and went into the first of two bedrooms.

It appeared to contain nothing more than a bed with a bare mattress and a chest of drawers along with an empty vase on the window sill and a chamber pot on the floor next to the bed. Going straight to the chest I found every drawer to be empty and then quickly looked underneath both the bed and its mattress without finding anything. Finally, I decided to check if there might just be a loose floorboard under which might be hidden what I was looking for, but a close inspection revealed nothing, even when I managed to push the bed to one side.

By now I was beginning to feel nauseous again. I was fearful, too, that I had taken a considerable risk for no good purpose and could only pray that the second bedroom wasn't just as empty. I was just about to step inside it when Olivia appeared.

'I've found nothing,' she told me.

'Nor I in the first bedroom I looked in. Help me search the second. The sooner we're out of here the better.'

As we entered it was immediately apparent to me that this must have been Jessica's boudoir. There were florid chintz curtains at the window, made of calico , a four poster bed made up with sheets, a blanket and pillows, a wardrobe, a travelling chest, dead flowers in a vase on the window sill, and, on a small bedside table, various bottles, containing what I took to be perfumes and powders.

'If we're going to find anything it will be here,' I declared.

'It doesn't look as if it's been touched since she died.'

'I agree, in which case we may just be in luck. Look in the wardrobe and I'll see what's inside this chest.'

Olivia flung open the wardrobe doors to reveal a number of dresses as well as shoes whilst I opened the chest. I found that it was mostly full of bed linen and there was no sign of any paperwork.

'See if there's anything under the wardrobe or perhaps even on top of it,' I said. 'I'll check the bed. I won't give up until we've checked the floorboards as well. If any of them are loose, what I'm looking for could just be hidden underneath.'

'One thing I can't see is any jewellery box,' Olivia said.

'That's been taken, for certain.'

'So any letters are likely to have been taken as well?'

'...unless they were hidden. Keep looking. There's still just a chance...'

Having looked under the bed my eyes were drawn towards a picture hanging on the wall above the travelling chest. The walls of the other bedroom had been completely bare and this single picture in Jessica's boudoir was a black and white print depicting a three masted sailing ship. I decided to look behind it and as I did so a thin bundle of paper, bound together by some blue coloured ribbon, fell onto the top of the chest in front of me. It was Olivia who spoke first.

'My God, Jane, this could be what you're seeking.'

As I picked the bundle up and undid the ribbon, I could immediately tell that it consisted of just three sheets of paper.

'Look at this, Olivia, they're love letters...see *My darling Jessica...*'

'And the signature?'

'*Your obedient servant, James Lovell.*'

At that moment I heard a banging sound and wondered if it might even be someone knocking on the front door of the house.

'Time we departed,' Olivia said anxiously.

'Yes, I want to be able to read these at our leisure.' And with that I thrust the letters down the cleavage of my dress.

12

A body in the river

The first opportunity I had to peruse the contents of the three letters, was when we reached my sister, Caroline's house. I only did so briefly but it was enough to tell me that whoever James Lovell was, he had been madly in love with Jessica. Frustratingly, the letters were undated and, at least at a first glance, gave no indication of where the man lived. All the same, as I came to the third letter and quickly read it, I noted that it was urging Jessica to come away with him and *escape the clutches of that cruel man.* Here, perhaps, was a motive for her execution. Graveney had somehow discovered that she was betraying him and had exacted the most terrible of punishments.

It had never been my intention to remain with my sister for long and although John was blessedly absent when we arrived, Caroline was quick to inform us that he was expected to return by two o'clock at the latest. It was the perfect excuse to depart as soon as we had eaten, whilst I explained that Olivia and I had some shopping to attend to before we returned home. However, though this was perfectly true, I had also made up my mind that I wanted to instruct Master Overbury again in the hope that he would be able to trace James Lovell.

'I mean to discover his whereabouts,' I told Olivia as soon as we had said our farewells to Caroline.

'I thought you'd say that.'

'You sound as if you're hostile to the idea.'

'Not so much that, Jane. Rather, let's just say that I am wary of the risk we'll be taking if we keep on with this. If Graveney is like some vengeful snake then we could end up dead like poor Jessica Martin.'

'But we've come too far to give up now, especially with a lead as good as the one these letters have given us. I see no reason why Overbury and his clerk couldn't trace this James Lovell, just as they did Graveney, and Lovell's testimony could be enough to hang Graveney, or at least cause him to be arrested.'

Olivia looked sceptical. 'Any knowledge that he might have of Jessica's fate may be no better than suspicion.'

'Perhaps, but we simply will not know until we ask him.'

'And if he does have any evidence against Graveney, why hasn't he come forward with it?'

'For all we know he may be too frightened to do so. At any rate, I say we should visit Master Overbury's chambers before we leave Exeter. It need not take us long.'

'Oh very well, if we must.'

As I entered the familiar surroundings of Master Overbury's chambers, his clerk rose to greet me with all his usual deference. If he was surprised to see me return, he did not let it show on his face, and with perfect politeness volunteered the information that his Master was in court and was not expected to return until late in the afternoon.

'I rather expected he might be, but it is really you, good Sir, who I think can be of most assistance to me on this occasion. You see I've now discovered that Jessica Martins, the woman I believe Hugh Graveney had executed, had taken another lover named James Lovell. I have his letters to her here on my person. They say nothing as to his place of abode but I'm confident it must be here in Exeter, or certainly close by, otherwise I struggle to imagine how they could ever have become acquainted. What's more I have a description of him, of sorts. Apparently, he was in his twenties, clean-shaven, and wearing gentlemanly attire. Do you think you could find him for me?'

'I see no reason why not m'lady but you say the man's name is Lovell?'

'Yes, quite so, James Lovell ...'

'It's just that the name's familiar to me... Yes, it comes back to me now. I'm sure he's the one whose body was found floating in the river Exe.'

'When was this?' I asked, my stomach turning a little at this unwelcome news.

'It be about eight weeks ago now.'

'So around the time that Jessica Martin was found hanged?'

'Yes, though I'd never seen any connection between the two events until now. Anyhow, it was the talk of the tavern I like to frequent on the waterfront. A drinking companion of mine was present at the inquest and told me the dead man had been identified as Lovell and that he was young and from an upstanding family in the city. As I recall, he mentioned that his father's a merchant like Graveney with a fine house in Goldsmith Street.'

'And the inquest's verdict, did he mention that?'

'Oh yes, he said it was accidental death. Apparently there were no marks on the body to suggest foul play and the lad couldn't swim. He also said that no one came forward to give any evidence as to how exactly he'd ended up in the river, but the conclusion was that accidental death by drowning was the most probable cause.'

I turned to face Olivia. 'This smells of foul play to me.'

'It could still be a coincidence, even if his body was found at the same time as the girl's. We should even countenance the possibility that he took his own life.'

'Out of grief, you're suggesting, having discovered that Jessica was dead?'

Olivia nodded. 'Though that would depend on whether he even knew she was dead. For all we know, he might have been the first to die.'

'Whatever, I don't see this as being a case of suicide, any more than I believe Jessica hanged herself.'

I turned to face Overbury's clerk, once more. 'I don't suppose the body had been in the river long?'

He shrugged. 'I've no idea, but if you're thinking days, or even weeks, I'd say that's most unlikely.'

'So, what do you propose to do now?' Olivia asked me as we walked away from Overbury's chambers.

'Ride home, of course. It's too late to do anything else today.'

'But thereafter? I mean, you're not going to let matters rest as they stand, are you?'

'No, certainly not. At the first opportunity I want to speak to James Lovell's family. They may well be able to throw some further light on what happened to James and whether he really did just drown by accident.'

'And what will you say to Thomas? He'll not take kindly to your pursuing this quest of yours, and if you're not honest with him, what excuse will you find for coming back here to Exeter so soon after today's visit?'

'I'll think of something, though God knows I don't like telling him lies.'

'So you'll tell him all about our criminality today, will you?' The tone of Olivia's voice had now become teasing.

'No, I can't! And don't you dare tell him anything either.'

'Fear not, Jane, I wouldn't dream of it. After all, it reflects as badly on me as it does on you.'

'But had we not broken in I'd never have discovered those letters and we'd be none the wiser as to James Lovell's existence.'

'And perhaps all the better for that. I still fear that the closer we come to unravelling this mystery, the more danger we may face.'

'But don't forget our purpose is to gather sufficient evidence to warrant an arrest. After that, let justice take its course.'

By the time we returned to Altringham Manor, I was no nearer to deciding on what excuse I might make to justify an early return to Exeter. True to my word I was also careful to say nothing to Thomas of what Olivia and I had discovered, so for all he knew I had entirely put behind me any interest in the sad fate of Jessica Martin.

For the next few days I then pondered whether I should be honest with him about my intentions, but in the end, for all that I knew it was deceitful of me, I decided to shy away from this in order to avoid any confrontation. Instead, when I next rode over to Fetford Hall, I told Olivia to expect another visit in a week's time in the early morning and to be prepared to depart for Exeter as soon as I arrived.

13

Another line of enquiry

Having left our horses at the livery stables, Olivia and I had little difficulty in locating the whereabouts of the Lovell's House in Goldsmith Street, albeit that we were somewhat discomforted by a heavy shower. It was accompanied, too, by a blustery wind, which threatened to blow our hats off our heads, while a passing cart managed to splatter our dresses with mud. This caused us to reach the front door of what a neighbour had assured us was the correct address in a somewhat dishevelled state. Undismayed, I then knocked firmly, and within a few moments the door was opened by a fresh-faced maid, who looked as if she might be no more than fourteen.

'I take it that this is the Lovell's residence; are either your Master or Mistress at home?' I asked her.

'Yes, ma'am, and who shall I say's asking for 'em,' the girl replied in a strong local accent.

'Tell them that Lady Tremayne, widow of Sir Paul Tremayne of Altringham Manor and Lady Courtney of Fetford Hall, have come to pay their respects and offer their condolences concerning their late son, James Lovell.'

The maid duly showed us into what was a spacious hallway of a substantial town house, which looked to me as if might date from the reign of Queen Elizabeth or possibly even a little earlier. Its three storeys and large windows were a testament to the wealth of whoever had had it built, whilst the fine wood panelling on its interior walls were a clear indication that this wealth had been fully maintained.

Moments later the same maid stood to one side to allow us to enter a wood-panelled parlour room that was now bathed in sunshine, the heavy shower having abated as quickly as it had arrived. I was immediately struck by the pleasant scent being given off by a large arrangement of wild flowers in a vase standing on a substantial, well-polished oak table. I thought that this was likely to be the work of the lady of the house, and looking around was struck by a painting hanging above the fireplace depicting a handsome young couple together with three young children. I assumed this could only be the Lovell family. Moments later, a gentleman entered the room.

'Good morning to you both. I am Edward Lovell, the father of the late James Lovell,' he said with a gentle Devon accent.

Appearing to be about fifty years old, with greying hair and neatly-trimmed beard, he was soberly dressed in black as was to be expected, but not, I surmised, a Puritan for he was wearing a starched lace collar, which I knew my brother-in-law, John, would have denounced for its vanity. I was also struck by the warmth of the smile that he gave me in greeting while looking me straight in the eye in an open and honest fashion. Behind this I thought I detected a certain melancholy but then that was hardly surprising.

'So, dear ladies, I am grateful to you for wishing to offer myself and my wife your kind condolences, but forgive me if I ask what causes you do so? Were you ever acquainted with him?'

'Sadly, Sir, we were not,' I said. 'We have, however, come to have some knowledge of a certain Jessica Martin and of the love that your son had for her.'

His eyes widened in surprise. 'Have you indeed. How is that, may I ask?'

'Of course, you may. I must explain that it was my friend, here, Lady Courtney, who discovered Jessica Martin's body hanging by the neck from the branch of a tree in woods close to Fetford Hall at the end of May…'

'But that's when James's body was discovered…'

'So I understand, and it is my firm belief that she was murdered, indeed executed, although for what reason I cannot yet say.'

'I told James that no good would come from him courting a courtesan like her.'

'I see. Did he also tell you then whose courtesan she was?'

'Yes, it was when he did so that I became particularly concerned.'

'You've no time for Hugh Graveney then, I take it?'

'Assuredly not. I think the man a thorough scoundrel, though I could not prove anything against him in a court of law. He's cunning and slippery as any eel.'

'And do you believe that he might even have been responsible for your son's death?'

'That I do not know, but I have my suspicions. Certainly, he has henchmen in his employ who I think are capable of committing acts of murder at his direction.'

'Well, I have grounds for believing that he ordered the death of Jessica Martin. You see, a coach he owns was seen in the vicinity of the woods the day before her body was discovered.'

Until now Edward Lovell had remained quite composed but now he began to pace up and down in an agitated fashion. 'The day before his body was discovered in the Exe my son told me that he had something important that he wished to discuss with me. I was busy at the time but we agreed to talk that evening. Then he went out and I never saw him alive again.'

'And he gave you no idea what this was about?'

'He said it concerned this whore of his as well as Hugh Graveney. I was about to go out on an important business matter and cut him short. I wish to God now I'd let him have his say there and then.'

'So, this is why you don't believe your son died by accident?'

'Indeed, and now you tell me that she died at the same time as he did, I'm even more convinced of it.'

'Is it true he could not swim?'

'Yes, it is. Yet I still don't believe his death was purely accidental.'

'And I'm curious as to how your son and Jessica Martin came to meet,' Olivia said. 'Did your son ever explain to you how this happened?'

'Yes he did, once. According to him it was quite by chance. Their paths frequently crossed as he would see her walking with her maid and thought her captivating. One day, I'm not quite sure how he contrived it, they fell into conversation, and I suppose the attraction must have been mutual. His infatuation with her was certainly a powerful one. My wife even thinks she bewitched him but I don't believe in such nonsense.'

'You say she had a maid?' I asked, excitedly.

'That's what he told me.'

'I don't suppose he ever mentioned her name to you?'

'Not to my recollection but he could have done to my wife, Margery.'

'And nor, I suppose, would you know what's become of this maid?'

'No, not at all, but you might care to ask my wife the same question. She's gone shopping as it's market day but I expect her to return at any time. If you care to wait for her, I would like to offer you both some refreshment.'

I glanced quickly at Olivia who gave me one of her knowing smiles. 'Yes, we would be happy to wait, and thank you, I would welcome a glass of beer, if you have some to hand?'

'And I,' Olivia added.

'I will see what can be fetched from the kitchen.' With that he walked to the parlour door and called out in a commanding tone of voice before coming back to us.

'Forgive me, but I in turn have a question to ask of you. I understand your concern that a young woman, whatever her station in life, may have been murdered…'

'I would say it amounted to an execution.'

'Perhaps it did, and all the more terrible for that, but even so what has that to do with you? I take it you did not know anything of this woman before her death?'

'No, Sir, that's true enough,' I answered him. 'We are pursuing the interests of justice against a most evil deed, are we not Olivia.'

'Yes, quite so,' Olivia affirmed although far more diffidently.

I began to think that I detected an air of condescension in Edward Lovell's manner towards both myself and Olivia. Perhaps he was thinking that we were mere meddling females straying into what was rightly a solely male preserve.

'I am a widow and a landowner in my own right,' I asserted, for all that this was no longer really true following my secret marriage to Thomas. 'Only last year I was instrumental in exposing a murderer and rapist who might have otherwise have continued to commit such vile crimes'

'And that is entirely to your credit, my dear lady. Please do not think me critical of your endeavour, I am merely curious.'

At that moment Margery Lovell made her appearance, greeting Olivia and me in a perfectly pleasant manner, although I thought I could detect an air of sadness about her that was almost palpable. Dressed in black as befitted a mother in mourning, she looked flushed as well as somewhat older than her husband, though again I wondered if the rigours of age were simply treating her less kindly.

'My dear, these ladies have come to express their condolences upon the death of James and have been able to bring some interesting news. They tell me that the courtesan he was so enamoured of is also dead in the most cruel manner and that this occurred at much the same time as James's. What is more, they think that she was put to death and that this could have been at the instigation of none other than Hugh Graveney.'

'That dreadful man,' Margery Lovell exclaimed.

'Quite so, my dear, and what they have now told me only serves to heighten my suspicion that he may have been responsible for James's death, too.'

'Yes, I would agree,' I said. 'There's no doubt in my mind that these two deaths are connected.'

A light tap on the door was then followed by the entrance of the same maid who had let us into the house , bearing with her a tray with two glasses and a jug of beer. On what was an increasingly warm day despite the rain, I was grateful to be able to quench my thirst before asking the question of Margery Lovell that was most on my mind.

'Your husband tells me that the dead woman had a maid and I wondered if your son might ever have mentioned the maid's name to you? It would only ever have been in passing, I expect.'

'No, I'm sorry. I don't believe he ever did. You must appreciate that his relationship with that whore caused me deep distress. I understand the ways of the world and that a pretty young woman can all too easily turn a man's head but he even spoke of marrying her and I told him in no uncertain terms that this was unthinkable. We are a respectable family of some standing in this city, are we not Edward?'

'Of course we are, my dear, of course we are. Though it saddens me to confess it now, when I learnt of his intention, I told him that I'd cut him off without a penny if he married her, for all that he was our only surviving son.'

Margery Lovell caught her breath at these words and Jane could immediately tell that she was on the point of bursting into tears.

'Forgive us for intruding upon your grief,' I said.

'It is a cross that we must bear. One day I hope to meet my son again in heaven.'

Meanwhile, the maid had re-entered the room carrying another glass, Margery Lovell having also expressed her wish to quench her thirst. However, having set the glass down she appeared to hover in the background as if reluctant to leave.

'You may go, Joan,' Edward Lovell told her firmly.'

'Excuse me, Sir, but I couldn't 'elp over'earing the lady's question to the mistress.'

'Yes, what of it?'

'Well, I think I know the maid. 'Er name's Nancy and I see 'er around the city. I saw 'er last week, in fact, in the market place.'

'How do you come to know her?'

'She be the daughter of a friend of my mother's, Hester Grey. We used to play together when we were children. Some months ago, when we 'appened to meet she told me she'd become a lady's maid in Paul's Street. I asked 'er who this lady was and she blushed and told me that she was the mistress of a certain gentleman, going by the name of Hugh Graveney. His name meant nothing to me, but, begging yer pardon, I've 'eard 'is name spoken of a lot since Master James died.'

'And would you know where this Nancy lives?'

'Well, I expect she still lives with 'er mother and father in North Street. Their address be number thirty-one, as I recall.'

I was determined to seek out Nancy as soon as possible in order to establish if she was capable of throwing any more light on what had happened and Olivia understood this perfectly without the need for any conversation between us. Edward Lovell, too, was also equally cognisant of this intention and made a point of wishing us well with our endeavours.

'I'd be grateful indeed if you'd keep me informed of what you may discover. I'm not without wealth and influence in this city and I'll willingly offer you whatever assistance I can. Graveney and I have been rivals for many years and I've never liked him, so let me make myself clear that if he was responsible in any fashion for the death of Edward, I want him brought to justice.'

14

A cargo of brandy

'I believe that Jessica's maid may well be able to throw yet more light on this affair,' I asserted boldly to Olivia as we made our way into North Street.

'I agree so long as we don't discover that she has mysteriously disappeared,' Olivia cautioned me. 'After all, should she have any vital knowledge of what took place I'd imagine that Graveney would know of this and want to shut her up.'

'There's that danger, I grant you. We can but hope that she's still alive and willing to talk.'

The terrace of cottages we were now approaching looked to my eye to be very old and little better than hovels, with thatched roofs in poor condition, blackened walls, and only single storey in height. The particular address we were looking for was the second to last of these and possessed a door barely five feet in height, which was in such a poor state that it was possible to see through its cracks into the dark interior.

I knocked once, hoping as I did so that this time I was about to discover a really crucial piece of information. Almost immediately a woman opened it, who looked old before her time and also malnourished, so thin was she in both face and body.

'Yes, what can I do for thee?' she asked in a gentle if slightly hoarse voice, which suggested to me that she could be consumptive.

'Excuse my intrusion,' I responded, 'but I'm looking for a girl called Nancy Grey. Might you be her mother?'

'Aye, I am, but ye'll not find 'er 'ere. She 'ave live-in work as a parlour maid at a gentleman's house, in Southgate Street. Ye can't miss it. It be built of red brick and be the largest in the street. What ye want with 'er?'

'It concerns her former mistress, Jessica Martin.'

'Um, from what Nancy's told me, she's nothing but a whore, so I'm glad she's free of her.'

'Indeed she is, Madam. Jessica died at the end of May.'

'Did she now. Well I mustn't speak ill of the dead then, God rest her soul.'

Under skies that were once again darkening with a threat of further rain, we quickly moved on in the direction of Southgate Street. Here, we easily came upon a fine-looking, brick-built residence, which appeared to date from the reign of King James. In stark contrast to the humble dwelling we had just visited, its large front door possessed a portico to afford protection against the elements, and my knock was soon answered by a young maid with freckles as well as some red hair protruding from underneath the cap she wore.

'We've come in search of Nancy Grey,' I explained whereupon the maid looked at me in surprise.

'But that be me.'

'It's about your former mistress, Jessica Martin. If we may, it's important that we ask you some questions about her.'

'Who's there, Nancy?' This question came from a woman looking to be in the prime of life, wearing a lilac-coloured dress, which to my eye was likely to be made of silk, and whom I took to be the mistress of the house. It was not only her dress that was striking, either, for she was quite tall for one of the fairer sex, with curly, auburn-coloured hair, and possessed of such well-proportioned features that I thought her quite beautiful.

Coming closer to the door the woman's face broke into a welcoming smile and I introduced both myself and Olivia before seeking to explain the purpose of our visit. 'We do not wish to intrude, of course, but we wonder if we might be able to speak to your maid? It need not take more than a few minutes and we believe that she may have knowledge of certain events that could help us resolve the mystery of what happened to the poor woman, Jessica Martin, whose body was discovered close to Fetford Hall, some two months ago.'

At these words Nancy let out a cry of anguish and burst into tears. 'I knew it, I knew it,' she wailed. 'How did she die?'

'I'm sorry to tell you that she was found hanging from the branch of a tree. There was a suggestion that it was suicide, but the coroner's jury were persuaded to enter an open verdict and I firmly believe she was murdered.'

'Well, you are both welcome to come inside, the mistress of the house told us, having introduced herself as Margaret Baker. 'You may have as long as you need to speak to Nancy, though you'll forgive my curiosity in asking you why you're pursuing this enquiry?'

'Madam, we are doing so in the interests of justice and because, if we do not, I believe no one else will.'

'Well, very laudable of you, I'm sure.'

We were then shown into a library with such an array of books on its shelves that I couldn't help but be impressed.

'My husband, Andrew, is a Judge of Assize,' Margaret Baker explained.

'I see. In that case I imagine he must know my lawyer, Gilbert Overbury,' I said

'Yes, he often speaks well of him… I'll leave you now. As I said, take as long as you need.'

For her part Nancy still looked distinctly upset so Olivia decided to offer her a handkerchief, which she gratefully accepted.

'When did you first start working for Jessica?' I asked her quietly.

'It be last autumn, m'lady. I'd been working as a scullery maid for Master Graveney at 'is house 'ere in the city and 'e suggested that I might like to be a lady's maid. 'E told me that 'e'd pay me more and that me hours of work would be more agreeable.'

'And was that true?'

'Oh, aye, and I liked my mistress, too. She was kind to me. I thought of her as a friend.' Again her lip began to quiver and she brought the handkerchief to her eyes.

'And what did you think of your Master?'

At this question Nancy screwed up her face. 'When I was but a scullery maid in 'is big house, I didn't see 'im much at all, and even when I did 'e just swept past as if I barely existed. Sometimes, I'd 'ear talk from other servants that 'e 'ad a short temper and I remember one saying that 'e'd been struck by 'im because 'e did something which displeased 'im. Once I remember 'earing 'im shout out in anger and then 'earing 'is wife crying. It made me wary of 'im and I was really surprised when 'e asked me if I'd like to be a lady's maid…'

'And once you took up your new position, what happened then?'

'For a while it went well. As I say, me and the Mistress liked each other. Mind you, she used to cry sometimes, saying that Master Graveney could be cruel and made her do things for 'is pleasure she didn't like. Once when she refused 'e 'it 'er and I could see the bruise on 'er cheek. And then-...well...'

'She met James Lovell, I suppose.' Nancy nodded. 'You see we found you through visiting his parents and speaking to their maid Joan, who said she knew you, and then your mother. Do you know that he's dead, too?'

Again Nancy nodded. 'That I heard. Drowned in the river by all accounts.'

'Do you believe that could have been an accident?'

'I suppose it could but when Master Graveney discovered that the Mistress was being unfaithful to 'im 'e was mighty angry. I wouldn't put it past him to have had Lovell killed...'

'Did you ever hear him utter any actual threats against Lovell's life?'

'Oh yes, I did, more than once. Mind you, if I'd been in 'is shoes I'd 'ave been angry, too, I expect.'

'Do you know how Graveney came to discover that your mistress was having an affair of the heart behind his back?' Olivia asked.

'From what the mistress told me, she and Lovell weren't careful enough. Someone in Graveney's employ saw 'em both together and reported this back to 'is Master. Perhaps 'e was already suspicious and sent 'is man to spy on 'em.'

'We've been quite surprised to discover that your mistress could read. We'd rather assumed that she was from a poor background,' Olivia commented.

'T'was the war that forced her into poverty, so she told me. It left 'er an orphan but when 'er parents were alive she was taught to both read and write.'

'So when did you last see your mistress?' I asked.

'It be close to the end of May. Graveney came to the house. 'E was in a mighty temper and told me my services were no longer required. 'E gave me a few minutes to get me belongings together, paid me a shilling, and told me to leave and stay away if I knew what was good for me.'

'And that's all you know?'

'No, there be more. Two nights afore I was dismissed 'e came to the house and I over'eard 'im accuse 'er of being a spy…'

'A spy! Why should he say that?'

'I didn't 'ear all that was said, but I did 'ear 'im say that the Lovell's be 'is enemies and wished 'im only 'arm. And then 'e said somet'ing about a landing of tea being surprised by troops. 'E said she must 'ave informed on 'im. She begged 'im that t'is wasn't true but 'e wouldn't listen. 'E seized 'old of 'er. There was a bit of struggle and then 'e left.'

'So did your Mistress say anything to you about this allegation against her?'

'Yes, she was most upset and I gave 'er what comfort I could. She repeated 'er denial of 'aving spied on Graveney…'

'You think it was completely without truth then?'

'Well, she did tell me she was present when a man, she did not know 'is name, spoke to Graveney about a certain ship.

'E named it the...the *Saint Claire*, and said that it 'ad arrived off the coast near Sidmouth and was ready to land its cargo o'brandy...'

'It seems surprising to me that Graveney would have such a conversation in front of Jessica,' Olivia commented. 'Did she tell you how this came about?'

'E used to take 'er out sometimes in 'is coach. I think she said the man approached them on a 'orse and 'e and Graveney then fell into conversation, which she could not 'elp but over'ear.'

'And that was all? I mean, she never spoke to you of anything else that she might have overheard?'

'No, she never did. I'd swear to that. But look I don't want ye telling anyone 'twas me that told you any of this. If Graveney be cruel enough to 'ave murdered both my mistress and 'er lover, I don't imagine 'e'd think twice about doing the same t'me.'

'So I take it you wouldn't be prepared to put your mark to any statement then?'

'No, nor would I go into court.'

'Even if you were offered protection? Remember, you're servant to a judge. Graveney wouldn't be able to touch you.'

'Wouldn't 'e now. I'm not so sure about that. I'd be forever looking over my shoulder.'

'Not once he's executed for his crimes.'

'Maybe not then, I grant ye, but it's what 'e might do t'me afore 'e was ever put behind bars that worries me.'

'Well, I still thank you for what you've been willing to tell us today. It has helped bring us closer to the truth,' I said.

15

Frustration

'So, what do you propose we should do now?' Olivia asked me once we had left the Baker's residence.

I shrugged. 'It's difficult. If Nancy won't give evidence against Graveney, we may be no further forward with this endeavour.'

'...Except that we now know that she was probably murdered, not just out of jealousy but because she was thought to be a spy.'

'Yes, and it's possible she was one for all that she denied it to her maid. What she learnt, whether by accident or design, of this landing of brandy, no doubt an exercise in smuggling, she could very easily have passed on to James.'

'But surely that would have led to Graveney being accused and so far as we know that has never happened.'

'Yes, that is a fair point, I grant you. However, even if she did, do not imagine that she would have been any more willing than Nancy has just been to swear on the bible to what she overheard. In that event, what information she might have given James could simply have been enough to ensure that a watch was put on the coast. It's possible, too, that he was hoping she might discover something even more damning.'

'Are you suggesting that he was just making use of her?'

'I don't know but it has to be possible that right from the very beginning their whole relationship was just a means of getting at Graveney…'

'In which case his father would surely have been a party to such a scheme…'

'Quite so. And more than that, he could even have been its prime instigator. Either way, I think we should go back and speak to him again. Mind, I don't know about you, but I'm feeling hungry.'

Once we had partaken of a simple meal of bread and cheese in a nearby inn, we duly made our way back to Goldsmith Street where I once again knocked on the Lovell's front door. I felt anxious not to make unfounded allegations. However, Edward Lovell had assured me of his desire to be of further assistance should we require it and in the first instance all we would be doing was informing him of what we had gleaned from Nancy. After that I would have to tread with care. The same maid as before showed us into the wood-panelled parlour and within a few minutes Edward Lovell joined us.

'This is an unexpected pleasure, dear ladies. I did not imagine you would return so soon,' he said with a welcoming smile.

'It is good of you to receive us again,' I said. 'I'm pleased to say we've been able to speak with Jessica's maid, Nancy, and I wanted to share with you what she has told us. It introduces a fresh aspect to this affair, which you might be able to assist us with.'

Lovell seemed to tense a little. 'Oh yes, and what might that be?'

'The maid told us that she overheard a conversation in which Graveney accused Jessica of being a spy, and, what is more, a spy on behalf of your family. He apparently said that he regarded you as an enemy.'

'That puts it somewhat strongly, I think. We have certainly been close rivals for many years as I have told you already.'

'She also said that what provoked this accusation of spying was the seizure by troops of a smuggled landing of brandy on the coast near Sidmouth. Further, Jessica admitted to being present when someone, probably a henchman of Graveney's, approached him with news of this landing. He even mentioned the name of the ship…the *Saint Claire*.'

'Yes, I'm aware of the seizure to which you refer.'

'I see. I must ask you if that's because you reported the landing?'

Lovell now looked at me angrily. 'I don't like the tone of your voice, Lady Jane'

'Forgive me, Sir, I do not wish to cause offence. All I am striving for is the truth. I must therefore respectfully suggest that you were in fact perfectly happy for your son to court Jessica, because the central purpose, perhaps indeed the sole purpose, was to extract as much useful information out of her as possible. Is that not so?'

Lovell opened his mouth to reply, his face still contorted with anger and then hesitated. He put his hands to his eyes and seemed almost on the point of collapse as he staggered forward slightly. When he took his hands away from his eyes, I could see tears in them.'

'Sir, I'm sorry to cause you such distress,' I said.

'Your words are like a knife to my heart but…I must confess that what you have suggested is largely true. The pain of it is that I will have to live with this truth to the end of my days. James and I were close. He was my only surviving son and very dear to me. He told me he'd encountered this attractive whore and discovered, I recall him saying it was from her own lips, that she was the kept mistress of Hugh Graveney, who had set her up in her own house with a maid to do her bidding. God forgive me, I thought this could be a heaven-sent opportunity to expose Graveney's machinations at last…'

'So you actually encouraged the relationship?' Olivia asked in a somewhat more judgemental tone than I expect she intended.

Lovell stiffened. 'Let us say that I did not discourage it. James was young and I was prepared to be indulgent towards his dalliances with whores, remembering my own youth. I said to him he needed to be careful, both of the dangers of the pox and of Graveney's anger, but that if he chose to ingratiate himself with the woman and could extract any information from her that might damage Graveney I would welcome it.'

'So he did indeed come to you with the information concerning the *Saint Claire* that Jessica had given him?'

'Yes, yes he did. We discussed it and agreed that whilst it was right that I report what he'd discovered it was also vital to protect Jessica. James was fearful she would be in danger if the source of this information became known and that he would not expect her to act as a witness against Graveney while she was still his mistress and beholden to him in every way. Indeed, he stressed that he had not encouraged her to spy on

Graveney and that she had volunteered what she had overheard because she was upset by the way he had treated her.'

Lovell drew breath. 'And there is something more that I must say. My son told me frankly that he had fallen in love with this woman and wished to marry her. He also said that he would not endanger her any further. I was angry with him and so was his mother but I believe it just made him more determined. I suspect that he wanted to rescue her and it was this that he wanted to talk to me about just before he died.'

'But why have you not sought to expose Graveney since your son's death?' Olivia asked. 'After all, you know that he was involved in smuggling.'

'Until now I've have had some compunction against doing anything to endanger the woman, believing that she was still alive. I also know that none of the men seized with the landing of tea have confessed to any knowledge of who owns the *Saint Claire*. They simply took orders from their captain, whilst the ship itself has sailed away.'

'But he had to be involved,' I insisted. 'The conversation that Jessica overheard must have been true otherwise the watch placed on the coast would have come to nothing.'

'Ah, but I've been mindful of the fact that Graveney's mistress never heard the word *smuggled* mentioned. She was bright enough to gather that this was probably what was intended, but according to James the words she heard said were that the ship had arrived off the coast and was preparing to make its landing of tea. I see nothing to prevent Graveney claiming that although it was indeed his ship and his cargo, he gave no orders for this to be smuggled ashore but rather to be properly brought into harbour.'

'Then who else would have done so?'

'Why the captain and crew of their own volition as an act of theft.'

'But that's preposterous.'

'Not necessarily. It's happened before, I can tell you.'

'I would still urge you to put your evidence before the Justices. Ultimately, it would be for a jury to decide where the truth lay.'

'But you forget Graveney's influence. I wouldn't think it beyond him to bribe his way out of trouble. Even if the Justice was resistant to his overtures, some jury members could well succumb to them, and don't forget either that there are many who don't even see smuggling as a crime.'

'When the landing of tea was seized were any men killed or wounded?' Olivia asked.

'By all accounts one of the smugglers had his arm shattered by a bullet but otherwise I think not. Even if convicted, I could see Graveney escaping with nothing more than a stiff fine, which he could well afford to pay.'

'Even so, it would still surely *clip his wings*,' I suggested.

'A little, I agree. I'll think on the matter, but I make no promises.'

I couldn't help but feel an acute sense of frustration as Olivia and I left the Lovell's house. We had come so far in unravelling the truth behind Jessica's death but now it seemed we could go no further. Edward Lovell might decide to bring a charge of smuggling against Graveney, but as he had made plain that might well not achieve anything whilst, above all, there still seemed to be insufficient evidence that any murder had been committed.

'I am wondering if we should go back to Nancy and seek to persuade her to give evidence against Graveney.'

'But what good would that do? It's not as if she heard him confess to murder.'

'Her evidence would still support Lovell's in any charge of smuggling. It would also help paint a picture of a man with a motive for murder.'

'Perhaps it would be better if we returned to Overbury and discussed what we have discovered with him?'

I shook my head. 'I'm not sure I see the point. He'd agree that she'd make a useful extra witness to a charge of smuggling but I can hear him telling us that any evidence as to murder remains entirely circumstantial. What we need is someone close enough to Graveney to know the truth of what really happened, who's prepared to turn against him. Remember, he won't have ever acted on his own. It was surely another man, or men, who actually strung Jessica up and dumped James Lovell in the river, having no doubt first knocked him unconscious .'

'But they're murderers themselves; they'd never say anything that might put a noose around their own necks.'

'No, but I expect they'll have wives and sweethearts to whom they might well make admissions when in their cups that they'd never utter when sober…'

'Just as likely they'll be hard men, to whom the keeping of secrets in any circumstances, drunk or sober, is second nature.'

'One or more of them could still be disaffected by Graveney. I fancy men like him make as many enemies as they do friends and can all too easily trample on others' pride, or fail to reward them as they would wish.'

'Even so, I doubt if anything less than a full pardon signed by the Lord Protector himself would make any of them give evidence against him. I tell you, Jane, give this matter up. You've done all that you can and more besides. Think of your son and your husband and be satisfied.'

I sighed. 'Yes, you're right, of course. It just rankles with me that a man like Graveney should literally be allowed to get away with not just one murder but two. And wait, we're forgetting something important, Nancy recalled that Graveney actually threatened to kill James Lovell…'

'But threats such as that are often made in a fit of anger; it does not follow that they are seriously meant. It still proves nothing…'

I held up a hand in resignation. 'True enough, I suppose.'

'Just let it be, Jane, just let it be.'

16

Alarming news

A few days later I was trying to enjoy the late summer sunshine by taking a little stroll around my rose garden. I was concerned that Lucas was not developing as I would have hoped and feared for his ability to survive his first winter, which I could only pray would not be too harsh. I was endeavouring, too, to reconcile myself to not being able to do anything more to bring Graveney and his henchman, whoever they might be, to justice. With the passage of time I expected my sense of frustration would abate, but for the present it continued to bring me restless nights and put me into a thoroughly poor humour.

This had played a small part in my becoming irritable with Thomas for drinking too much and taking too little care of himself. When he had made amorous advances towards me, I had shoved him off, complaining that he stank of strong beer and sweat and needed to take a bath. In response he had sworn at me and gone off in a sulk. That had happened only an hour previously, and I had seen nothing of him since, so I assumed he had gone fishing, as he did most days at the least excuse. I was coming to understand that he was a man who enjoyed his own company, and could be solitary to a fault, especially if I said anything which upset him.

I heard the sound of approaching footsteps and turning round saw that it was Mary coming towards me holding in her hand what looked to be a letter.

'This has come for ye, m'lady. The rider who's brought says it's from Edward Lovell.'

'The rider's been offered some refreshment, I trust?'

'Yes, m'lady. He's presently in the kitchen.'

Taking the letter from Mary, I quickly broke the seal.

Dear Lady Jane

I send you my felicitations and wish to inform you that I am still considering whether to lay a charge of smuggling against Graveney. Further, I thought that you should know without delay that I have received a message from Mistress Baker informing me that her parlour maid, Nancy Grey, has gone missing and that she is concerned for her welfare.

Her message tells me that after your visit Nancy was distressed and told her that she was fearful that what she had told you might place her in danger. She spoke, too, of the fate of my son, and explained that you found her through enquiries with myself and our maid, Joan. We have some acquaintanceship with the Bakers and Mistress Baker's message asked that I passed on the news to you of Nancy's disappearance. Her message ends by saying that her husband has spoken to the Sheriff and alerted him to the possibility of foul play.

Certainly, I share Mistress Baker's concern, and fear that even if Nancy's life is not in danger there must remain a possibility of her being taken abroad and sold as a slave to the corsairs. This may well both surprise and horrify you but I believe that Graveney is involved in piracy and is not above such a practice. To my certain knowledge he owns a merchantman, the Bellerophon, presently anchored in Topsham Harbour and I am taking steps to have a watch placed on it as well as upon his house here in Exeter. I will keep you advised of any further developments.

Your obedient servant,
Edward Lovell, Esquire

I was taken aback by this news, feeling an intense sense of guilt at the reflection that it could well have been my actions that had led to Nancy's disappearance and possible death. It was entirely probable that it had quickly come to Graveney's attention that the house he had set Jessica up in had been broken into, and that could well have made him suspicious of the possibility that someone, most likely Edward Lovell, was seeking evidence implicating him in the crime of murder. This, I could only assume, had been enough to encourage him into seeking to eliminate the one person still living who was likely to have some knowledge of the accusations he had made against Jessica and the threats, too, he had made against James Lovell.

By the time Thomas reappeared, his face reddened by too much exposure to the rays of the sun, and complaining of a headache, which I put down to an over-consumption of strong beer, I had decided that I must return to Exeter at the earliest opportunity. Rather than admit my true purpose, I merely told him that I once more intended to visit my sister, Caroline.

'But it's no time at all since your last visit,' he complained.

'I told her that I would return regularly, bearing in mind that she is pregnant again.'

'And regardless of the fact that you and her husband, John, dislike each other so much?'

'We are careful to avoid each other's company and I will only stay for a few hours.'

'So when will you go?'

'Tomorrow, at first light, I think. I'll take Mary with me.'

He gave me one of his quizzical looks and for a moment I feared he was going to question me further. 'Oh very well, if you must,' he said instead.

In many ways I would have much preferred to take Olivia with me, but I feared she might well remonstrate with me. Nor could I expect her to be ready for an early departure without due warning because I was anxious to give myself the maximum amount of time to visit both Edward Lovell and Master Overbury.

In both instances I was determined to use all my powers of persuasion to encourage them to take action. In the case of Edward Lovell, he would surely now understand the importance of pursuing a charge of smuggling against Graveney, whilst at the same time I was determined that Overbury should now support me in bringing a charge of murder against him.

I spent a somewhat restless night continuing to feel guilt over Nancy's fate but also a sense of unease as to whether I had acted too impulsively in deciding to return to Exeter so soon. I could hear Olivia's voice in my ear telling me repeatedly to *let it be, just let it be.* After that, I remembered little else until I was woken by sunlight streaming into the bedroom through the gap I had deliberately left between the curtains. I could also feel the weight of Thomas's body next to mine and gently eased myself out of bed. It was as well that the late summer weather was still set so fair, for had I woken to a wet and overcast morning I feared my resolution to make this journey again so soon might have been all too quickly extinguished.

It was already later than I would have preferred, and, by the time Mary and I finally set off on our journey, later still. Thomas, meanwhile, having drunk far too much beer the previous evening, remained in a nearly insensible state and gave me no more than a semi-conscious groan when I assured him that I would return by nightfall. I had deliberately said nothing to Mary about the purpose of our visit to Exeter, just as I had never previously taken her into my confidence concerning the investigation Olivia and I had carried out into Jessica Martin's death. Now I pondered if the time had come to do so.

'Mary, there's something I need to say to you,' I finally began.

However, even once I had told her, I realised there remained one thing more that needed to be said. 'And you must understand, too, that so far as anyone at Altringham Manor need be concerned the sole purpose of our journey today is to visit my sister, Caroline, and my nephew, Michael. In truth, though, I intend to visit both Edward Lovell and my lawyer, Master Overbury in order to discuss with them the disappearance of Jessica's maid, Nancy. Perhaps, after that, if there is sufficient time, I may call briefly on my sister... And there's no need to look at me in such surprise, Mary. Master

Thomas has not been altogether approving of my endeavours so I prefer that he remains in ignorance of what I intend doing today. We understand each other, I hope?'

'Of course, m'lady.'

Upon our arrival in Exeter, once we had left our horses at the livery stables, I kept to my plan of going first to the house of Edward Lovell. By now the weather had clouded over somewhat, but it remained warm, whilst the long summer had caused there to be an excess of flies and noxious smells emanating from both animal and human activity. It made me feel pleased to live in the countryside where the air was far fresher and there was less reason to fear the rapid spread of disease.

The closer we had come to Exeter the more I had worried that I would be unable to speak to either Lovell or Overbury because both would be too busy. Certainly, there was always a risk that Overbury would be in court. It would be ironic and also frustrating if in the end the only person I was able to see was my sister, but I was almost reconciled to this possibility as I came to knock on Lovell's front door. Sure enough, too, the maid who answered was quick to inform me that her master was out at present.

'But 'e's expected to return within the hour, m'lady...If you'd care to wait?'

'No, but do tell your master that I called and that I will be back. I am anxious to speak with him.'

Mary and I then made our way to Overbury's chambers where his clerk informed me that his master was not in fact in court but presently attending on another client. 'They've been together for a good half an hour, m'lady. I don't expect they'll be much longer.'

This time I decided to wait and within a quarter of an hour my patience was rewarded as I heard the door to Overbury's inner sanctum open and heard his familiar, well-spoken voice bidding his client farewell. An elderly man, his hair and beard turned a silver white, then walked slowly by me on his way out of the building before Overbury came to greet me, smiling warmly.

'Lady Jane, this is an unexpected pleasure. You wish to speak with me?'

'Yes, if you can kindly spare me a few minutes of your valuable time?'

'Most certainly.'

'You see, there has been another development, which much concerns me.'

Although as seemingly chaotic as ever, with paperwork scattered in all directions, I appreciated the ambience of Overbury's inner sanctum with its wood-panelled walls and many volumes of dusty legal tomes. It was also something of a relief to be able to speak to him in confidence in a way which I did not dare to do with Thomas, knowing how unsympathetic he had become to what he regarded as a dangerous obsession. I had also come to trust Overbury's judgement and was hopeful of persuading him that this time Graveney had gone too far.

'I can understand your distress at what has occurred and you have every right to be suspicious,' he told me once I had finished telling him about Nancy's disappearance, as well as the background to this and my sense of guilt that I might be to blame for her fate. 'However, I don't see that this as yet materially alters the situation. You still have no positive evidence that Graveney is behind what has occurred, whilst, if I were to present a case to either the Justices or the Sheriff based on your testimony, how am I to explain how you have acquired the knowledge that you have without revealing that you trespassed on Graveney's property and caused damage to it by breaking a window?'

'But it was the only way I could think of to try to get to the truth of what occurred and had I not done so I would never have discovered the letters. Look, I have them with me.' And with that I pulled them out of the pocket of my riding coat, which I had chosen to keep on.

Overbury proceeded to peruse them and then looked up once more. 'I grant you that this is evidence of her amour with James Lovell…'

'At a time when there can surely be no doubt that she was Graveney's mistress. What's more, Edward Lovell can give evidence of everything he was told. There is no question in my mind that Jessica was executed, not just because of her love for Edward's son, James, but because he thought her a spy! And now Nancy has disappeared because my breaking into Graveney's house has alerted him to the fact that she remains a threat to him, given what she knows.'

'Following the logic of your argument, you would have thought he would have previously eliminated her in much the same way you believe he eliminated Jessica and James?'

'Perhaps until now he saw no risk of anything she might say being used effectively against him. Now, following the break-in, he's decided that she might do so, after all.'

'Yes, that's plausible, I suppose, but all this is still a tissue of suspicion when it comes to bringing any charge of murder…'

'You'd agree, though, that Edward Lovell ought to lay a charge of smuggling against him?'

'I agree that he could seek to do so, yes. Certainly, the seizure of the landing of brandy appears to lead back to Graveney's door, although, from what you tell me of Edward Lovell's thoughts on the matter, I would share his concern that he might not get very far with the accusation. If I were you, I'd also be very careful about your own continued involvement in this matter. If Graveney is as dangerous a man as you fear, and gains any knowledge that you are primarily responsible for trying to bring him down, he might well seek his revenge.'

17

I'm not feeling very well

My meeting with Overbury had not been as successful as I would have wished but I was not greatly discouraged. Most positively, I would not fail to tell Edward Lovell that my lawyer supported a charge of smuggling being brought against Graveney, and that after what had now apparently happened to Nancy, he should hesitate no longer in bringing what he knew to the attention of the Justices. I was also disinclined to pay too much heed to Overbury's cautionary advice.

At first, however, although Lovell was perfectly courteous, he made it clear that he still had significant doubts about pursuing any case against Graveney on the grounds of smuggling.

'I regret that my reservations remain as they were and I am still not convinced that any such charge would prevail. But look, I believe that we are now playing for even higher stakes. If we can but apprehend some of his henchman in the act of trying to take this girl aboard *The Bellerophon* we might well be able to substantiate a charge of kidnapping against him.'

'Surely, she's already dead,' I exclaimed. 'Perhaps thrown into the river like your son, James, strung up like her former mistress, or, more likely, just lying in undergrowth somewhere with her throat cut.'

'There's every possibility of that, I grant you. All the same, I fancy he would have decided to have her questioned, perhaps even threatened with torture, before going that far. After that, he could well have decided that selling her to Corsairs was a better option than killing her. Of course, it's occurred to me that if he's had her questioned, he now knows of your involvement in this affair as well as that of Lady Courtney. I'd be very careful, if I were you.'

'My word, sir, you're the second man in less than an hour to give me that same warning.'

'Then all the more reason to take heed of it.'

'And how do you come to suspect him of having dealings with Corsairs?'

'It's mostly rumour, I must confess, but the odd unguarded comment has also been overheard in taverns, and some of his henchman are dark-skinned enough to be Moors although they do not dress like them. My suspicion is that he trades goods with them, tea and the like, taken by piracy, and in return his captain has a safe harbour to put into when he needs it.'

'Then Graveney's no better than a Corsair himself!'

'I agree.'

'But would he really go so far as to sell an Englishwoman into slavery, and why should the Corsairs pay up when they can snatch women a plenty for nothing on one of their raids?'

'I believe she'd be treated as if she were cargo. In other words sold or bartered along with a consignment of tea or wool. But look, if the girl is conveyed to Topsham harbour, I've put my men there under instructions to endeavour to affect a rescue before she can be taken on board ship.'

‘That’s bold of you, I must say. If Graveney’s men put up any sort of resistance it could well result in deaths on both sides. What’s more, I can envisage them threatening the girl’s life to protect their own.’

‘Should it come to that the Justices will be alerted so they would soon find themselves surrounded, either by constables or troops.’

‘Even so, if they could manage to get her aboard ship, they could still slip anchor and sail away, couldn’t they?’

Lovell shook his head. ‘I’ve a ship of my own in harbour and I’ve alerted the captain to the situation. He’s ready to obstruct any attempt *The Bellerophon* might make to reach open water.’

‘Then you would appear to have covered every eventuality.’

‘I’d not go that far. I’ve done what I can and now we can but wait.’

‘Yes, but for how long exactly? Graveney could keep her under lock and key indefinitely if he chose to. And even if he does try to get her out of the country, I fancy his men would only make their move in the dead of night.’

‘I’m prepared to have a watch kept on the harbour for a fortnight at least. By then, if the girl is in fact already dead, her body may well have been found.’

For a few moments there was a silence between us as I looked out onto the street and pondered what I should do next. Perhaps, after all, there was time to visit my sister before returning home.

‘But you know,’ I said, turning my eyes towards Lovell, ‘if I were Graveney, assuming that you’re right and the girl still lives, the last thing I’d do is hold her in my own house here in Exeter, which she could well recognise, or, for that matter, seek to take her out of the country by way of Topsham …'

'Did you not just say, Lady Jane, that I had covered every eventuality?'

'Yes, but I was too quick to do so. If the girl still lives, the chances are she's being held somewhere in the country that means nothing to her. What's more, if I was intent on selling her to Corsairs, I'd have her taken to a cove somewhere and then rowed out to *The Bellerophon*, or some other ship that Graveney owns; perhaps even the *Saint Claire*, wherever that might be at present.'

'What you say makes sense, I must confess.'

'And from what my sister's been able to tell me, given her husband's Graveney's doctor, he not only has his house here in Exeter where they've been entertained by him, but also owns a country estate somewhere near Honiton as well. Nancy could very easily be held in a cottage there. Though wait, my sister's also told me he owns a row of fishermen's cottages in Topsham. If any are unoccupied, it's possible she could be there instead. All the same, I'd still say it's more likely that she's being held in the country.'

'Do you think you could establish exactly where this estate is?'

'It's possible my lawyer might be able to find this out for me. Making suitable enquiries in Honiton might also prove fruitful, and as you're watching his house there must also be the option of having his coach followed. Should it leave the city through the East Gate then the chances are it will be heading for the estate…' At that moment I was unable to suppress a yawn, and it struck me how tired I had become.

'Forgive me, I'm somewhat fatigued. I must leave you in order to pay my sister a visit before returning home. What will you do now, may I ask?'

'If she's being held in any fisherman's cottage in Topsham, then it should be possible to find her. Otherwise, I'll consider what you've suggested about having his coach followed…'

'But you'll still not bring a charge against him of being a party to smuggling?'

'Let's wait and see if Nancy can be found first… If not, then I may yet seek to do so.'

Feeling reasonably content that I had now done all that I could, I duly paid Caroline a brief visit, explaining away my late arrival with the vague statement that I had had business to attend to and this had delayed me longer than I had intended. At least John was out on his rounds and I was pleased to find both her and Michael in good health. Then, after a stay of barely an hour it was time to leave, and, having collected our horses from the livery stables, Mary and I rode the short distance towards the East Gate. It was as we were approaching it that I was barely able to suppress a gasp of surprise. Only a short distance ahead of us I could see a black coach being pulled by two horses, one of which was as black as the coach itself.

'Mary,' I said quietly, having pondered this development for no more than a few moments,' I do believe that the coach ahead of us belongs to Hugh Graveney, the very man whose actions brought me to Exeter today. I mean to follow it as far as Honiton, if necessary. Perhaps, if needs must, even a little further.'

'But m'lady, if ye do that, we'll not be 'ome afore it's dark.'

'Quite possibly not, but that's a risk I'm prepared to take. With luck, its destination will be well before Honiton, in which case we may still just be home in the light. I mean us to keep our distance from it, too, so however slowly it travels we must remain well behind it, just so long as we don't lose sight of it altogether.'

'And what if it halts, m'lady?'

'Um...we'll have to halt, too, but God willing it won't come to that. We've not yet seen the onset of any autumn rain so the road should still be in a fair condition.'

In the event, with the weather remaining clement, the coach made quite rapid progress, its driver clearly being under instructions to encourage the horses to keep to a fast pace. As a consequence, even though we kept well back, I could still hear him applying a crack of the whip and urging the horses forward, so that within two hours, with the evening coming on, we were due north of Ottery St Mary and only some five miles west of Honiton.

By now, though, the relentless pace was beginning to take its toll on the horses leading the coach, and for all the coachman's continued cracking of the whip, they were travelling at a noticeably slower pace. This was something that I could only welcome as I was conscious of Hera beginning to tire and of Mary's horse becoming even more distressed.

'I think my horse might drop if we don't stop soon,' Mary complained.

'Ease back on the reins then. We're on a straight enough stretch of road and I don't mind if the coach is barely within sight.'

We continued like this at no more than a trot with the coach gradually gaining on us to the point that it was little more than a dot in the distance until I saw it almost halt and then slowly turn to the right in a southerly direction.

'Come on, we don't want to lose her now,' I declared, encouraging Hera forward into a canter. 'And don't worry if you can't keep up with me, Mary, I fancy the coach has taken the lane that leads to Alfington.'

By the time I reached the turning, the coach had been out of sight for nearly a minute and Mary was now some way behind me. 'I'm riding on,' I called out to her. 'Follow me as best you can.'

The lane proved to be narrow and tree lined on both sides. Further, as I continued along it at no more than a steady trot for the best part of half a mile, I became increasingly frustrated and even fearful that the coach had somehow disappeared into thin air. Then, as I came round a bend, I just caught sight of the rear of the coach turning off the lane through an open gate, which I imagined must be the entrance to a house or estate.

Instantly, I brought Hera to a halt, but, even as I did so, a man appeared at the entrance and looked in my direction. I was sure he must have come from the coach, presumably with the intention of shutting the gate behind it, and my instinctive response was to turn Hera round and go back the way I had just come. However, I was soon cursing under my breath as I realised I had done the one thing I'd been at pains to try and avoid, namely drawing attention to myself in a manner which might well suggest that I'd been deliberately following the coach.

As I rode on I could feel myself being overcome by an overwhelming sense of lethargy, which far exceeded the tiredness I had felt whilst in Exeter. It worried me that I was sickening for some dreadful illness, and it required all my determination not to slip out of the saddle onto the ground.

'Are ye alright, m'lady? Mary's voice sounded both concerned and strangely distant to me despite the fact that we were now almost side by side.

'I'm afraid I'm not feeling very well. Mind you, at least I saw the coach pass through some gates. I'll need to inform Edward Lovell what we've discovered but for now let's try and get home while there's still some light.'

'Forgive me, m'lady, wouldn't it be better if we went through Alfington and then Ottery St Mary?'

'Um, yes, I suppose it would. It's just…' I didn't in fact say it but I was somewhat reluctant to ride by the gate that the coach had passed through for fear that we might be accosted for one or more of Graveney's henchmen. However, I decided to shrug this off. At the same time my lethargy seemed to be intensifying. Suddenly, I felt myself slump forward in the saddle, momentarily losing consciousness.

'I…need…water,' I managed to say before feeling myself falling. The ground seemed to be coming up to meet me, I heard a scream that was strangely distant, and then I blacked out completely.

18

Lady Olivia's diary

I was sitting in the long gallery at Fetford Hall, glancing out of the window occasionally and daydreaming of my lost love; the man I would have happily married and borne children by if he had not been so cruelly taken from me in a bloody civil war. Now I was reconciled as best I could be to dying an old maid, finding consolation in the love of my family, my friendship with Jane, and my Christian faith.

Meanwhile, my sister-in-law, Becky, now three months pregnant, was in good health, and I was delighted for her as well as looking forward to becoming an aunt for the first time. I was minded, too, to ride over to Altringham Manor to give Jane the good news, but that very morning the weather had broken with a thunderstorm accompanied by a heavy downpour of rain and a dramatic fall in temperature, presaging the arrival of autumn. I had therefore decided to put my mind to some needlework but as midday approached my concentration was flagging somewhat.

I then thought I heard the sound of a whinnying horse and glancing out of the window once more saw that a male rider was approaching, undeterred by the elements, for all that he and his horse appeared thoroughly soaked. I almost immediately recognised him as being Jane's steward, Harry Parsons, and felt an immediate sense of alarm, thinking first of Lucas, given that it was Harry's wife, Melissa, who was wet nursing the child.

'Oh my God!' I cried, putting my hand to my mouth and rising to my feet. This had the effect of startling my mother, Constance, who had fallen asleep in a chair opposite me.

'What on earth is it, Olivia?' she asked me.

'I fear something awful has happened. It may be…' Failing to complete the sentence for fear that by doing so I might be tempting faith, I instead pointed out of the window and then hurried towards the front door of the hall. I had it open even before Harry had dismounted and called out to him as calmly as I could.

'Good day to you, Harry. What on earth brings you here in such foul weather? Not bad news, I trust?'

'I fear it may be, m'lady. Two days ago my mistress set off for Exeter, accompanied by her maid, saying that she intended to visit her sister and would return by nightfall. Unfortunately, we've seen nothing of her since and Master Thomas has sent me here to enquire of you whether you've seen anything of her?'

'No, nothing at all, I'm afraid. I expect she's been delayed in Exeter for some good reason.'

'I do hope so, m'lady . Master Thomas has asked me to proceed there without delay, assuming you had no news of her.'

'Let me come with you. I can be ready to leave in less than thirty minutes, I swear it.'

Harry looked doubtful. '…But the weather's bad, m'lady.'

I glanced westwards and shook my head. 'No, it's already brightening,' I declared optimistically. 'Anyhow, my hat and riding coat will protect me.'

In the event, I was ready to leave in little more than twenty minutes, accompanied by anxious good wishes from both Constance and Becky as well as a look of concern from James. 'Take care, sister,' he said knowingly. I had been frank with all of them about what I and Jane had discovered about both Jessica Martins and James Lovell.

'Of course I will,' I assured him.

'If what has happened here has any connection with the likes of Hugh Graveney, make certain that you do.'

'I promise I will,' I said, with a wave of the hand, before Harry and I rode away on a journey that would take us some two hours in conditions that continued to be blustery and wet, although by the time Exeter came in sight the rain had finally stopped. We had also been sustained by some bread and cheese and a flagon of beer, which Constance had insisted on supplying us with. The latter was strong enough to make me feel a little light headed and also helped to relax me somewhat, notwithstanding my growing sense of anxiety over what might have become of my dearest friend.

We made our way directly to Caroline's house, having enjoyed a companionable enough journey together, and even as I dismounted gratefully from my horse I decided to remain optimistic.

'God willing, Jane will be here to welcome us. I expect she's suffered no more than some minor ailment or mishap, which has indisposed her.'

Even as I knocked on the door and heard footsteps approaching my optimism began to slip away, however, and it took just one question, put to the maid who appeared, to cause it to evaporate completely.

'I was hoping that Lady Tremayne and her maid might be here?'

'Oh no, m'lady. They were here for a time two days ago, but not since.'

Caroline soon appeared and was mortified when I had to inform her that Jane and her maid had failed to return to Altringham Manor and that their whereabouts were completely unknown.

'Did she make any suggestion to you that she did not intend to ride straight home?' I asked her.

'No, not at all. It was late afternoon when she left and she was not with me for more than an hour or so.'

'So, did she tell you she'd been anywhere else first?'

'As I recall, she said she'd had some business to attend to with her lawyer...'

'Gilbert Overbury, you mean.'

'Yes, I think that was the name she mentioned. She gave me no details and I did not press her. I must say that I thought she looked both tired and somewhat anxious but for what reason I cannot tell you. What on earth could have happened to her? Surely, if some dreadful mishap had befallen her and her maid, we'd have received some news of it by now?'

'Yes, you would think so unless...'

'You're not thinking they might have been... I mean, victims of some foul play?'

'I pray not, of course. Look, I am going to try and speak to Jane's lawyer and there is someone else as well I have in mind to whom it would be worth making an enquiry.'

'Who is that?'

'Edward Lovell, the father of James, whose body was found floating in the river Exe. Jane and I discovered that he was the lover of Hugh Graveney's mistress, Jessica Martin, and that she was the woman whose body I discovered hanging from the branch of a tree in woods near Fetford Hall. We were suspicious that Graveney had a hand in both their deaths and we spoke with Edward Lovell about our suspicions….'

Caroline gave a horrified gasp. 'Are you suggesting that Hugh Graveney might also have a hand in Jane's disappearance?'

'I am fearful that it could be possible, yes.'

'Oh why in God's name do the two of you involve yourselves in such terrible matters. Last year Jane could so easily have been killed by that dreadful man, Turnbull.'

'Jane is impulsive, as you well know, and has a keen sense of justice. I try to restrain her when I can but it isn't easy.'

'Um, she is not merely impulsive but wilful, too.'

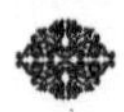

I entered Edward Lovell's house with a rising level of apprehension about the fate of my best friend that threatened to reduce me to tears. I might easily have gone first to Gilbert Overbury's chambers, which but I had a keen sense that coming here first was likely to get me closer to what had happened. I then needed to take several deep breaths before finding the courage to knock on his door, only for the maid who answered it to frustrate me with news that her master was out on business. Nor did she know when he would return.

'Might I be of assistance to you?'

The question was asked by a woman whom I took to be in her fifties and the lady of the house. She had an air of calm authority about her, and whilst wearing a black dress of mourning, had a gold ring on her wedding finger, and around her neck a gold chain and locket.

'Good day to you, I am Lady Olivia Courtney, a close friend of Lady Jane Tremayne. I am wondering if you can tell me if she visited here two days ago? It's just that I am extremely concerned for her welfare as she and her maid have disappeared.'

'Oh dear, I am very sorry to hear that. I am Louise Lovell and my husband told me that she and her maid were indeed here when you suggest. She came in response to a letter he sent her…'

'Did he tell you what the letter said, may I ask?'

'Yes, it told her that Judge Baker's parlour maid, Nancy Grey, if I recall her name correctly, has gone missing. My husband has been most concerned for her welfare and I understand that he and Lady Jane discussed what might have become of her.'

'And did he by any chance also tell you what conclusion, if any, they might have come to?'

'Yes, he said that it was Lady Jane's opinion that if she was not already dead, she might well be a prisoner of Hugh Graveney's at his country house. He said she thought that this was somewhere near Honiton and that his coach ought to be followed in order to establish exactly where. He agreed with her that this was quite possible and told me that he was prepared to do as she suggested.'

At this news I felt my fear for Jane's safety grow even deeper. If Nancy was Graveney's prisoner then in all probability she would have been threatened into telling one of his henchmen what she knew, not only of his hatred of James Lovell, but also of what she had revealed to both Jane and myself. In that event, he might well have come to perceive Jane as a threat.

'There is more that I can tell you,' Louise Lovell added.

'Oh really what is that?'

'My husband has thought it possible that Nancy Grey might be taken on board one of Hugh Graveney's ships, *The Bellerophon*, which is anchored in Topsham harbour. However, he told me that Lady Jane thought it more probable that she would be rowed out to a ship offshore under cover of darkness…'

I was puzzled. 'Forgive me, I don't quite understand why she would be taken onboard a ship?'

'My husband believes that Hugh Graveney may be in league with certain Corsairs and is capable of selling Nancy to them as a slave.'

'My God, surely not!'

'Some years ago now, when in his cups, a sailor who'd been on board one of Graveney's ships started bragging that it had been used for piracy on the high seas and sailed out of a North African port.'

The thought that Jane, too, might now have been kidnapped and could therefore be at as much risk as Nancy of being sold into slavery, made my stomach turn over with fear. Everything I knew about Jane's character was also telling me that she was more than capable of having tried to find Nancy through her own initiative and that left open two likely possibilities, the first that she was being held somewhere in city.

'I can also tell you that my husband has had a watch put on both *The Bellerophon* and Graveney's house here in Exeter.'

'And that has revealed nothing as yet, I assume.'

'Not up to this morning, no.'

This information suggested to me that it was more likely that Jane was being held elsewhere. I also thought of one way of establishing this with some measure of certainty. Thanking Louise Lovell for her kind assistance, I told her that I intended to make enquiries with the keeper of the East Gate. 'Hopefully, he may be able to tell me if he remembers Lady Jane leaving the city.'

'And will you return once you have done so?' Mistress Lovell asked. 'I expect my husband to return within the hour and I imagine that he would like to speak with you.'

'Yes, most certainly, I will.'

The gatekeeper scratched his head at my urgent question. After all, as he then pointed out, there were so many comings and goings through the gate and the days quickly merged together.

'It would have been late in the afternoon, only two days ago,' I emphasised.

'The black coach passed through the gate, I remember that.'

'Really! Which way was it going?'

'Out of the city; yes, definitely out.'

'But not two women on horses? They'd would have been riding side-saddle and Lady Tremayne, you should remember. She's a handsome woman with a fair complexion.'

'Yes, it comes back to me now. I did see her, of course I did, and it was no time at all after the coach had left. She even turned her face towards me, gave me a nod and wished me a good day.'

19

Pursuit

I was duly encouraged by what I'd discovered and still accompanied by Harry, decided to return to Edward Lovell's house immediately. He had still not returned, but I decided to be patient, and within a quarter of an hour he did so and was visibly shaken by what I had to tell him.

'It is clear to me that Lady Jane and her maid followed Graveney's coach but what happened thereafter we can only speculate upon,' I said. 'My own surmise, however, is that somehow or other they were taken prisoner and are probably being held somewhere in the country.'

'Unless by now they are either both dead or have been placed under cover of darkness aboard a ship lying offshore. Even as we speak, it may already have set sail for the Barbary coast,' Lovell replied sombrely.

'Do you seriously believe that Graveney is unscrupulous enough to be in league with Corsairs, of all people?'

'I can only tell you what I've heard said. I cannot be certain that it's true but if he's capable of selling stolen goods to the Corsairs then why not people, too. My fear is that they'd pay a handsome sum for someone as fair as Lady Jane.'

'Then Graveney's country house near Honiton needs to be located and a watch put on it as soon as possible. Hopefully, it's not already too late to save her along with her maid, Mary, and also Nancy.'

'Yes, I agree, and I'm willing to offer the assistance of some of my retainers. You should also know that the coach has returned to the city. I have received a report to that effect within the last hour...'

'And was Graveney onboard?'

'Yes. He and his wife alighted from the coach and went inside their house.'

'So, he's no doubt left others to do his dirty work for him. If Jane and the two maids are still alive, I worry that they might even have been hidden away in some remote cottage, in which case our chances of finding them before it's too late are slim. Still, we can but do our best. I now intend seeing Lady Jane's lawyer, Gilbert Overbury. He and his clerk have, I believe, an extensive knowledge of the whole of South Devon, and might have some idea of where the house we seek is to be found.

'And in the meantime, I'll ensure that a watch is still kept on the Graveney's house here in Exeter. If by any chance the coach returns to the country, then it might be possible to have it followed.'

By now it was late in the day and I was feeling weary. However, I did my best to shrug this off, being concerned that if I did not hasten, I might find Overbury's chambers had closed.

'You are welcome to take supper with us,' Louise Lovell said. 'And indeed we can offer you both beds for the night.'

'That's most kind of you, but I really do not want to impose.'

'Not at all, it would be a pleasure.'

'Very well. We should be back within the hour...'

Upon reaching Overbury's chambers on foot, having left our horses in the Lovells' stables, I found its front door to be both closed and bolted. I was about to turn away, vowing to return the following morning, when Harry spoke up.

'There's a man still at his desk, m'lady.'

'So there is. It's Overbury's clerk.'

With that I tapped urgently on the window and a few moments later the door was opened.

'Good evening, m'lady, I'm afraid we're now closed for the day.'

'I'm sorry, but this is urgent. I believe Lady Jane and her maid have been kidnapped. Is your master here?'

'Yes, m'lady. Please come in, by all means.'

'Who's there at this time of day?' The question came from Overbury himself, his head appearing around the door leading into his inner sanctum. 'Oh, Lady Olivia, what on earth has happened? You seem distressed.'

'I am, sir, I am. I fear that Lady Jane is either dead or on her way to slavery.'

'When she was here two days ago I warned her to take care.'

'Well, she's now disappeared along with Mary, her maid. The keeper of the East Gate recalls seeing her leave the city immediately behind Graveney's black coach. She must have followed it and then fallen into his hands. I've come here to ask you if you or your clerk might have any idea where Graveney's country house is to be found. All I know is that Graveney once indicated to Jane's sister, Caroline, that it was near Honiton.'

Overbury shook his head. 'Nothing comes to mind, I'm afraid.' Then he looked at his clerk who to my frustration also shook his head. I was left with no choice but to return to the Lovells, vowing to set out for Honiton the following morning. Before leaving Overbury's chambers, however, he expressed scepticism at the notion of Jane being sold to Corsairs.

'They can seize women for nothing when they make one of their raids so why pay any money for them?' he asked.

'Lovell thinks that Graveney trades pirated merchandise with the Corsairs and would include Jane, Mary and Nancy in the price.'

That's an interesting notion, I must say, but I wouldn't be too certain that it's true.'

As Harry and I made our way back to the Lovells' residence, I wondered whether to accept their invitation or ride back to Altringham Manor. My concern was that half the journey would have to be undertaken in darkness and whilst I could imagine Thomas being desperate for news of Jane I would not be able to bring him any comfort. In fact, quite the reverse. This was enough to make up my mind for me, especially as I was both tired and hungry. We would remain in Exeter for the night and ride to Honiton in the morning, though with whom exactly we would make enquiries once we arrived there I was by no means certain.

After a somewhat restless night in a bed I had found much too hard for my taste, Harry and I both rose early. We then partook of a light breakfast of bread, butter and cured ham, and were on the point of departure when I heard a loud knocking on the front door.

'There has been a development,' Edward Lovell soon informed us. 'A horseman has been seen to leave Graveney's stables and ride off in the direction of the East Gate. It must be possible that he's heading for his country house.'

'Then he needs to be followed before it's too late.'

'He is probably out of the city by now.'

'I hope we can still catch him, if we hurry.'

'Go with care, though. You may be placing yourself in the same danger as Lady Jane.'

'I have Harry Parsons here.'

'Who's unarmed…Look, Jack Casey, who has just brought me this news is a loyal servant and able to ride and shoot. You see he served in parliament's army. I can have a horse saddled for him as quickly as your own and equip him with a pistol, too.'

Ten minutes later, accompanied by Harry and Casey, I was ready to depart and in less than another ten minutes had reached the East Gate. Casey then asked the gatekeeper if he had seen a lone rider leave the city within the last half an hour.

'He be a dark-skinned fellow, riding a dapple grey mare of about fourteen hands.'

'Yes, I do, but it be a good thirty minutes ago now, that's for sure.'

The three if us set off in pursuit at a galloping speed at first, although I was all too aware that we would not be able to maintain this for long.

‘If we continue riding at this pace we’ll soon exhaust the horses. Better to go at a steady canter and hope the man we’re following is travelling a little slower so that we gradually gain on him before it’s too late…’

‘And that he keeps to the high road, m’lady,’ Harry added.

‘Yes, and that. I’m reckoning he has at least a three mile start on us but with luck we can whittle that down to nothing at all by the time we come in sight of Honiton. If we don’t catch him we’ll just have to make enquiries in the town, which was what I intended anyway.’

I estimated that at our present speed, we could be in Honiton in a little less than three hours, which might not be enough to overhaul the man we were pursuing. After an hour’s riding the horses still seemed fresh, so I decided that the time had come to force a somewhat faster pace. I could not know if it would be enough but the closer we came to Honiton, the more I was willing to tax both my horse’s stamina and its speed, knowing that it would be able to both take its ease and drink its fill once we entered the town.

Harry and Casey’s mounts were also able to keep pace with mine, and it was as we were approaching the bridge over the river Otter to the north of Ottery St Mary that I spotted a lone rider, still some distance ahead of us.

‘That must be him,’ I cried. ‘See, his horse is a dapple-grey!’

‘I think he’s halting m’lady, probably to let his horse take a drink from the river,’ Harry said.

‘We must halt too then. I don’t want him to know we’re following him.’

‘But he may have already seen us, m’lady. We should be careful not to arouse his suspicion.’

'Very well, let's just walk on slowly. If he's still at the bridge when we get there, I'm prepared to pass the time of day with him but we won't halt. All that matters is that we don't lose sight of him completely.'

Just as we reached the bridge, the man who had appeared to keep his back to us all the while we had been approaching, turned his head. I was immediately struck by the darkness of his skin and the keen look in his eyes.

'Good day to you,' I said pleasantly whereupon he doffed his hat to me, revealing a head of black hair to match the colour of his skin.

'And a good day to you,' he responded with an accent which indicated to me, that as his skin colour had suggested, he was foreign born.

And then we rode on at the same walking pace until the bridge was out of sight. I glanced nervously behind us but could see no sign of the rider we had just passed following us.

'What should we do?' Harry asked.

'Just ride on. He'll come soon enough, I'm sure he will.'

Unless, I thought, he had been so suspicious of us that he'd decided to ride back towards Exeter. Still we rode slowly on until finally, when I was on the point of thinking the worse, I heard the sound of a horse cantering along behind us and within half a minute we were overtaken by the rider of the dapple-grey mare. He acknowledged us again by merely bringing a hand up to brim of his hat. We were also close to a bend in the road so he was soon out of sight.

'Let's ride on a little faster now,' I said. 'But we don't need to do so at more than a gentle canter. He shouldn't get far ahead of us now unless he chooses to break into a headlong gallop.'

I also felt an instinctive sense of caution. If the rider had been suspicious of us, and was armed, then he had already had one perfect opportunity to take us by surprise, and yet failed to do so. All the same, he could still be about to spring an attack on us as we came round the bend.

'I'd feel safer, too, if you drew your pistol and cocked it,' I said to Jack Casey who looked at me in some alarm. 'Merely as a precaution. We can't be too careful.'

In the event, my fears proved to be groundless and by the time the rider came into view again he was well ahead of us.

'Look,' Harry exclaimed. 'He's turning off the high road.'

'There's no need to ride any faster, though,' I said. 'And Casey, please continue to keep your pistol cocked.'

It was quickly apparent that we had reached the lane that led to the village of Alfington and I had a keen sense of Jane having come this way less than three days previously. I could only guess at how she had then fallen into Graveney's grasp.

20
Gone for ever?

'If he even begins to suspect that we're deliberately following him, we may do more harm than good,' I insisted. 'So let's just continue at no more than a gentle trot and even if we do not see him again, we should be on the lookout for a large country house. We'll then enquire in Alfington who its owner might be.'

'And if we do not see such a house, m'lady,' Harry asked.

'Then we'll still ask the locals here if they know of one, and, if so, who its owner might be, and where we might find it.'

'But what if he rides on well past the village without our knowing it?' This time the question came from Casey.

'If necessary, we'll have to make enquiries in Ottery St Mary. Still, I fancy the house is nearby, otherwise why travel this way at all, and why should Graveney have ever told Lady Jane's sister and brother-in-law that his house was to be found near Honiton.'

It was as we were approaching the village, without having caught any sight of the dark-faced rider we had been following, that I noticed some gates to our left and beyond that a fine-looking, red-brick house, built in the Jacobean style. The gates also stood open and although there was no sign of any rider, I surmised the man we'd been following had had time to disappear out of sight.

'I'll be bound this is where he's come to,' I declared, although in truth I could not be certain. 'Let's ride on into Alfington, I expect there'll be an inn there, where we can make our enquiries.'

As we entered the village, I was pleased to see what I was looking for and to be able to slip out of the saddle. As a woman, I would have hesitated to enter the inn on my own but was fairly relaxed about doing so with Harry and Casey alongside me. Even so, I was still entering what was very much a male preserve and I was conscious of lascivious glances from one or two of the half a dozen or so men who were present. Undaunted, I approached the bar, behind which a red-faced man of middle years was standing, whom I took to be the landlord.

'Pray, can you help me?' I asked. 'I'm searching for the house of the merchant, Hugh Graveney. I understand it's near to here. Can you perhaps give me directions?'

'I think he be the man who owns the big house between here and the high road. From which direction have ye been travelling?

'From Exeter along the high road, and then we turned down the lane to here.'

'Then ye'll have passed the house on your left.'

'Ah, I did wonder if that might be the house I'm looking for. I'm obliged to you.'

While it was satisfying to have established the whereabouts of Graveney's country house, almost beyond doubt, the question remained as to what to do next. There was also no certainty that Jane, Mary and Nancy were being held prisoner in the house itself, or for that matter were all being held under one roof. What was more, without a careful reconnaissance I could not know how many outbuildings there were including habitable cottages. Worse, if we attempted to enter Graveney's land we were almost bound to be seen and with one pistol between us possessed only a very limited ability to defend ourselves.

'We need reinforcements as quickly as possible, I declared as soon as we had left the inn. 'Casey, you should now return to Exeter. Tell your master that we've located the whereabouts of Graveney's country house but can hope to achieve nothing without the support of several armed men. We need them to come here to the village before darkness falls today. In the meantime, Harry and I will see what more we can discover. Leave us your pistol, if you will?' Casey looked at me doubtfully. 'Come, do as I ask. For the sake of his dead son, I know your master will continue to provide me with every assistance, and your pistol will be returned to you soon. You have my word.'

Once Casey had departed, having handed over his pistol, my first priority was that Harry and I should take care of our horses, by ensuring they were able to drink from the village trough. We then looked to assuage our own thirst and hunger by returning to the inn and taking seats next to the window affording us a view over the village green where we had left our horses tethered to a post. I also remained uncertain about what to do for the best.

'Bringing armed men here is all very well, Harry, but if we then march up to the front door of the house and demand the release of Jane and the others, it's likely to remain shut in our faces, however loudly we insist on being allowed entry. We can't then force our way in without breaking the law and anyway, even if we ignored that reality, might find they've been hidden elsewhere. I'd like to get a better view of the house and its grounds, if that's possible. I'm particularly interested in any out buildings or cottages we might be able to see.'

'If we're not careful, m'lady, we might arouse suspicion. Think, if that dark-faced fellow were to see us...'

'Yes, he would recognise us, I agree. Oh dear, this has turned into a nightmare. I'd far rather instruct Overbury to request a search warrant of Graveney's house, except I fear it would all take too long, and for all we know Graveney's men might be preparing to smuggle Lady Jane out of the country this very night.'

What also frightened me even more was the possibility that we were too late anyway because this had already happened, but this was not a fear that I cared to express

'Look, we'll take a ride back along the lane and see if we can gain a better view of the house and its grounds. Admittedly, on the way here I could see little or nothing beyond the stone wall and many trees that surround it, but from this direction we may see a vantage point that's helpful to us.'

Half an hour later as we made our way back along the lane, we were at first still denied any view at all of the house and its grounds. Then, though, just as I had hoped, we reached a point where the lie of the land just enabled us to gain a view not just of the house but of more besides.

'If it were winter time we'd be able to see far more, of course,' I said. 'All the same, I can still make out a stable block to the right of the house and, yes, it's two storeys' high, so there could well be living space for more than just horses.'

'The house has attics, too, m'lady,' Harry pointed out.

I contemplated its three storeys for a few moments. 'Yes, for the servants, of whom there are bound to be some, so I still think that Lady Jane is more likely to be in the stable block.'

I was beginning to think that once Lovell's men arrived, it might be possible to attempt a rescue, by breaking into the stable block. Of course, it would still be a considerable gamble and might achieve nothing, but I decided that it still represented a better option than trying to storm the house.

There was now nothing left to do but wait for Lovell's men to arrive and I was grateful for the fact that the weather was still set fair with no hint of rain. At first we simply turned our horses round and rode them at a walking pace almost as far as Ottery St Mary before finally turning back again towards Alfington. By then it was late into the afternoon and by the time we reached the village green, I was hopeful we might not have too much longer to wait. I was increasingly restless, though, and once the horses had drunk again from the trough, I made up my mind that we should ride slowly back in the direction of Exeter in the expectation of meeting up with Lovell's men.

Harry looked somewhat askance at such a suggestion, but it was not his station in life to disagree so we set off. Yet, we had not long returned to the high road when it was not any group of riders we saw approaching us but a black coach with two horses, one of which was also black. The animals were being ridden hard at a galloping pace thanks to a liberal use of the whip by the coachman.

The road being quite narrow, we were obliged to bring our mounts to a halt to allow the coach to pass us, and as it did so I had a fleeting view of the bearded face of a man looking out at me. The thought that this must be Graveney made me shudder. I also felt instinctively that there could only be one reason why he was travelling in such haste.

I thought of pursuing the coach, given that Harry was armed, but then changed my mind. Another man had been sitting next to the coachman, who could also well be armed as could Graveney.

'We need to gallop on, too, Harry,' I said, giving him a knowing look. 'Hopefully, we'll meet up with Lovell's men soon.'

In the event, it was to be another half an hour at least before I finally caught sight of a body of four horsemen coming towards us, and quickly realised that Edward Lovell himself was leading them.

'We came as fast as we could,' he told me. 'I needed to summons men from Topsham and only the three men I've brought with me have both mounts and arms.'

'Whilst, I fear the worst, sir. Thirty minutes ago and more, we were passed on the road by Graveney's coach, and I'm sure he was on board. He means to take Jane and the others to the coast tonight, I'm certain of it.'

'That makes sense to me. I'm told the Bellerophon up anchored and left port this morning when the tide was in its favour.'

'Then we have no time to lose. Even as we speak they may already be on their way.'

'In that case we should look to head them off. It's more

than likely that *The Bellerophon* will be waiting offshore at Sidmouth.'

We were close to a lane that led south towards Ottery St Mary and from there to the coast, passing both Altringham Manor and Fetford Hall. I also felt confident that we could travel faster than any coach, especially one carrying passengers. Edward Lovell, however, was less certain as he and his men had already ridden their horses hard and they were beginning to tire. As it transpired, it took us nearly an hour to reach the coast by which time evening was coming on and although the weather remained fine, the light was just beginning to fail.

I scanned the horizon for any sign of *The Bellerophon* but at first could see nothing. Then Edward Lovell pointed eastwards.

'Look, that's her, I expect. She's waiting off Branscombe!'

The fact that this was some five miles away made me almost groan with dismay. 'In God's name, we may be too late to save them!'

By now the horses were seriously weary and in need of water. Once their thirst had been satisfied in a nearby stream, they were revived enough to be able to canter, but they were still beyond being forced into a gallop, so it was another half an hour and nearly dark before we finally reached Branscombe.

'Look!' I said. 'There's a boat just coming alongside *The Bellerophon*.'

I then watched in horror as a rope ladder was thrown over the side and first one and then four more figures ascended it. The sea was calm enough, but the light was now so nearly gone, and the ship so far out from the shoreline, that it was hard to distinguish whether anyone climbing on board was either male or female. Yet, I was still convinced that at least two of the figures were skirted and I even thought I heard the distant sound of a scream of fear carried on the wind, which made my stomach turn with dread. I was so utterly dismayed that it brought me close to tears until I began to feel a burning sense of anger and looked about for any sign of the coach that could surely not be far away.

'There, there it is!' I cried out furiously. The coach with its two horses was travelling back inland and I caught no more of a glimpse of it through the failing light before it disappeared behind a long line of trees and was lost in the darkness. 'We should go after it and force the devils to admit to what they've done,' I declared vigorously.

Edward Lovell, though, was less than enthusiastic. 'They're bound to deny everything and even if we could force admissions out of them, I know that Graveney would say they were given under duress and therefore worthless. Anyway, think how dark it now is, and my horse, for one, is totally spent.'

'But Graveney himself could be on board the coach!'

'No, he'd keep his distance from such dirty work, I'm sure he would, and don't imagine we could force any admission out of him, even at the point of gun.'

'So he's got away with it then. First murder and now the kidnapping of three women who he's happy to sell into slavery. It's utterly wicked!'

And then I thought, too, that it would have to fall to me and Harry to tell Thomas what had befallen Jane. No doubt he'd be devastated to the point of feeling utterly bereft.

Caroline, too, would have to be told the worst, which would inevitably lead to her husband, John, knowing too. I could imagine him being full of self-righteous criticism of Jane for having brought it all upon herself by her determined meddling in affairs that were really none of her concern. It really was the worst of all nightmares, and when it struck me like a hammer blow that I was unlikely to ever see my closest friend ever again, I simply could not hold back the tears and wept unashamedly.

21

Aftermath

Following the failure to rescue my dearest friend, I was in a profound state of shock. My family, too, had reacted in horror to my news of what had happened when I had returned there the previous night, accompanied by Harry along with Edward Lovell and his men, all of whom had been accommodated for the night. Now, over breakfast, a fraught debate took place as to what, if anything, could still be done to bring a case against Graveney, and distressed as I was, I quickly seized upon one particular fact.

'Graveney's men must be holding Hera and also the other horse that Jane's maid was riding!'

'Unless they've been slaughtered and cut up for their meat or buried,' James remarked gloomily.

'And even if the horses are still alive, there can be no hope of searching for them without a warrant,' Edward Lovell added.

'I need to return to Exeter and ask Master Overbury for his advice,' I said. 'Mind you, I know what he'll say. *All your evidence is still circumstantial.* I also dread having to tell both Thomas and Caroline what's happened. He'll be angry beyond words, I expect, and she'll be utterly distraught. For all that she's married to a Puritan, she and Jane were still close…'

And then, of course, there was Lucas. To all intents and purposes he had now lost his mother while still a babe-in-arms, for all that in the short term he at least had Melissa to wet nurse him. Thomas, too, would also now be left in difficulty following Jane's disappearance although I had every confidence in Harry being able to manage the estate in order that outgoings could still be met. And then as well there was Caroline's brother, Francis, who so far as I was aware remained in ignorance of Jane's marriage. Sooner or later he would have to be informed of her fate, and I could only be grateful that responsibility for that task rested with Caroline rather than myself.

Having to face Thomas with the news that Jane was gone was a distressing prospect that I could have left entirely to Harry but decided I could not avoid. In the event, when we arrived at Altringham Manor, Edward Lovell and his men having returned directly to Exeter, I did not even have to open my mouth for him to realise that my news was bad.

'I can tell from the expression on your face that you are able to bring me no comfort,' he said in a slurred voice, betraying the fact that he had been drinking heavily.

'That is so. I'm afraid I have every reason to believe that she's been taken abroad along with her maid. Graveney's ship, *The Bellerophon*, was off the coast at Branscombe. We saw a boat go alongside it and I'm sure two women at least were taken on board. We also caught sight of Graveney's coach heading back inland but by then it was getting dark.'

'Then he must be held to account for this outrage.'

'I would like to think that he could be. I'm prepared to return to Exeter to tell Jane's sister what's happened and I also intend to speak again to the lawyer, Master Overbury, and urge him to make an appeal to the Justices, or as needs be the Sheriff, to at least issue a warrant for a search of Graveney's country house. After all, it's quite possible that he's still in possession of Jane and her maid's horses. What's more, Edward Lovell has told me that after what has happened, he's finally made up his mind to make out a case of smuggling against Graveney. Admittedly, he still has reservations about how successful he'll be, but it's something he's willing to try.'

'And meanwhile I continue to be trapped here, Goddamn it!' Thomas snapped. 'I feel…I feel so impotent.'

'Jane would want you to protect Lucas's interests, so far as you possibly can. I'm certain of that.'

'And so I shall, I can assure you. However, for the moment he's no more than a babe and best off in the care of his wet nurse.'

After that there was little more to be said between us so I decided to head for Exeter. First, though, I had to spend a painful few minutes in the company of Melissa and Lucas.

'I have to be frank with you that the boy may never see his mother again,' I said sombrely.

'No, surely not, m'lady!'

'We have to face up to that probability, I'm afraid, for all that I pray fervently that it may be otherwise.'

Harry was then insistent that I let him accompany me to Exeter. 'For safety's sake, m'lady. Graveney likely knows of your involvement in Lady Jane's investigations.'

'You've given me help enough as it is, Harry…'

'That's as maybe, m'lady, but I'd feel bad if anything were to happen to you now for want of an escort.'

'Very well then, I'm grateful to you.'

The closer we came to Exeter the more I was filled with mixed emotions. Much as I hated having to tell Caroline what had now happened, I was anxious to still get the job done and then speak, if I could, to Master Overbury. I fancied he would be full of his usual caution, saying this or that was circumstantial, or that we lacked firm evidence, but I was determined to be insistent that he at least present a case, being confident that James would be responsible for his fee, whatever the outcome.

By the time I came to knock on Caroline's door, having left our horses at the usual livery stables, it was well after midday and I was in need of sustenance. 'We'll not outstay our welcome, Harry. Hopefully, this should take no more than a few minutes and then we can take our ease at an inn.'

Somewhat to my discomfort, although a maid answered my knock, I had barely stepped over the threshold when I was confronted not by Caroline but by her husband, John.

'Good day to you, Lady Olivia,' he said politely enough. 'Do you bring us news of my sister-in-law?'

'Yes, indeed I do and I am afraid it's not good…'

As I uttered these words Caroline appeared, looking utterly distraught, and I proceeded to explain as briefly as I could what had occurred.

'But you can't be certain she or her maid, or this other woman, were those you caught a distant glimpse of boarding the ship,' she asserted.

'Not absolutely, no, but I cannot see who else they would have been. Jane and her maid must have followed Hugh Graveney's coach to Alfington, and in some way, I know not how, been seized by his retainers. His ship then appears off Branscombe, and no sooner do we see these women being taken on board than we also catch sight of a black coach with horses disappearing into the gloom...'

'I knew it would come to this,' John interjected self-righteously. 'Your sister's a meddler, and no mistake, forever interfering in matters that should be none of her concern. It would be bad enough if she were a man but for a woman to act as she has done beggars belief.'

'She still did not deserve this fate, John,' Caroline responded, choking back her tears.

'I did not mean to suggest that she did. I merely assert that she has been exceedingly foolish.'

'I think your criticism is misplaced,' I said with a rising sense of anger. 'I doubt if that rapist and murderer, Turnbull, would have been exposed if it were not for her endeavours and Graveney is also undoubtedly an evil man. I now intend visiting Master Overbury to instruct him to lay a charge before the Justices against Graveney of kidnapping and murder.'

'You must act as you see fit, of course. And what of that renegade husband of Lady Jane; I suppose he's still skulking around at Altringham Manor?'

I was rather caught off guard by this sudden question and hesitated before replying. '...He's still there, yes, as he's every right to be.'

'And has he the right to plot to overthrow the Commonwealth that our Lord Protector has created?'

'I don't believe he's plotting anything. I simply meant that he has the right to reside in his own home.'

John grunted and then looked around for his coat. 'Well, thank you for calling. I really need to set off on my rounds, I'm late already.'

'And I'm sorry to be the bearer of such sad news,' I said, looking towards Caroline, who was still in tears.

Having been shown the door in a perfunctory fashion by John, I had barely stepped outside when my anger at his attitude began to boil over.

'Insufferable man!' I exploded to Harry. 'He couldn't even bring himself to show his wife any sympathy.'

Having eaten well at one of the city's inns, we then went to Master Overbury's chambers. I was prepared for a long wait, knowing that he might well be at court, and it was to be two hours before he returned, by which time I had grown thoroughly bored and frustrated whilst Harry had fallen soundly asleep.

One glance at Overbury's face suggested to me that he was tired and probably not in the best of humours. All the same, he still managed a kindly smile the moment our eyes met, and ushered me into his inner sanctum as soon as I begged his indulgence, explaining that it concerned the fate of Lady Jane.

'I bring the worst of news. She and her maid have, I am certain, been taken aboard Graveney's ship, *The Bellerophon*.'

'You mean you actually saw their faces?'

'No, but it was definitely women who were being taken on board. We could make out their skirts and they looked young. And then we saw Graveney's coach…'

I went on to explain in a little more detail but could tell that Overbury was still concerned that the evidence wasn't certain enough.

'Look, it's surely possible that Graveney is still holding both Jane's horse and her maid's.' I insisted. 'Jane's mare, Hera, is a fine horse, and he'd surely hesitate before having it killed and cut up for horse meat. An urgent search needs to be made of his stables both here and at Alfington. My brother, James, will meet your fee for making an appeal to the Justices or, if that fails, the Sheriff, for a warrant to be issued allowing the Constables to carry out a search.'

' . . . Very well, I will do it for you, but you must understand that the plea may well be rejected. You are now the only person who can bear witness to most of these allegations and the existing evidence is still circumstantial. What's more, Graveney continues to enjoy powerful connections. I do not say that they give him immunity from prosecution, but certainly those in authority in this county may still be very reluctant to take any action against him.'

'I understand all that, Master Overbury. I merely say that we owe it to Lady Jane to try. Edward Lovell has also now agreed to make out a case against Graveney of smuggling, which may also aid our cause.'

'Perhaps, but I would urge you, Lady Courtney, to take care for your own safety. Graveney has already shown himself to be the most dangerous of men.'

I held up a hand. 'That I also appreciate. It is why I have brought Jane's steward with me to act as my guard. We shall leave the city as soon as possible and trust that no one with evil intent has any designs upon us.'

22

I'm so sorry, m'lady

'Here, m'lady, drink this.'

I looked sombrely at Mary and then took the mug from her, grateful to be able to quench my thirst, for all that the hops in the beer had a sharp, bitter taste, which made me splutter a little. My head was still throbbing somewhat and I did not yet feel myself but I was nonetheless much better than I had been, at least in body, if not in spirit. I was lying on a hard mattress in a cold room, the door to which had been locked, and possessed of only a small window to give any light.

'I'm so sorry, m'lady, I didn't know what else to do, really I didn't.'

I had lost count of the times I had heard this lament and it was beginning to irritate me.

'I know that, Mary. Nothing that's happened is your fault. Try not to distress yourself too much.'

'But what's going to 'appen to us, m'lady? I'm scared, really I am.'

I knew what she feared might be about to happen to us, but it was a fate I preferred not to speak of. Instead, I tried to be encouragingly optimistic. 'God willing, we'll be rescued and soon.'

'I think 'e means to do away with us. After all, 'e murdered my mistress and her lover, too, I expect.'

I turned to face Nancy, who was sitting opposite me on a tiny bed. 'If he intended that, I think we'd all be dead by now.'

'So what then; does he mean to keep us 'ere as prisoners for ever?'

'I don't know what he intends, but you can be certain people will already be searching for us. My good friend, Olivia Courtney, for one.'

I closed my eyes, resting my head against the wall, and took another sip of beer. I turned over in my mind the events of the last few days and cursed my ill fortune at being overtaken by sickness and delirium. I feared that I had only myself to blame for overtaxing myself when my body had not yet fully recovered from giving birth. The thought, too, of being separated from Lucas, perhaps indeed of never seeing him again, was enough to make me catch my breath.

'Are ye alright, m'lady?' Mary asked anxiously.

I opened my eyes and grimaced. 'I was thinking of Lucas. I know I must remain strong for his sake.'

Then I closed my eyes again and sighed. After my fall from my horse, I had remained in a groggy state for some hours but retained a vague recollection of being picked up by a well-built man who had carried me in his arms as if I was a child through the gates leading to Graveney's house. An authoritative male voice had then snapped out orders, after which I had been carried past the house and through another gate leading into what had smelt like stables, before being taken up a flight of stairs and into the room where I now lay.

I had slept for upwards of twelve hours and it was only when I'd begun to wake up the following morning that I'd realised I was sharing the room not just with Mary but Nancy, too.

'Are we all prisoners now?' I had asked weakly, whereupon Mary had burst into tears and begged my forgiveness.

'When ye fell off yer horse m'lady, and then didn't stir, I ran to the house in search of help.'

'And you said who we were?'

'I said m'lady 'ad been taken ill. The man, Master Graveney it be for sure, knew who you were. 'E was mighty fierce I can tell 'e. 'Alf scared me t'death 'e did.'

Since our imprisonment no one had entered our room save a man who had brought us food and drink and emptied our piss pot. A surly looking individual with a pock-marked face, suggesting to me he was a survivor of the pox, he had been totally uncommunicative. At first I had been too weak to even attempt to engage him in conversation in order to protest at the situation in which I now found myself. Once I began to feel better and sought to do so, he simply turned his back on me without a word and walked out of the room. Any thought I might have had of the three of us managing to overpower him was also deterred by the sight of a second man standing immediately outside the door, holding a sword in his hand.

Now I faced the prospect of another cold and uncomfortable night as well as the dread that we might never be rescued.

With the coming of a new day I awoke feeling cold, stiff and thirsty, too. As soon as I tried to stand I also realised how unsteady I was on my feet. My head was spinning as well as throbbing gently, and I knew I was still far from recovered from whatever illness it was I'd contracted. I worried, too, that if I continued to be confined in such poor conditions with such meagre fare to eat and drink, whatever measure of recovery I'd made since my fall from my horse, would be reversed. Above all, I knew it was essential that Olivia, and whoever she could summons to assist her endeavours, came quickly to our rescue, so with every hour that passed I continued to pray fervently for our safe deliverance.

Had I been in a better state of health I knew that my confinement, affording as it did such a limited view of the outside world, would have driven me to distraction, like some caged beast. As it was, however, I was mostly content to lie back and try to rest. At what I judged to be about midday we finally received our first visit of the day, only to be provided with some tolerable soup and half-stale bread together with more strong beer.

'How much longer are we going to be confined here?' I asked but my question was answered by nothing more than a shrug of the shoulders and a grunt.

After that the day gradually slipped by until I became aware of the sound of horses. Going to the window, which afforded only a limited view of the stable yard, I just caught a glimpse of Graveney's black coach. It looked to me as if it had just arrived and I wondered what this might herald. Within less than a quarter of an hour I then heard the sound of footsteps on the stairs leading to our place of confinement, followed by the sound of a key being turned in the lock.

‘Get up, now, it’s time to leave!’ These words were spoken in a foreign accent that I found hard to place, by a dark-skinned man who I thought rather handsome save that his eyes were cold and his expression haughty. I wondered, too, if he was a Moor. He carried no weapon but there was another man behind him with a sword in his hand that was suitably intimidating.

‘Where are you taking us?’ I asked.

‘You’ll find out soon enough. Now come, there’s no time to lose.’

The three of us were then bundled down the stairs, out into the yard, and told to get inside the coach. I hesitated, as much through a feeling of unsteadiness in my legs as any reluctance to comply with this order, whereupon the dark-skinned man grabbed hold of my arm.

‘Let go of me!’ I cried. ‘Don’t you realise I’m unwell.’

‘Just get inside the coach. Then you you’ll be able to rest.’

I did as I was told, and Nancy and Mary followed me inside along with the dark-skinned man, whereupon the coach then immediately departed. The ensuing journey was one that I found thoroughly uncomfortable as the lane we travelled along was narrow and in a poor state of repair, despite which the coachman still forced the horses into a gallop. This made the coach sway alarmingly at times as if we were at sea, making Mary begin to groan and complain that she felt sick.

‘In God’s name, lean out of the window if you’re going to throw up,’ the dark-skinned man told her. Moments later, she did just that.

For my part, I did not feel so much sick as dizzy, and the further the coach travelled the more I feared that I would pass out. All I could do was close my eyes and pray that the journey would soon come to an end, which eventually, after about an hour, it did. However, this was not before Mary had been sick out of the coach window a second time, and Nancy, too, had also begun to complain that she was feeling sick.

It was the growing noise from seagulls, which first alerted me to the fact that our journey was likely to be coming to an end as well as helping to confirm my worst fear that we were about to be put on board a ship and taken abroad. A glance out of the window indicated we were now entering a village that I vaguely recognised. It crossed my mind to call out for help but as if reading my mind the dark-skinned man issued a stark warning,

'Keep your mouths shut or you'll feel the back of my hand.'

The coach then continued on its way out of the village until I got my first sight of the sea, which in the late afternoon sunshine was looking perfectly calm. Shortly thereafter the coach halted and the dark-skinned man ordered us to get out. It was obvious to me that we were close to a beach whilst out to sea I could make out a ship's masts.

At the point of a sword, the three of us were then made to walk to the beach where a small boat was waiting in the shallows to take us out to the ship. I was still so unsteady on my feet that I struggled to keep up and knew that any thought of trying to run away was out of the question. The prospect of being cuffed also deterred me from seeking to cry out for help, and anyway, as far as I could see, the beach was deserted. Furthermore, the nearest dwelling I could make out was some distance away.

Accompanied by the dark-skinned man, we had to wade through some shallow water to clamber on board the boat, and were then rowed out to the ship by two oarsmen, leaving me to stare back at the coastline and wonder when, if ever, I would set foot in my own country once more. The prospect, too, of being separated for ever from both Lucas and Thomas as well as Olivia was terrible enough to bring me to the verge of tears.

When we reached the ship, I was feeling so weak that I found it a real struggle to climb the rope ladder in order to get on board, so needed the assistance of one of the two oarsman, who climbed it with me. Along with Mary and Nancy I was then shown to a small cabin in the bow of the ship, which was to be our prison for the duration of our journey. Instead of beds we would have to sleep in hammocks, and although our cabin was above the waterline, our porthole was tiny, making the space we occupied seem especially dark and claustrophobic.

I was convinced that Olivia, for one, would have done her best to rescue us, but whatever her endeavours might have been, they had proved to be totally ineffectual. Even as night came on, the ship up-anchored and sailed away, heading, so I feared, in a southerly direction towards the Mediterranean Sea and the Barbary Coast. If the dark-skinned man was indeed a Moor, it had occurred to me that he might well have links to the Corsairs, in which case the plan could well be to sell us into slavery. It was a truly awful prospect.

23
Storm clouds

We had been at sea for barely more than a day and already the journey was becoming intolerable. None of us had ever sailed before so even a fairly gentle swell was enough to induce feelings of nausea. Then, as the wind got up and the sea became rougher, first Mary and then Nancy were both sick out of our porthole, and I knew it might not be long before I was as well.

The ship was also beginning to creak a little as it was tossed about ever more vigorously by the strengthening wind. Finally, I could contain myself no longer, but had barely reached the porthole before I threw up. At the same time my face and hair were soaked by sea water and moments later a sailor burst into our cabin.

'There's a storm coming,' he announced. 'No porthole can be left open!'

He proceeded to close the porthole's shutter before departing again, plunging us into almost total darkness. It proved to be an increasingly nightmarish experience as the sea tossed and turned the ship with ever greater violence in the howling wind. Soon, it creaked so loudly that I feared it was bound to break asunder, sending us all to a watery grave.

Mary literally began to tremble with fear while Nancy preferred to curl up on the floor of the cabin like some wounded animal. It was behaviour that encouraged me to try and demonstrate that I was made of sterner stuff for all that I was really just as terrified.

'We must be brave,' I said as calmly as I could. 'I expect the storm will soon pass.'

Except that if anything the noise around us seemed to grow yet fiercer. Then there came a terrible grinding noise. The wind was still blowing as loudly as ever but the ship was no longer being tossed and turned so I wondered if we might have run aground, presumably on some rocks.

'God save us, m'lady,' Mary cried out. 'We're going to drown, I know we are!' There was a hysterical edge to her voice, which made me seize her hand.

'No we're not, don't say that, don't even think it. I believe we've run aground. That could yet be our salvation.'

Mary stared at me as if I was unhinged, which perhaps I was. Yet, all I knew was that if the ship had indeed run aground it would surely have to be abandoned, which might well save us from ever being transported to the Barbary coast to be enslaved. For what seemed an interminable length of time, but in reality was probably no more than four to five hours, we waited as the ship continued to remain stuck fast to the rocks whilst the storm raged on.

At first sleep was out of the question, but after a time, huddled together with Mary and Nancy on the cabin's floor, I began to doze a little. When I woke, I sensed that the storm had abated somewhat. The ship was still creaking, though, as I also heard an indistinct voice shouting out commands. Then the door to the cabin opened and I recognised the dark-skinned man.

'We're abandoning ship. It's beginning to break-up. Come with me.'

As we made our way on deck, I realised that dawn had not long broken. It was possible, too, to make out some tall cliffs along with a narrow beach beneath them, only a short distance away. The storm had clearly driven our ship onto rocks where it had stuck fast, the waves and wind taking a relentless toll. It was noticeable, too, that the tide was right up the beach so I surmised that the crew must have hoped that as the tide came in so the ship would float free. Unfortunately for them, they'd clearly been disappointed in any such expectation, though they had at least been able to launch the boat, which had brought me and my companions aboard.

As I looked again towards the beach, I could see some figures standing there, and assumed they were members of the crew who had already used the ship's boat to reach the shore. Now it was the turn of myself and my companions to leave the ship, which meant each of us in turn having to descend the rope ladder. With storm force winds and crashing waves, this proved to be a hazardous exercise for all three of us. It was accomplished only with the help of strong male arms and screeches of fear on the part of Nancy, who went first, followed by Mary.

Going last, I had time to steel my courage, but also appreciate that the arrival of a particularly heavy gust of wind, along with a powerful wave, might leave me clinging to the rope for dear life. Worse, I might all too easily be thrown into the water with every likelihood of being carried out to sea and drowned. Somehow, though, I managed to reach the relative safety of the boat without undue difficulty save for a thorough soaking from heavy spray. Then, once the dark-skinned man had also joined us, the oarsmen put their backs into the task of rowing us ashore.

The thick, woollen riding habit that I wore, offered me some measure of protection against the elements, but even so it was still raining steadily enough to make me feel drenched; my teeth chattering because of the cold. Mary and Nancy looked equally forlorn, but I still gave thanks for our survival. I even had a sense of elation at the thought that we might now be able to achieve our freedom.

I had never before set foot on French soil but as a child I'd been taught to speak its language so had a number of books in my possession written in French, which I was able to read fairly fluently. I was therefore quite confident that I would be able to converse in the language, but was left wondering whether any crew members were similarly capable of doing so. I wondered, too, what exactly they now intended to do.

As I looked back towards the ship I could see that its rigging had been seriously damaged by the storm and that one of its masts had even snapped in two. Even if it could be floated off the rocks on which it had floundered, it would therefore require substantial repairs. I suspected, too, that it was probably badly damaged below the waterline, and therefore in distinct danger of sinking, sooner or later.

Any hope that I might have had of simply walking away from the beach along with my companions, was quickly dashed when we found ourselves put under guard at the point of a sword before being ordered to sit down on some rocks close to the waterline. We were all cold and wet to our skins, but at least both the rain and wind were beginning to ease off to the point that I soon noticed several breaks in the cloud. When the sun then broke through from the east, I even thought that we might soon see a rainbow. When it duly appeared, this helped to further lift my mood.

Yet I was not entirely without apprehension, as some distance away along the beach I could see the dark-skinned man in animated conversation with a taller, middle-aged man, with a thick beard and something of a swagger about him. I'd seen him on the bridge of the ship when I had been taken on board, and assumed he was probably its captain. The dark-skinned man began to gesticulate quite vigorously, jabbing his finger in my direction while the captain shouted back, so it was obvious that my companions and I were the principal object of their altercation.

It struck me like a hammer blow that they might even be contemplating our murder. If so, whilst what had just happened might yet prove to be our salvation, it had also exposed us to an even greater danger. To our captors we must surely still represent a valuable cargo but at the same time, too, a liability. After all, they couldn't allow us to escape lest we not only made accusations against them here in France but also ultimately in England against Hugh Graveney. One solution to the predicament this created was, I realised, to either simply slit our throats, or take us back out to sea and throw us overboard to drown.

I continued to stare in fear at the altercation taking place in front of me , wondering if my very life was now hanging by a thread. Meanwhile, apparently oblivious to the danger they were in, Mary and Nancy were huddled together for warmth, their heads down. A short while later, the captain turned on his heel and strode back towards the water's edge, shouting out an order as he went, which caused the boat that had brought us ashore to be rowed back towards the ship.

I didn't believe that anyone remained on board, but while it remained afloat, I could see the sense of trying to salvage as many useful items from it as possible. It was a relief, too, to have been left undisturbed. For the next hour the three of us remained where we were as the boat returned to the ship a second and then a third time.

It was as the boat was returning from its third journey that I then spied some strangers coming onto the beach via a steep pathway. They were six men of various ages led by a man wearing a gentleman's attire, who looked to be in his mid-fifties, with greying hair and a moustache. As he reached the beach he called out.

Salut, nous sommes arrive a offrir notre aide.

Somewhat to my surprise, the ship's captain promptly responded in fluent French and a conversation ensued, which I had difficulty in following. This was not only because I was some distance from it but also because the Frenchman spoke rapidly with what I assumed must be a strong Breton accent. I was, though, able to make out mention of *le village de Porspoder.*

Meanwhile, at least one barrel of beer had already been offloaded from the ship along with some supplies of food, and I also gathered that the captain was making a request for both fresh drinking water and bread. At the same time, he was able to produce what looked like silver coins from a bag, which for all I knew might well have been French *Ecus.*

Assuming he had given up any hope of re-floating his ship, I also imagined that one of the Captain's first priorities would be to try to send a messenger to Hugh Graveney in England, perhaps in the hope that another ship could be sent to pick them up. For that to be possible he would have to be looking to purchase at least one horse, though he might not be carrying enough silver or even gold on his person to be able to do so. All the same, should that be the case, he surely had the option of selling off at least some of the items, which had been brought ashore.

Of course, it was likely to be several weeks, or more, before any other ship came to our rescue, and in the meantime we would need somewhere to live and also require the means to sustain ourselves. If, as I suspected, *Pospoder* was no more than an isolated fishing village, the best option might be to purchase more than one horse and perhaps a couple of carts, too, in order to head for the nearest port where it might well be possible to gain passage aboard a ship bound for England.

Anyway, whatever their intentions, what troubled me most was how were they now going to be able to cope with continuing to hold the three of us prisoner. It was surely, too, an absolute certainty that Graveney would not want to see any of us set foot again in England.

This brought me back to my fear that we were in serious danger of being done away with unless it was possible to find some means of escape. Further, it did not elude my attention that while the captain continued his conversation, the dark-skinned man had decided to stand very close to where my companions and I were sitting, and had placed his hand on the hilt of a sword. I did, though, still have the option of ignoring the threat that was implicit in this gesture by simply calling out for help in French, for all that there was a risk this might just provoke him into some extreme act of violence. In the end, caught in two minds as to what to do for the best, I hesitated for too long, by which time the party of Frenchmen had begun to leave the beach, soon disappearing the way they had come.

I felt increasingly nervous that this isolated place on what I thought must be the tip of Brittany could be the last place on earth I ever set eyes upon. It made me contemplate a sudden dash for freedom, except that I knew my chances of getting more than a few yards were slight in the extreme. Alternatively, I could make an appeal to whatever shred of humanity our captors possessed by going down on my knees and begging for mercy, save that a certain sense of pride inclined me against demeaning myself in such a fashion.

'On your feet!' The order was barked out by the dark-skinned man, causing me to flinch and my companions to stir from their torpor in surprise. 'I said on your feet!'

'What do you mean to do with us?' I asked, while at the same time reluctantly obeying his command.

He grunted at me and shrugged his shoulders. 'That's yet to be decided. For the present we're taking you to a village, nearby. We've been offered shelter there.'

The walk into the village was less than half a mile but I quickly felt tired and thoroughly bedraggled as well as dirty, too, from not having had a change of clothes let alone a wash since I had set out from home to Exeter. This now seemed like a lifetime ago but was in fact less than a week. However, at least the sun was shining; its warmth helping to dry me out and make me feel less cold.

Our place of shelter proved to be the village church, which looked to be hundreds of years old and was both small and gloomy inside. Its priest, who was a shrivelled, elderly man, was at his door to greet us, giving my companions and me a solicitous smile as we entered, which I returned in kind. I was tempted to ask for his help, but had the dark-skinned man immediately behind me, and remained nervous of what his reaction would be if I said anything to anger him.

Freshly baked loaves, the aroma of which made me realise just how hungry I was, were soon brought to the church in a basket by a young, dark-haired woman, accompanied by an older woman with a pitcher of water and pewter cups. There was barely enough bread to go round, but once we'd eaten what there was, I for one was completely overcome by exhaustion, quickly falling asleep.

I woke with a start, wondering at first where I was. The church door had just been thrown open, allowing in a stream of light, and looking up I saw the dark-skinned man staring at me lustfully. Up until that moment I had given no thought to the possibility that he might have sexual designs upon me but now it struck me that the three of us were as vulnerable to the possibility of rape as we were to murder. Perhaps, indeed, he could not quite make up his mind, which he would most prefer to subject us to. Of course, it could well be both! This reflection was sufficient to make me even more desperate to escape, if only I could find both the courage and the opportunity to do so.

24
A chance encounter

I was feeling more bedraggled than ever as once again dark clouds gathered and it began to rain. The three of us were sitting together in the back of a small cart, which along with the horse that was pulling it, I assumed our captors had been able to purchase from the farmer whose barn we'd all slept in the night before. Both had definitely seen better days.

The cart was very rickety, making our journey uncomfortable, and the horse looked under-nourished, old and tired. I had been intimidated, too, by the threat from the dark-skinned man to make me suffer if I so much as opened my mouth. Worse, any hope I might have had of using the cover of darkness to make a bid for freedom had been thwarted by our captors taking turns to stand guard over us.

Now I could only guess at where we were heading, but what was noticeable to me was that not all the ship's crew had accompanied us, and in particular there was no sign of its captain. I could only think that *The Bellerophon* was still intact and that there remained some hope of being able to salvage her. It was also obvious that we were heading inland, and I surmised in a south easterly direction, although it was hard to be certain as the sky was blanketed with rain clouds.

Our progress was inevitably slow, but at least after a while the rain began to abate, and eventually the sun broke through the clouds to confirm the direction in which we were heading. Not long afterwards we came in sight of what appeared to be a town, which a signpost told me was called Saint-Renan. By now it was well after midday and Nancy, for one, was beginning to complain of thirst. Once we entered the town, its main well was soon located, from which water could be drawn, whilst a bakers was able to provide a quantity of fresh bread.

It was a Wednesday, the town was quiet with few passersby, and the three of us were not even allowed to leave the cart. Nor did we linger long and were soon on our way again, continuing in the same south easterly direction for less than an hour before we once again came within sight of the sea. We were approaching what appeared to be a broad estuary or inlet and I then caught a glimpse of some distant habitation on the coast, perhaps a fishing village or even something larger; it was hard to tell.

Nancy was beginning to complain with increasing desperation that she needed to relieve herself and begged that she might be allowed to do so before she was forced to soil herself. At first her appeals were stubbornly ignored. Then she was told to 'shut up' as we would be at our destination within half an hour, but still she whined on until we entered a wooded area whereupon the cart was brought to a halt and she was allowed to get out.

'Might I also be allowed to relieve myself?' I enquired

'Alright,' the stubbornly anonymous, dark-skinned man told me. 'Mind you, try to escape and I'll make you suffer for it. Is that understood?'

I nodded, and then eased myself off the back of the cart.

My feet had barely touched the ground when I heard a scream and looking around saw that one of the seamen was in the act of trying to rape Nancy.

'In the name of Allah, keep your dick inside your trousers,' the dark-skinned man swore. He then strode up to the man in order to pull him off Nancy before cuffing him over the head as well as kicking him with his boot.

I threw my arms around Nancy to comfort her, and within a few minutes we were on our way again, the incident serving as a salutary warning to all three us of the level of risk we faced of being assaulted and raped. For my part, I could also see the irony in the dark-skinned man acting as our protector, even while threatening to make me suffer if I made the least attempt to escape. More than ever, though, I was still determined to take that risk, and was increasingly convinced that it would have to be sooner rather than later.

Apart from whether I should seek to do this in consort with Mary and Nancy, the main question on my mind was whether I should seek to make an appeal for help on behalf of the three of us in French to some passing strangers, who might realistically be able to come to our aid. I had contemplated such a strategy before, but the right moment had never quite presented itself, or, even if it had, I had still hesitated for too long. I knew that I had to throw off any apprehension and act boldly, but that was always easier said than done.

Within another quarter of an hour we came in sight of much more than a mere coastal town. A sign informed us that its name was Brest, while I could see a curtain wall, which reminded me of Exeter. Furthermore, from the number of masts I could make out it was clearly a port of some importance. Entering such a place would surely present me with the opportunity I was looking for. Yet, to my growing frustration, our captors took no risks. First, we halted before entering the city and waited, while the dark-skinned man, along with one of his cronies, went on ahead. An hour then passed before they reappeared and when they did so they produced a linen sheet.

'We're going to keep you under cover until we reach our destination,' the dark-skinned man said. 'You're to lie down.'

I looked at him defiantly. 'No, I won't.'

'I said lie down or I'll take my fists to you!'

Very reluctantly I complied with his demand as did Mary and Nancy. To be forced to lie under the sheet was yet another humiliating experience and a thoroughly unpleasant one, too, as we had to lie face down with our feet facing the rear end of the cart. Worse, to prevent us from moving, three seamen placed their feet on top of us.

'I can't breath!' Nancy complained.

'Course you can!'

'I can't, I can't!'

One of the seamen then produced a knife and used it to tear the sheet a little. 'That'll give you enough air. Now be quiet or else!'

The cart then moved forward at the same walking pace as before and I could only gather where we were from the sounds I could hear as well as certain smells I could detect, some far more pleasant than others. It was when I heard the sound of an English voice, seemingly quite young and cheerful, and with an educated accent, that I knew I just had to seize the moment and began to scream.

'Help me, please help me! I'm a…'

At that moment I felt an awful blow to the back of my head and screeched out in pain before almost passing out.

'What's going on here?' It was that same educated English voice, sounding concerned.

'Mind your own business!' The dark-skinned man growled back.

'Who are you holding under that sheet?'

'Fuck off, will you, unless you want a fight.'

'I'm Lady Jane Tremayne, I'm being held against…' Once again I was struck on the back of the head and once again screamed out in pain. I could also hear the crack of the whip and the cart beginning to move along more quickly.

'You won't get away with this,' the same English voice cried out. It was no longer so close, though, as the cart's wheels clattered over the cobbled street at an even faster pace before slowing down to take a right turning and then, after briefly speeding up again, slowing down even more sharply. This time it veered to the left and moments later came to a standstill. The sheet was then taken off us and I realised we had entered a courtyard. My head was throbbing with pain and when I felt the back of my head I could feel a bump that was also wet with blood.

'Oh dear, m'lady, ye're bleeding badly, ye really are,' Mary exclaimed.

'I'm alright, Mary, don't you worry.'

In truth, I was nothing of the kind, and as I tried to alight from the coach I began to feel faint. I would have collapsed to the ground, had Mary and Nancy between them not supported me, and they had to continue to do so as we were ordered to enter a door to our left and to then to climb a flight of stairs. Once we had managed this we were then taken into a room dominated by a double-sized bed and a large chest. There was also a small table next to the bed with a candle on it but little else. I felt the need to lie down and collapsed onto the bed just as the door to the room was closed behind us and I heard the sound of a key being turned.

For all my hopes, we were still very much prisoners, and I couldn't help wondering what sort of place we had arrived at and how our captors had come to know of its existence. I wondered, too, who the Englishman was with the educated sounding voice and what he might now be thinking. He'd certainly heard me call out, albeit that the sound of my voice would have been somewhat muffled, and for all that he'd been threatened could even have followed us. Whether he could actually do anything about our plight was quite another matter, however.

'What d'ye think they mean t'do with us, m'lady?' Mary asked anxiously.

I did not reply at first, preferring to gingerly feel the wound to my head and also glance out of the room's tiny window, which overlooked nothing more than the courtyard below. Then I sighed.

'They don't intend to let us go, that's for certain. I can only imagine that they expect to be able to put us on board another vessel, although how that's to be achieved I've really no idea. Perhaps, they mean to send a message to their Master in England, asking that one be sent. Yet, if that's their plan, it's bound to take some while to bring it to fruition.'

'And in the meantime, we're no better off than we were before,' Nancy added ruefully.

'I wouldn't say that. At least we're on dry land and there's a chance that Englishman I called out to, whoever he is, might be able to come our aid.'

It was perhaps a slim hope but it was still one I was determined to cling to for want of anything better. Meanwhile, the room we were confined to was cold, damp and dark, and the bed possessed nothing more than a stained mattress, which I suspected might contain lice. With my head still aching from the blows it had received, I had no desire to stand up, so continued to lie on the mattress with my back against the wall before closing my eyes. The prospect of being confined in such a place for days on end was not one to be welcomed but I was determined not to give way to despair.

'Should no one come to our rescue, then, whenever they next move us, we have to be prepared to seize whatever opportunity arises that might enable us to achieve our freedom,' I asserted to my companions.

'Aye, like ye seized yours on the way 'ere and were struck over the 'ead for your pains,' Nancy said sarcastically.

'We have to take that risk, yes. Otherwise, we may still find ourselves being sold into slavery. Do you want that fate?'

'...No,'

'Well then. When the right moment comes give me your support and we may yet get out of this.'

After a few tedious hours we were provided with some watered down wine and stale bread and each escorted in turn to a foul smelling privy on the other side of the courtyard. I asked if we could be provided with blankets and was simply told 'no.' I tried to steel myself to endure what I feared would be a long, cold night, during which the three of us would have to huddle together for warmth. In the event, it had been dark for less than an hour when we were visited again and told to get up as we were leaving .

'Where are you taking us this time?' I asked.

'You'll soon find out.'

25

Au nom du Roi Louis

As the three of us emerged into the courtyard, we shivered in the face of a fresh wind, which had sprung up, and saw the farm cart waiting for us.

'Quickly, get them on board,' the familiar voice of the dark-skinned man called out of the darkness before stepping forward into our line of vision, whereupon we were duly made to do so. We then departed into the night with the carthorse moving forward across the cobbles at no more than a steady walking pace; the sound of its hooves magnified by the silence all around us.

This time our journey was a short one of somewhat less than ten minutes taking us only so far as the quayside. Here we were ordered out of the cart and made to go on board a two masted vessel with a low draught to the water. I felt an almost overwhelming sense of despair that any chance we might have had of achieving our freedom now seemed to have disappeared completely. Then we were ushered below decks into an empty cabin, even smaller than the one we had been confined to on *The Bellerophon*, with a tiny, shuttered porthole.

Quite where this vessel had come from and so soon was a total mystery to me and I confessed as much to both Mary and Nancy who eyed me glumly. 'I'm sorry,' I said. 'I find it hard to believe how they can have acted so quickly to get us on board another ship.'

I expected that it would up anchor and sail away at any moment. Yet, as the minutes slipped by, I heard no sound of any movement whatsoever, just, at first, muttered voices, coming from the deck above us, followed by a deafening silence. I could only assume that they therefore had no plan to depart before dawn at the very earliest and feeling overwhelmed by tiredness slumped to the floor. Here I was destined to spend an uncomfortable night, huddled together for warmth with my two companions, and drifting in and out of a fitful sleep.

I was woken with a start by the sound of shouting. The cabin was still shrouded in darkness but I could hear the shriek of a seabird and sensed from this that dawn must have broken.

'What's happening?' Nancy asked. 'Are we leaving?'

'No, wait, I think..' I pricked my ears and could tell that the shouting was angry in tone and becoming angrier. The voices, for there were more than one, were naturally speaking in French and as I adjusted my ears to what was being said I felt a surge of hope. 'I think, no I'm certain, God be praised, someone has come to our rescue. He's demanding to be allowed to come on board *au nom du Roi Louis*. He must be a Constable. The Englishman, whose voice we heard yesterday, must have alerted him to what was happening, and somehow they've found out where we are!'

It soon became clear, however, that our captors had no intention of releasing us without a fight. A shot rang out, the noise thunderous enough to make several seabirds shriek in alarm, and then I heard someone scream. It was impossible to tell at first who had fired, but within a matter of seconds I could feel the boat begin to move, leaving me fearful that it was the Constable who had been shot and that our captors were now making good their escape.

There was more bellowing and angry shouts from above as the ship continued to move slowly forward, heading, I could only assume, for the open sea. The commotion going on above us then seemed to reach a crescendo, followed by an awful crunching sound making the boat shudder. I had been standing up but the force of the impact was such that I was thrown backwards, landing in a heap on top of Mary who promptly screeched in pain and apprehension. As the ship then began to settle in the water, I had a terrifying sense that it was about to sink, and Nancy started to panic.

'Let us out,' she screamed, going to the cabin door and banging on it. 'Let us out or we'll drown!'

I looked towards the shuttered porthole just as water began to come through it. I could easily open the shutter but that would just bring more water in and the porthole was simply too small to be able to squeeze through. Anyhow, I couldn't swim and knew that Nancy or Mary couldn't either. In desperation, I wondered if there was anything we could use to break down the door, but there was nothing. All we could do was continue to scream for help and hope that we were not going to be left to drown.

'For pity's sake don't leave us here,' I shouted, feeling even as I did so that I was on the verge of losing my nerve completely and becoming hysterical. Finally, as the amount of water coming into the cabin was beginning to become a flood, a key was turned in the cabin door's bolt and the dark-skinned man stood before us.

'Alright, alright, you can cease your screaming, I was never going to let you drown. Now out of here, quickly. We've launched the small boat and there's room in it for all of us.'

As he spoke he waved a pistol, which he was holding in his right hand, in our general direction. The sight of this made me flinch and I recalled the shot I had heard. I was instinctively convinced that he must have fired it and felt deeply afraid of him as I made my way up to the deck of the ship, which was now beginning to list, making it difficult to stand upright. After the dankness of the small cabin we had been confined to, it was good to breathe fresh air again, and as I glanced around, my eyes were inevitably drawn towards the ship with which we'd evidently collided.

It was close at hand and at right angles to us, its prow badly damaged, which suggested that its captain had deliberately rammed our ship in order to prevent its escape. Looking around I could also see that we had not travelled far from the quayside, and were still inside the wooden walls of its harbour. The boat we were expected to clamber into was indeed tiny, so we were surely unlikely to get very far in it if the ship which had just prevented ours from leaving the harbour was able to pursue us, or, for that matter, some other ship's captain was able to do so. To make matters yet more difficult a strong breeze was blowing, making the sea decidedly choppy, and once eight of us had entered the boat, I was anxious that it might begin to take in water and begin to sink.

The boat possessed four sets of oars and the sun having broken through the cloud, the oarsmen bent their backs to the task of rowing the boat in what looked to me to be a south easterly direction towards land, which I guessed was a couple of miles away. Upon reaching it, I could only imagine that our captors hoped to once more acquire a horse and cart before setting off in the direction of some alternative hide-away to the one we had not long left behind.

We made slow but steady progress, the coastline we were heading for growing gradually closer. I kept hoping that we would soon be pursued but at first there was no sign of this happening. Then, when we were still not even halfway towards our destination, one of the oarsmen, who was facing in the direction in which we had come, made an exclamation.

Merde, ils nous suivent!

I immediately looked back and saw that a three masted ship had just left the harbour and was heading in our direction.

'We can still outrun her,' the dark-skinned man insisted, also speaking in French. 'She's too big to come too close to the shoreline.'

At first, I wasn't even convinced that the ship was pursuing us, whilst, even if it was, I certainly had no idea whether it was likely to overhaul us before we could reach the shore we were aiming for. Our oarsmen were certainly finding their task to be an increasing struggle in choppy waters, but, for whatever reason, the ship's progress seemed to be agonisingly slow with the result that it seemed to be making very little impression on our lead. Nonetheless, there came a point when the oarsmen were so close to exhaustion that our boat was almost at a standstill, whereas the ship, having put on more sail, was definitely gaining ground on us.

'Come on, damn you,' the dark-skinned man yelled at the oarsmen, 'keep rowing, the beach is very close now.'

He was right, too. Worse, I could tell that the ship pursuing us was slowing down, its captain no doubt fearful that he might run it aground in shallow waters . Yet all was not lost, as I was soon able to make out a boat being lowered into the water, which would be capable of pursuing us all the way to the beach.

By the time the three of us were made to leave the boat and take a few steps through shallow water to reach dry land, the boat coming after us was within hailing distance. As I glanced back I could also see a man standing up in its stern, cupping his hands together in front of his mouth.

Arretez au nom du Roi Louis, he bellowed. 'You will not escape us.'

The dark-skinned man's response was to draw his sword and seize hold of Nancy by the arm. Then he held the sword across her throat.

'Let us be or she dies,' he bellowed back.

'And if you murder her, you'll be executed for your pains,' came the immediate response. 'Surrender and you can expect to be shown mercy.'

The dark-skinned man spat into the sand. I could see that the boat pursuing us had ten men on board and I assumed they'd all be well-armed, giving them overwhelming superiority. Surely, there was nothing to be gained by prolonging my misery and that of my companions. Alas, the dark-skinned man didn't see it that way at all.

'Come on, let's get out of here,' he barked. 'There's still time.'

The beach was quite broad with a gentle incline leading to a line of trees, which would certainly afford some cover, but whether we could hope to successfully hide from our pursuers was surely doubtful.

Vous etes fou, I screamed at him, losing my temper. 'You're mad, can't you see your position's hopeless. Leave Nancy be!'

I took a step towards him as I spoke, angrily trying to shove off the man holding my arm. The dark-skinned man looked at me furiously and in doing so lowered his sword whereupon Nancy tried to break free of his grasp but didn't quite succeed

'Let her go, let us all go, you bastard,' I shouted, hitting out at him with my fist, whereupon he dropped his sword and punched me hard on the jaw so that I collapsed to the ground, groaning with pain. Even as I went down I heard the crack of a gun being fired and was barely on my knees before I heard a scream of agony. I could see a man in the stern of the boat had taken aim with his pistol and managed to shoot one of our captors in the arm. He was also now so close to the shoreline that within moments he was able to make his way through the shallows onto the beach itself, only a short distance from where I was still lying on the ground, while the man who had been shot continued to cry out; his left elbow completely shattered.

To my utter dismay, the dark-skinned man then snarled with rage and picking up his sword proceeded to run Nancy through the lower abdomen with it.

'Didn't I say I'd kill her,' he shouted and for a moment it looked as if he might try to kill me as well, but he then thought better of it and instead began to run away. At the same time the man who had been holding onto Mary held his hands up above his head in a gesture of surrender, and after only a slight hesitation his two uninjured companions did the same. Meanwhile, I did what I could to comfort Nancy, but it was obvious that the sword thrust had been a fatal one as her life's blood began to soak the sand and she soon expired in my arms.

It had been an utterly callous murder by a cruel man, which left me feeling both distressed and angry. I could only hope that he would not be allowed to escape and was pleased to receive news of his fate from the youthful officer in charge of the rescue party, which had come to the aid of myself and my companions.

'I am Lieutenant Tenier of his Majesty's frigate *Saint Antoine*,' he told me, speaking in French. 'The Moor is dead. When we came upon him he refused to surrender and was cut down. I very much regret that he could not be prevented from murdering this poor woman. Were you friends?'

'No, I wouldn't say that,' I responded, also in French. 'You see, we were both kidnapped because we knew too much about certain events in England. I am very grateful to you and your men for coming to our rescue although I am somewhat confused as to how you came to do so.'

'I can only tell you, Madame, that my Captain witnessed what happened in the harbour. First, the shooting of a man on the King's business, and then the ramming of the ship you were on by a merchant vessel. We were about to depart anyway so he ordered that we pursue your boat.'

'Then I am so grateful to your captain for his initiative, and indeed to everyone who has come to our aid. It has been a most terrible ordeal, it really has.'

26

I need to get home

'Sir Roger Claybourne, at your service.'

The instant these words were spoken, I was certain I recognised the voice. It was the one I had heard and called out to when we had first arrived in Brest. Its tone was also well modulated and the face behind it clean-shaven and mature enough to suggest to me that he was well into his thirties, but still strikingly handsome with a confident gaze and a solicitous expression. He was not especially tall, wore his hair long, and as he removed his hat with a flourish and bowed to me, I saw that he had the beginnings of a bald patch on the crown of his head. His clothing, meanwhile, was that of a gentleman but looked decidedly well-worn, having clearly seen far better days.

Mary and I along with Nancy's corpse had been brought back to Brest on board the *Saint Antoine* and Sir Roger had approached us the moment we disembarked. My immediate assumption was that he was a royalist in exile and aside from the natural affinity this gave us I felt a profound sense of gratitude at the thought that I must owe our freedom to his initiative.

'I am Lady Jane, the widow of Sir Paul Tremayne of Altringham Manor near Exeter in the County of Devon,' I told him. He died at Worcester fighting for our rightful King.'

At this Sir Roger's eyes lit up. 'M'lady, I remember him well. A fine man, I'm sure. We had the honour to serve together under General Leslie. My condolences on your sad loss.'

I gasped a little. 'You didn't by chance…'

'No, Lady Jane, I did not. In fact until now I had no certain knowledge of his death. However, so many men fell that day fighting for the King, I must confess it comes as no surprise to me. I was most fortunate in being able to escape with only a slight flesh wound and, like the King, to avoid capture.'

'You should also know, Sir, that I have remarried…'

At this he raised his eyebrows. 'And who is that fortunate man?'

'His name is Sumner…Thomas Sumner. He, too, is a staunch royalist. We have married in secret and a warrant has been issued for his arrest. He lives with me at Altringham Manor with only the knowledge of my retainers and a few trusted members of my family and friends.'

'So what has brought you to the dire straits, which I have helped to rescue you from?'

'That, Sir Roger, is a rather long story. Suffice it to say that I and my two companions fell foul of a powerful and unscrupulous individual who I believe was prepared to see us sold into slavery. We might even now have been in the hands of Corsairs, had the ship on which we were being held as prisoners not run aground. I also count myself doubly fortunate to have heard your voice. I will be forever in your debt for coming to our aid.'

'I had my servant, Gabriel, keep watch on the house to which you were taken, and alerted the Mayor of the city, nothing more.'

'Even so, Sir Roger, I am most grateful to you.'

'Pleased to be of service, I assure you.But tell me, I understood that three of you were put on board the ship that was anchored here…'

'I regret to say that Nancy was murdered. Her body has been brought back here on the *Saint Antoine* for burial.'

'That is sad news indeed. Was she a friend?'

'No, she was the maid of a young woman, whom I firmly believe was also murdered. It was because of what she knew of the events leading to that, and what I and my maid, Mary, here, came to know, that caused us to be kidnapped and smuggled out of England, I now need to return there as soon as possible in order to expose the man responsible for everything that has happened to us.'

'You know this person then?'

'I know of him only too well although I am yet to actually speak to him. He has overreached himself on this occasion and now I intend to see that justice is done. Can you help me do so? Of course, I have nothing but the clothes I stand up in.'

'Lady Jane, I will give you every assistance I can, but I must tell you that I and my wife and children are only surviving as exiles on the charity of my cousins. You see, one of my grandmothers was a Breton by birth. My cousin, Jacques Chabot, has given us a cottage to live in on his land for which we pay no rent, whilst I was able to bring a little money with me when we fled from England, but that is now nearly gone. Gabriel stays with me and my family out of loyalty, not because I can afford to pay him, and helps me farm the land that my cousin has also kindly set aside for us. He is a generous man, who would never let us starve, but our lives are still but a shadow of what they would have been had it not been for the wretched war.'

'You can still give us shelter, I hope?'

'I will speak to my cousin. I am sure he will be willing to do so.'

'Thank you... And wait, of course, I do still possess something of value. I have my wedding ring on my finger. See, it is made of gold and has a small diamond... It is the one that Paul gave me. If it will pay for my passage to England along with Mary's then I will gladly sell it.'

'But it must have...'

'Yes, some sentimental value, of course. All the same, I must get home. I have a baby son, Lucas, who's less than six months. I know his wet nurse will be taking good care of his needs but I already miss him terribly and had thought...well, that I might never see him again.'

For all his protestations of poverty both Sir Roger and his servant possessed horses, which he explained were owned by his cousin, and these were used to convey the four of us back to his farm, which proved to be situated about five miles inland from Brest in a north easterly direction. We were not, however , able to depart until arrangements had been made for Nancy's body to be placed in the city's principal mortuary and I worried that for want of any money she would end up being interred in an unmarked pauper's grave. It was a sad fate, for sure, but one I felt powerless to do anything about.

By the time we reached our destination evening was coming on and the weather closing in, with increasing amounts of rain and wind having made our journey thoroughly uncomfortable. I felt exhausted and worse could feel myself becoming feverish. I feared a repetition of the ill health, which had so recently struck me down, although it felt far longer given the series of events which had since occurred. With the help of a pillion-saddle, which Sir Roger had obtained from livery stables I had been able to sit behind him, while in the same fashion Mary had sat behind Gabriel. Now, as the moment came to dismount, I found myself stumbling as soon as I had done so and complained of feeling both dizzy and hot.

'I need to lie down , Sir Roger,' I said so he helped guide me towards the threshold of the Chabots substantial farmhouse where we were met by both Jacques Chabot and his wife, Marguerite. After a rapid explanation by Sir Roger of what had taken place, we were greeted with much friendly concern, but I felt so exhausted I was barely able to respond.

Pardonnez-moi, je suis malade, I muttered and was quickly helped up a narrow flight of stairs by Marguerite, who showed me into a small room with nothing on its walls but a crucifix above the head of its single bed. Mary then assisted me to take off my dress and lie down, still wearing my chemise. I then fell into a deep sleep, only to begin to wake in the early hours of the morning, still feeling hot and feverish as well as desperately thirsty, and at first, completely disorientated.

'God, where am I?' I called out before everything that had happened the previous day came rushing back to me.

'It's alright, m'lady, we're in a farmhouse. don't you remember?' Mary responded out of the darkness where a bed of sorts had been made up for her on the floor, consisting of a sheet, two ample blankets and a small pillow.

'Yes, it all comes back to me now. I need to drink. Is there any water?'

'There's a jug of weak cider here, m'lady. I've tried some. Here, I'll pour you a glass, though it might be hard to see what I'm doing in the dark.'

By morning my condition had worsened as I became more feverish. I moved in and out of consciousness and lost much sense of time and place. So ill did I become that the next thing I remember with any clarity was the arrival of a doctor, who upon examining me recommended that I be bled. I was too ill to protest at a process I had long thought to be of questionable value and not surprisingly it left me feeling weaker than ever. I could also tell from Mary's increasingly anxious expressions that she feared for my very life.

I was fortunate that Marguerite Chabot proved to be an intelligent and caring individual who despite the burdens of her brood of five children was prepared to ensure that I was as well nursed and fed as possible. Without her ministrations supporting Mary's best endeavours I might well have succumbed, but as matters transpired after a week or more I began to rally.

By the twelfth day of my ordeal I was finally on the road to recovery, feeling able to eat and drink unaided, and no longer being at all feverish. However, I was still so weak that another two days went by before I was able to get out of bed and dress myself with Mary's assistance. I was full of a profound sense of gratitude for the care I had received, but with every hour that I felt stronger my impatience to return to England without yet further delay increased. As soon as my fever abated I was also quick to realise that my wedding ring was no longer on my finger.

'What has happened to it?' I asked Mary.

'Why, m'lady I was told it would have to be sold to cover the doctor's fees as well as the expense involved in keeping us both well fed.'

'Has all the money obtained from the sale been spent then?' I asked in alarm.

'I don't know m'lady, you'd best ask Madame Chabot.'

This I did at the earliest opportunity, being much relieved to be told that although the ring had indeed been sold it had raised a handsome sum, a fair part of which remained unspent.'

'Enough to pay for our passage home to England, I would hope.'

'Oh yes, I would have thought so,' Madame Chabot reassured me.

When I at last felt well enough, I dined with both the Chabots and Sir Roger and Lady Claybourne. It was a convivial occasion and I was much taken by Lady Claybourne's good looks, auburn hair, and vivacious manner, despite her straitened circumstances, although her grasp of French left much to be desired. In different times we might well have become good friends but as it was I remained preoccupied with thoughts of home and was quick to enquire whether any ships they knew of sailed regularly from Brest to Topsham, or failing that Plymouth. I was greeted by shakes of the head, but Sir Roger assured me that he would make urgent enquiries on my behalf.

Further, Jacques Chabot promised that, if necessary, he would convey me to Roscoff on the northern coast of Brittany. He seemed confident, too, that I would be able to find a ship bound for either Plymouth or Topsham, whose captain would be willing to take women passengers on board in return for a suitable payment.

Another five days were to go by, during which, whilst my health continued to improve, my sense of frustration also reached a fever pitch, before Sir Roger was finally able to inform me that a French merchant ship was in port, which was due to leave for Southampton the following day. To get home from there would still involve a journey of nearly a hundred miles, but Sir Roger was able to assure me that the payment he had agreed with the ship's Captain would still leave me with enough money to pay for the coach journey as well as food and lodgings.

'Remember that I was paid in gold Louis for your ring and I'm certain you will be able to make use of these in England. The ship will also be leaving shortly after dawn but I can still get you onboard in time.'

'I will forever be in your debt for all that you have done for me, Sir Roger…'

'It has been an honour, I assure you.'

27
Bad news

It was now early October and my journey home had been a long, uncomfortable and exhausting one, causing me to worry that I would suffer another relapse into poor health. True to his word Sir Roger had brought me and Mary to the port in good time to board our ship. However, adverse tides along with rough seas, which had given both of us seasickness, had caused our crossing to Southampton to last all of three days. We'd then had another day's wait before being able to travel on to our destination by coach. Still, that had allowed us to take our ease a little, whilst the inn we had stayed in for a night had been perfectly adequate.

The journey to Honiton and beyond had then taken all of five days and had proved as an unpleasant experience as the sea crossing, given the poor state of the road. The inns we'd stayed in had also been adequate save for one grim place, which had offered no hot food. Worse, its beds had been hard as nails. Finally, having been dropped off by the coach on the road between Honiton and Exeter, we'd had no choice but to complete our journey on foot until Altringham Manor finally came in sight.

We made a bedraggled pair, our dresses dirty as well as torn in places, our hair and bodies in dire need of washing. Yet, I just felt an overwhelming sense of relief at having returned safely despite everything we'd endured, and couldn't wait to be reunited with my loved ones, for all that I feared that Thomas would admonish me for my reckless behaviour.

As we first approached the Manor House, I had no reason to think that anything had changed in the five weeks or so that had elapsed since I last set eyes upon it. True everything was very quiet but there was nothing unusual in that. After all, it was late afternoon, a normally quiet time of the day. Nonetheless, when I knocked on the front door, expecting a prompt response, there was none at all, so after a couple of minutes of growing frustration I knocked again yet more loudly. Still, there came no response, so I decided to call out.

'Hello, is anyone there? Hello. Hello!' This time the continuing silence seemed almost deafening to my ears. 'Christ in heaven, Mary, I don't understand this. Where is everyone?' I felt a dreadful fear in the pit of my stomach that something must be terribly wrong but did not admit to this. Instead, I merely said 'come with me' before setting off in the direction of Harry and Melissa's cottage, dreading the thought that I might not find anyone there either.

Once we arrived at its door, I banged on it with just a hint of desperation, and thus far more loudly than I would normally have done. Immediately, an infant inside started crying and I was convinced it must be Lucas.

'Hush child, hush,' I heard Melissa say. 'Who's there?'

'Melissa, it's me, it's Jane…'

'Oh m'lady! God be praised! We thought you lost for ever.'

Melissa threw the door open, holding Lucas in her arms, and I took him from her gratefully, planting kisses on his head, and rejoicing at our reunion.

'He looks well and for certain he's put on weight.'

'Oh yes, m'lady, 'e's getting stronger by the day, and 'e's a healthy pair of lungs on him, I can tell 'e.'

In confirmation of these words Lucas began to cry loudly and I did my best to soothe him. Meanwhile, Melissa's two youngest children appeared, gathering around their mother's skirts, but there was no sign of Harry, leading me to ask where he was.

'He's in the fields, m'lady. The harvest has been a good one, I'm pleased to say.'

'That's good news, indeed, but tell me, why does no one appear to be in the house? I knocked twice, the second time as loudly as I could, and still no one answered.' Melissa now looked at me in a distraught fashion. 'Well, is something wrong?'

'Oh m'lady, I'm afeared to tell 'e that soldiers have been 'ere again. They....'

'Oh my God, they didn't....'

'I'm so sorry, m'lady, they took Master Thomas away. He was dressed simply as always, and went to the cottage as soon as they came in sight, but they didn't just search, they questioned everyone closely. I don't know what it was gave 'im away. Perhaps 'is voice.'

'When was this?'

'It be a week ago, now.'

'And where did they take him, do you know?'

'I don't, m'lady, I'm sorry.'

My mind was racing at this dreadful news, wondering if anyone might have betrayed Thomas.

'And did they enquire about me?'

'Not then, no, but two days later they came back. Harry said that 'e was shown a warrant for your arrest, so 'e told 'em that 'e 'ad reason to believe you'd been kidnapped and taken abroad, You see, after you went missing, Lady Olivia tried to find you. She even rode to the coast and saw some women being taken on board ship. She thought they must be you and Mary, here, but by then it was too late to rescue you. Their officer also said 'e'd orders to seize the house and estate in the name of the Lord Protector. 'E demanded to be given the keys of the house and locked it up. Then they left again.'

'So where have Alice and Toby gone?'

'Alice has gone to her widowed sister in Sidmouth, and Toby, back to his parents.'

'And meanwhile Harry's just been left to run the estate?'

'Yes, m'lady, we've tried to carry on as normal...'

At that very moment Harry appeared, looking weary, or so I thought. At the sight of me, however, his eyes lit up with pleasure.

'M'lady, this is a miracle indeed. How on earth did you manage to escape?'

'Sheer good fortune, Harry. First our ship ran aground off the coast of Brittany and then when we were taken to Brest I heard an English voice. It was that of a royalist in exile, Sir Roger Claybourne. He persuaded the authorities to come to my rescue. There was one tragedy, though. Nancy was killed, run through with a sword by one of our captors. And now I return to discover that Thomas has been arrested and the house and estate seized...'

'Yes, m'lady, I'm mighty sorry that you had to return to such bad news. The officer who came to take possession of the house told me that the entire estate is likely to be sold but that's bound to take some time, I suppose.'

'And meanwhile, there's a warrant out for my arrest, too, I understand…'

'Aye, m'lady, for harbouring a known renegade.'

I was in a state of shock at this latest development. I had returned home counting my blessings, and fully expecting to be reunited with both Thomas and Lucas, only to discover that disaster had struck. Frustratingly, the arrest warrant with my name on it also meant that I might well be thwarted in my desire to bring Hugh Graveney to justice.

Mary, though, remained free to point the finger at him even if I did not, but even here I could see a difficulty. Once she came forward with accusations, she could expect in turn to be questioned about my fate. She could, I supposed, still try and pretend that she alone had returned from France, but I doubted if she'd be believed, in which case I could expect either soldiers or constables to come in search of me.

It followed that I'd be left with little choice but to flee Altringham Manor, for all that this would mean leaving Lucas behind as well. Of course, he would continue to be safe in Melissa and Harry's care, but when I might be able to see him again was something I could only guess at. I wondered, too, where I could hide and although I fully intended to pay a visit to Fetford Hall, the last thing I wanted was to place anyone there at risk of being accused of sheltering me. I began to imagine myself being forced to return to Brittany and asking the Chabot family if they would take pity on me.

I worried, too, about Mary's vulnerability as Graveney's sole accuser. After all, he was perfectly capable of seeking to silence her. Certainly, I could hardly blame her if she lacked the courage to speak out against him, whilst she would surely need protection, even if she did so.

'I must go to Fetford Hall to speak with Lady Courtney and her family,' I told Harry. 'I'll need a horse, though, having lost poor Hera, but I'll see it comes back to you.'

'Of course, m'lady, it's yours to take anyway. I must also tell you that Lady Courtney's been here within the last three days. She wanted to see your son and naturally I told her everything that's happened. She was most upset, I must say.'

'I see. Well thank you, Harry. And Mary, you'll be wanting to be reunited with your family in the village, I'm sure.'

'Yes, very much so, m'lady.'

'You also appreciate that Thomas's arrest, along with the warrant that's been issued for my arrest as well, changes everything. If any charge is to be brought against Hugh Graveney it can only be at your instigation...' At these words Mary looked positively nonplussed. It brought home to me just how young and innocent she still was as well as being so poorly educated that she could neither read nor write. 'What I mean is that you will have to lay a complaint before the Justices. I cannot do it for you.'

'I dunno if I want to do that, m'lady. Can't I stay with you?'

'You have served me loyally, Mary, and, believe me, I am grateful for that, but you need to understand that I face imprisonment for sheltering Thomas and may have to go abroad again to avoid that fate. At the same time, I don't want Hugh Graveney to go unpunished for his crimes. Harry here could take you to Exeter to see Master Overbury and he would assist you, of that I am confident...'

'Forgive me for saying so, m'lady,' Harry added, 'but he'll no doubt require paying for his services and all your money is presently locked inside the house. It could even…'

'What, are you suggesting it's been seized?'

'I don't know m'lady, but it's possible it could have been.'

'Then we need to find out. You know I keep it locked inside a box under my bed and the key to it inside an old jar on my dressing table. Mind you, both could still be easily found, or the box's lock simply forced open. There's a little jewellery as well, of course. I pray it hasn't been taken, too.' And with that I felt my finger, which had held my wedding ring until so very recently.

'The doors to the house couldn't easily be broken open, m'lady.'

'Then a window will have to be broken instead, either at the side of the house or round the back. Whatever the Lord Protector might proclaim to the contrary, it's still my home!'

I felt a rising sense of anger, not to say a measure of desperation, at the thought that on top of everything else that had befallen me I might now have been reduced to penury. As it was, Harry soon produced a hammer and together we set off for the house.

All its windows were lattice ones and after selecting one at the side of the house, Harry knocked out the glass in a panel nearest to where the window's handle was located. He was then able to open the window and with some difficulty clamber inside, reminding me of the illicit entry that Olivia and I had made into Hugh Graveney's house in Exeter. With his help I was also able to follow him.

I had steeled myself against the possibility that I would find that the entire house had been turned upside down but to my relief the downstairs appeared completely undisturbed. With a rising sense of hope we made our way upstairs and into my bedroom.

'Thank God,' I declared, having gone immediately to the bed and pulled out the box from underneath it. 'It's still locked.'

'I'm pleased, m'lady.'

'Look Harry, are you willing to support Mary? There could be danger involved. If Graveney were to get wind of our return, I wouldn't be at all surprised if he didn't try to have her silenced.'

'You can count on me, m'lady. I'll see to it that she gets to Master Overbury.'

'And the sooner that's done the better,Harry. What also concerns me is that she's bound to be questioned about my whereabouts. It's best, I think, that she's honest and admits that we returned here together. She can then say that I left, which will be the honest truth. Once I've visited Fetford Hall and spoken with Olivia and her family I will in fact return to see Lucas.'

'Of course, m'lady.'

'I'm also loath to go far until I know Thomas's fate. When you visit Overbury in Exeter with Mary, you must ask him if he knows what has happened to him. As needs be, I'm sure his clerk can make enquiries. Now, I need Mary to help me. A fire must be made to give me hot water to wash with and then I must change out of these clothes.'

28

Help is at hand

The stormy nature of the weather reflected my mood as I rode towards Fetford Hall. On the one hand, it felt good to be riding a horse again, to feel clean, my hair washed and properly brushed, and to have finally been able to discard the attire I had been forced to wear constantly for more than a month. On the other, my emotions were all at sea as I feared for Thomas and when, if ever, I would see Lucas again if I really did decide to flee back to France without him.

I was frustrated, too, by the turn of events, which had first rescued me from the prospect of enslavement only to then cause me to lose my home and face the risk of imprisonment. Meanwhile, whether Graveney would ever pay for his crimes also now rested on the shoulders of a vulnerable, illiterate, eighteen year old servant girl.

Upon my arrival, my reunion with Olivia proved to be a sweet moment of pure joy. I was certain that I would never forget the look of astonishment turning to utter delight when she first set eyes on me again. The rest of the family were similarly moved and there was much hugging and exchanging of kisses on the cheeks, and even the shedding of a few tears on Constance's part, before I could begin to explain the course of events which had brought me home.

'And now it seems that I will have to flee again or face

imprisonment, while at the same time my home is utterly lost to me,' I added. 'What's more I don't understand what brought soldiers to the doors of Altringham Manor yet again, and with more determination than ever, if it wasn't as a consequence of someone informing on Thomas.'

'I was appalled to learn what had happened when I visited Lucas just a few days ago,' Olivia said. 'Have you any suspicion as to who might have been responsible?'

'I could ask you the same question, dear friend?

'What, you don't think Hugh Graveney was behind this?'

'It's possible, yes, but tell me, as I understand you did all you could to find out what had happened to me and come to my rescue, did you in the course of doing so tell my sister that I had gone missing and then been spirited abroad?'

'Yes...I did. And as I recall...'

'John was there when you did so?'

'Yes...My God...You don't think...'

'I'd like to see him confronted with the question, that I can tell you. It was hard enough for Caroline to constrain him from informing on Thomas when he first learnt we were married. Once he gathered that I'd been taken abroad never likely to return, I can well imagine him deciding that the time had come to act.'

'Even if I confronted him with the accusation, he'd likely deny it.'

'Yes, perhaps he would. On the other hand he might be self-righteous enough to say *yes and be damned* to the question.'

'Either way, what good would be achieved by confronting him.'

'Just the satisfaction of seeing the indignant look on his face, but then that pleasure would have to be yours as I can't risk going anywhere near Exeter. Even if I dressed like a beggar woman, I'd likely be recognised.'

'And I've some news for you, too. I instructed Master Overbury to write to the Sheriff reporting the circumstances of your disappearance and the belief that you'd been kidnapped and taken abroad. The letter pointed the finger of suspicion at Graveney and urged the Sheriff to issue a search warrant of his country estate to see if yours and Mary's horses could be discovered there…'

'And what's been the response?'

'Total silence, I'm afraid. Master Overbury has told me within the last week that he has sent a short letter of reminder…'

'Hum, the likelihood is that Graveney has the Sheriff in his pocket.'

'And there's more, too. Lovell has also raised an accusation of smuggling against Graveney and been informed that the matter is being investigated, so he has written to tell me.'

'And that remains the position?'

'I assume so, for I've heard nothing more.'

'Well, I'm determined to still see Graveney brought to justice even if I can take no action against him personally. Nancy may be dead, God rest her soul, but that still leaves Mary to point the finger. Harry's also prepared to take her to Master Overbury and see that her mark is put to a disposition accusing the man of being responsible for her kidnapping.'

'And what mention will she make of you?'

'She need make little mention of me at all but, if questioned, I've told her to be honest and say I returned to Altringham Manor with her, only to depart again as soon as I learnt that there was a warrant issued for my arrest.'

'That will still put the authorities on the alert for you.'

'True, but by then I'll have slipped out of the country again. At least I found the box, containing such savings as I have, had not been tampered with in my absence, so I still have some means at my disposal.'

'No, Jane, surely you don't have to do that,' Constance appealed to me. We'll give you shelter, won't we, James?'

'Of course, you know we'd be happy to, Jane.'

'And then put your own security at risk. No, it wouldn't be fair.'

'But what about Lucas, if you go abroad again, will you take him with you?'

I shook my head. 'For the present he's safe enough in Melissa and Harry's care and as to the future I would beg you, Olivia, to be a mother to him in my place.'

'Do not make too hasty a decision, Jane, is all I would ask,' Constance said. 'At least enjoy what hospitality we can afford you for a few days. You look worn out.'

'Very well, as I mentioned, I have been very sick. I worry that it's a condition that might keep recurring.'

'You need to build up your strength and while you stay with us you can continue to visit Lucas whenever you wish.'

'I will do that, though Harry's assured me he'll take Mary to Exeter within the next five days, and once he's done so I'll not be able to linger here for too much longer.'

'Jane, I must say that I think you exaggerate the danger you face,' James asserted. 'It's true, of course, that there's a warrant out for your arrest, but I doubt if anyone will be in much hurry to act upon it. After all, you're hardly a dangerous renegade, just a wife protecting her husband. You might even have a defence to any charge brought against you on the basis that you were merely obeying his wishes as your legal spouse. Stay with us and bring Lucas, too, as soon as you wish to, and you'll be safe enough, I reckon.'

'You'd still be putting yourselves at risk, though.'

'Only a little, I think, and life's a risky affair in any event as we all appreciate, I'm sure.'

'Just do not make too hasty a decision on the matter,' Becky said, joining in the conversation for the first time.

'No, I won't and I'm grateful to you all for your support. I must say that I fear so much for Thomas. If he's indicted on a charge of high treason he's bound to be executed.'

'But he wasn't a ringleader in the failed conspiracy against Cromwell's life, was he?' James asked.

'No, not so far as I am aware, but he was still a party to it. Even if he isn't executed he could still be imprisoned for life, or perhaps transported to the Indies. Either might well amount to a death sentence. Anyhow, I will think very seriously about your generous offer. God knows, having just returned from France, I really do not want to have to turn round and go back there if I can avoid it.'

Within the hour we sat down to enjoy a meal together and the more I ate and drank and joined in the convivial conversation, the more I recoiled at the prospect of having to say goodbye before fleeing into exile. All the same, I also reflected upon the reality that once Mary admitted I'd returned to Devon, if the authorities had any desire at all to arrest me, then Fetford Hall was surely the first place they'd look.

My position within the Courtney household would therefore have to mirror the one that Thomas had for the most part enjoyed within my own and in the event of any Constables or soldiers arriving, I would have to be promptly and effectively hidden. The alternative might be to pass myself off as a servant but even if I dressed in a manner appropriate to such a station in life and kept my hair under a cap, I was so well known in the area that someone would be almost bound to recognise me.

'If I were to accept your kind invitation to stay with you as a guest…'

'As an honoured guest as well as a dear family friend,' Constance interrupted me to which I responded with a smile and a nod of the head.

'As I was about to say, I need some assurance from you that in the event of the worst happening, you would be able to offer me a hiding place, where I would be unlikely to be found.'

At that moment James spoke up. 'I can think of somewhere. When the house was built a far older one was demolished. In its day it was a fortified manor house, not only with cellars but also a tunnel, which is still accessible, and runs down to the river. A thorough search of the house might well reveal all, but by then you could be well gone.'

'Yes, but gone where?'

'Close to where the tunnel ends we keep a small boat with oars. You could row yourself downstream in no time at all. I can't believe any search party would follow the river bank for any distance. After an hour at the most you could row back again.'

'But I've never rowed anywhere in my life...'

'Well, it's easily done. I could teach you in no time.'

Having slept on the idea, I announced over breakfast that I had decided to accept their hospitality and would take a chance on being able to hide in the event of anyone coming in search of me. In the end what had persuaded me more than anything else was the thought of being able to remain close to Lucas. Of course, once he was brought to stay with me there was a danger that his presence might give me away, but when I expressed this concern James sought to reassure me.

'If you had to escape through the tunnel, you could take Lucas with you.'

'But once he starts crawling it would be hard to row and manage him as well. I would need help. Look, my maid, Mary, has said that she wishes to stay with me. Would you mind if I brought her here as well; that is once she has done what I have asked of her and brought Graveney to justice?'

'No, of course not. She'd be welcome.'

'It would mean another mouth to feed...'

'No matter, this is a large house and we have the means.'

Once again I expressed my gratitude before announcing that I would be returning to Altringham Manor to see Lucas and tell Mary what had been decided.

'I will also be asking Harry to enquire of Master Overbury if he has any knowledge of where Thomas is being held. If it is in the High Gaol in Exeter then I would like to think it might be possible to get a message to him, assuring him of my love and that I am safe and well. In fact, I'm sure if I asked Harry, he would visit him for me. I just dread to think how he must be suffering. I know he grew to feel that Altringham Manor was like a prison, but wherever he is now will be far, far worse!'

'Let me ride with you?' Olivia asked. 'It looks to be a fine day and I'd love to see Lucas again.'

'Of course, Olivia, you'd be more than welcome.'

It felt like old times when we both set out together and I drew as much consolation as I could from Olivia's company in the face of a growing sense of despondency over Thomas's fate.

'I really fear that he will be executed,' I confessed. 'God, to think that I might be left a widow a second time. It hardly bears contemplating. To think, too, that John might have betrayed him. I'd still like to confront him with the accusation and see his face.'

'Well, as that's not possible, I remain prepared to do it for you,' Olivia asserted. 'In fact I could ride to Exeter with Harry and Mary in order to do so.'

'That's kind of you, Olivia, but I really can't ask that of you.'

'Nonsense, I'd be happy to do so, whatever his response might be.'

'Very well then, if you must.'

29

Olivia travels to Exeter

Jane waved us farewell as our little party set out for Exeter, and I could sense Mary's trepidation from the nervous expression she wore constantly on her face. I thought it fortunate, in fact, that I had been so insistent on accompanying both her and Harry to Exeter, as I believed that without my gentle but firm encouragement Mary might have declined to leave at all.

Matters were also not helped by the inclement weather. Autumn rains had now set in with a vengeance and it had been raining heavily, on and off, for three successive days, a fact which would not only make our journey uncomfortable but also slower as the road became ever muddier. To compound our difficulty Harry's stallion would also have to bear not just his weight but Mary's, too.

It had occurred to me that I alone should accompany Mary but after due discussion it had been agreed that it would be safer to have a male companion with us as well. Further, to help ensure we reached our destination before midday, dawn had not long broken when we departed. It was then fortunate that within half an hour the rain began to ease off and then stop altogether, thus enabling us to make faster progress.

The further we travelled the more uneasy I became at the prospect of confronting John. I wondered, indeed, what had ever possessed me to suggest such an idea. By the time the walls of the city came in sight I was positively hoping that he would be out on his rounds so that I would honestly be able to inform Jane that my attempt to speak with him had failed.

What also troubled me somewhat was the awkward issue of what to say to Caroline about Jane's situation. I had naturally discussed this with Jane and it had been agreed that it was only right that she be informed that her sister had returned from abroad. Beyond that, though, we'd decided that I would not admit to any knowledge at all of her circumstances in John's presence. Further, even to Caroline alone I would say no more than that she was in hiding

Once having entered the city, we went first to the livery stables, and having left our horses there continued on foot to Master Overbury's chambers, quite prepared for the likelihood that he would be in court. In the event, though, I was informed by his clerk that he was presently engaged with a client in his inner sanctum and would probably be free to see me in about half an hour, possibly a little longer.

I decided that this just gave me time to walk the fairly short distance to Caroline and John's house. If only Caroline was at home then I would speak briefly to her in confidence about Jane. Otherwise, I would try and find the courage to confront John with the accusation that he had been responsible for betraying Thomas.

Upon my arrival the door was answered as I expected by a maid who informed me that John was out on his rounds, news that I received with an almost audible sigh of relief. Caroline, though, was at home and the instant she appeared I apologised for disturbing her but added that I had something important to tell her.

'I wanted you to know in strictest confidence that Jane has returned safely from abroad.'

'Why that is wonderful news but you do know, don't you, that a warrant has been issued for her arrest?'

'Yes, I do and she's aware of what's happened. I'm not able to say anything more save for the fact that she sends you her love. She'd also be particularly grateful if you said nothing to your husband about what I've just told you.'

'Why shouldn't I?'

'Her fear is that he might report her to the Justices.'

'I would never let him do that, I assure you.'

'Even so, I would still be obliged if you would keep this news to yourself.'

At that moment we heard the sound of someone entering the front door and then saw that it was John, dressed as usual in his puritanically dark garb. Both of us tensed a little and he looked anything but pleased to see me.

'Lady Courtney,' he said sharply without bothering to offer me any good day. 'What brings you to my house, might I ask?'

'I was hoping to speak with you.'

'Really. About what, pray?'

'I want to ask if it's your doing that soldiers came to arrest Thomas Sumner?'

John stared at me wide eyed, first with shock that I should ask such a question of him, and then with an expression of growing anger.

'Certainly not. How dare you suggest such a calumny against me!'

'Forgive my forwardness but ever since I heard what had happened the question has been troubling me. I had to be certain... For my peace of mind.'

'Well, now you have your answer and I must make it clear that you are not welcome in this house so please leave.'

'Alright, I wish you both a good day.'

So, it had been much as Jane had predicted, I thought, as I stepped out onto the street, although I had seen no curl of the lip, merely a flash of indignant anger, which might or might not have been genuine. In any event, the visit had taken no more than a few minutes and when I returned to Master Overbury's chambers once more it was to find that Harry and Mary were still waiting. I smiled gently at them both.

'That didn't take long. I was able to speak to both Caroline and her husband.'

'Good, m'lady. You look troubled, if you don't mind me saying so,' Harry responded.

'Do I really. Yes, well, let me just say that I was not looking forward to my conversation with Caroline's husband and the question I needed to ask him made him quite angry. It was not an unexpected reaction, but I was still shown the door, so it has left me feeling, if not troubled, then certainly a little flustered.'

Harry was respectful enough of my superior status in life not to seek to question me about what it was that had made John angry, although he must have been curious. Instead, we simply lapsed into silence and another ten minutes at least went by during which I was conscious of a growing level of hunger. This was hardly surprising, given that we had eaten nothing more than a small quantity of cheese and somewhat stale bread before seven o'clock in the morning, and it was now past midday.

Finally, the door to Overbury's inner sanctum swung open and out walked a thin faced, rather tall individual, with a pointed beard and grey, wispy hair, who departed with no more than a glance in my direction. Overbury then appeared, and, recognising me, immediately smiled and swept me a bow.

'This is an unexpected pleasure, Lady Courtney, how may I be of service?'

'I am here on behalf of my friend, Lady Jane, and this is her maid, Mary, very recently returned from France. Harry, Jane's steward, you've met before, as I recall.'

'Indeed I have and I wish you a good day, sir,'

'You'll appreciate,' I continued, 'that Mary and Jane were both kidnapped and taken abroad. By sheer good fortune their ship then ran aground off the French coast and they were subsequently rescued from their captivity. Mary can testify to this and to her having been held in the country house of Hugh Graveney.'

'Can she, by God. And as to Lady Jane, where is she?'

'Also returned, but you may have heard that there is a warrant for her arrest.'

'No, I haven't, though I'm aware that Thomas Sumner has been arrested. He's currently languishing in the High Gaol.'

'Would it then be possible for you to get a message to him offering the reassurance that Jane has been able to return to England and is safe and well?'

'That could be arranged, certainly. I'm also not going to ask where Lady Jane is at present, but if you are seeking my assistance in bringing a charge against Hugh Graveney based on her maid's evidence then she must expect to be questioned about her mistress's whereabouts.'

'Quite so, Master Overbury. All she can say, though, is that she's no longer at Altringham Manor.'

Overbury looked fixedly into my eyes and I detected a faint smile. 'So you're saying she could be anywhere; perhaps even on her way back to France?'

'Precisely that.'

'And I take it that this girl can neither read nor write?'

'No, but she can place her mark on any testimony that you care to prepare for her, and will willingly give evidence in court. Is that not so, Mary?'

Mary nodded nervously. 'Yes, m'lady.',

'My brother, James is also willing to cover your fee for your services,' I assured Overbury.

'Good, good. I'd also advise that this girl needs to be kept safe at all times until she's given evidence in court. We both know what Graveney's capable of. I can make sure that her mark is witnessed by a notary under oath, but there's really no substitute for her giving evidence in court if Graveney's to be convicted of anything. My clerk here can take down her testimony and then she will need to go before a notary. As soon as that's done I will personally accompany her to the Justice and request that he immediately issue a warrant for Graveney's arrest.'

'Can you do all this in the space of an afternoon?' I asked.

'With my clerk's assistance, I can but try. It will mean putting other work to one side but you are fortunate that I am not due in court again until the day after tomorrow.'

Overbury's clerk went quickly to work and within the hour had prepared a testimony, to which Mary placed her mark. By this time, however, I was feeling almost weak with hunger and Overbury suggested that we adjourn to a nearby inn. 'They serve a decent stew,' he declared.

Leaving his clerk in charge of his office, Overbury led the way towards the inn. By now the weather had closed in again and it was spitting with rain while a keen wind had also sprung up encouraging us all to keep our heads down. Out of the corner of my eye, though, I still caught sight of three men coming towards us at a fast pace. Turning towards them I realised that they were not only all wearing hats, which was to be expected, but had also covered their faces so only their eyes and foreheads were visible.

I screamed in alarm and then, before I could do anything more, two of the men pounced on Overbury and Harry, knocking them both to the ground, while the third, taller and stronger looking, seized hold of Mary and started dragging her away. I tried to stop him but he flung out an arm with a clenched fist that struck me so hard on the nose that I felt it begin to bleed. I reeled back in pain, conscious as I did so that Mary was struggling desperately with her attacker. However, he was simply too strong, and struck her such a blow to the head that her legs buckled, enabling him to pick her up as if she was a rag doll.

One of his two accomplices then waved a knife in a threatening manner in Harry and Overbury's direction. 'Try to come after us and ye'll get this through yer guts,' he shouted in a strong Devon accent, standing his ground just long enough for the man carrying Mary to disappear from sight.

Then he slowly backed away, still holding out his knife as if he was prepared to use it if he had to.

'You won't get away with this,' Overbury retorted. 'We know who your Master is and I'll see you hanged for what you've just done.'

Their attacker's response was to simply turn and run off, taking the same route as the man carrying Mary.

'Go after them,' I said to Harry.

'I don't think it's worth it,' Overbury declared. 'They've already had time to disappear down some dark alleyway and I'd be very wary of the man who threatened us with a knife.

'But we can't just let them get away with this! Carrying Mary will have slowed their progress and passersby will surely have seen them, too. Just be careful, Harry.'

He nodded and set off in pursuit, but Overbury remained unwilling to follow him.

'Graveney's not going to get away with this,' he declared. 'The three of us can all testify to what has just happened and my clerk took down a testimony from the maid before we left. I'm still going to put a case before the Justice that there's enough evidence against Graveney to justify his arrest.'

'I just wonder how anyone knew we were here?' I asked.

'Someone in Graveney's employ must have seen you upon your arrival in the city, presumably recognised you for who you were, and then alerted Graveney. I wouldn't be surprised if the news threw him into a panic, causing him to act too hastily. Now he's going to pay for it.'

'Perhaps, but Jane, for one, will still be utterly mortified if Mary's murdered.'

30

In the name of the Lord Protector

I was growing increasingly impatient for news from Exeter as it was now the best part of a day and a half since Olivia, accompanied by Mary and Harry, had departed, and I had expected them to return the previous evening. Having regained entry to my house, I had made the decision that I would sleep in my own bed and had woken in the morning to the sound of rain, which had continued falling ever since. To pass the time I had still had the pleasure of enjoying Lucas's company and was delighted by the progress he had made while I had been absent. Clearly, he was continuing to put on weight, his complexion was healthy, and he was feeding well.

Finally, as midday approached I heard the sound of horses approaching and looking outside saw that Olivia and Harry were returning. I went immediately to the cottage door to offer them a welcome.

'But where's Mary?' I asked.

'I'm sorry, Jane, but she's been taken again,' Olivia told me.

'Taken! But how?'

'Three masked men attacked us in broad daylight in Exeter, snatched her away while one of them threatened us with a knife, and then disappeared. We were with Master Overbury at the time, his clerk having taken down Mary's testimony, and he went straight to the Justice. It was two hours before he was able to speak with him, but once he'd done so, the Justice was persuaded to issue a warrant for Graveney's arrest and also a search of his house…'

'And what has been the outcome of that?'

'Nothing as yet, I'm afraid. Graveney was not at home and there was no sign of Mary. However, the keeper of the East Gate was then questioned and said that he recalled Graveney's black coach leaving the city about three hours previously. The chances are that Mary was on board and that she's been taken to Graveney's country house. Armed Constables have been dispatched there today and Overbury promised to send a message to Fetford Hall as soon as he has any news for us.'

'I still don't understand how this happened. How did the masked men know where to find you?'

'I can only assume that we were spotted entering the city and then followed. Overbury thinks that Graveney panicked.'

'Christ almighty, poor Mary could be dead by now.'

Olivia placed a hand on mine. 'We can only pray that Graveney intends to spare her that fate . More likely, he'll be looking to have her spirited out of the country again.'

'But if he's cornered, I could well imagine him looking to trade her life for his freedom.'

'Which would surely never be agreed to.'

'Well, I just hoped the Constables have been dispatched in sufficient numbers. Otherwise, Graveney could escape with Mary still in his grasp.'

'I've more news for you, too. Thomas, your husband, is presently in the High Gaol in Exeter. Overbury's said he can arrange to get a message to him that you've managed to return to these shores safe and well. And I spoke with both your sister and her husband. I accused him of having exposed Thomas and he flatly denied it.'

'Did you sense that he was lying? Did he look you in the eye?'

'He did and expressed considerable anger at such an accusation being made against him. How genuine that was I really cannot judge.'

Half an hour later, Olivia and I set off for Fetford Hall with me riding Harry's horse. I had found it difficult to separate myself from Lucas and looked forward to the time that he would be able to join me. At the same time, my anxiety over Mary's fate was growing in intensity, and I could only pray that she would be released unharmed and Graveney finally brought to justice.

As we approached our destination it struck me forcefully that for all the harm he and his minions had caused, I was yet to ever meet him and had little idea what he even looked like. He remained just a name, an evil eminence with power over others, but no substance as a human being of whom I had any personal knowledge. Furthermore, even if he were to be indicted for kidnapping and murder and sent to the gallows, I was in no position to attend either his trial or his execution, so there seemed to be no prospect of that reality ever changing.

After enjoying a meal of ox tongue soup flavoured by nutmeg followed by the remains of a herring pie, made all the more convivial by James having brought up a bottle of best claret from the cellar, Olivia and I began to play the harpsichord together. Constance then withdrew to her bedroom, complaining of a slight headache, while Becky suggested to James that they play a game of cribbage. My head was spinning a little with the amount of wine I had drunk and I was finding it hard to concentrate. Tiredness, too, was beginning to affect me, causing me to yawn rather loudly. Olivia smiled at me sympathetically and then tensed.

'Who are those men approaching the house?' she asked, pointing out of the window.

I turned my head and saw that there were four of them on foot and that they all carried swords. They were within a few yards of the front door. I immediately sensed that they posed a threat and rose to my feet, cursing the fact that no one had seen them sooner.

'I don't like this...'

'Open up in the name of the Lord Protector, or we'll break down the door,' a gruff sounding voice shouted out. 'I've a warrant to search this house.'

'I'm going to take you down to the cellar,' Olivia said, seizing hold of my right hand. 'James, don't let them in 'til I've had time to do so.'

She then took me towards a flight of stairs that led to the kitchen and even as we reached it I could hear more fierce banging and shouting, too.

'Quickly now, there's not a moment to lose,' Olivia said.

The kitchen was occupied by both the family cook and the scullery maid, who looked at us in alarm. Olivia merely brought a finger to her lips before leading me into a pantry where she pulled open a narrow door barely five foot high and we then descended again down some six stone steps. The trouble was that we were now in darkness and Olivia had to feel her way across the cellar until she reached another narrow door.

'There's a bolt here somewhere. if I can slide it back, the door should open. Just make your way down the tunnel and you'll come out by the river.'

'Do you then expect me to row away? I don't think I can.'

'No, there are woods close by. Hide yourself there until I or James come for you. Now, I must go back.'

With that Olivia drew back the bolt, the door swung open, and I entered the tunnel.

31

Olivia's anger

As fast as I could I returned the way we had just come. I barely had time to cross the kitchen and ascend the stairs to the main part of the house when I was confronted by a plainly dressed, heavily built man with a beard, a crooked nose, and cruel looking eyes, carrying a sword. He immediately seized me by the arm and ignoring my protestations frogmarched me into the long gallery where I saw James sitting in a chair, and holding a hand to his head, which was oozing blood from a wound. He was clearly in some pain, whilst Becky, sitting next to him, looked quite terrified.

Standing close by her was another plainly-dressed man holding a sword whose demeanour looked to be just as threatening as the man who had just seized hold of me. In contrast, the man standing next to the fireplace was finely dressed and appeared to be every inch a gentleman with a well-trimmed beard and features regular enough for me to consider him quite handsome, save that he was rather thin lipped and his eyes betrayed almost no emotion.

'Master, I discovered this woman ascending stairs from below,' the man, who was still holding my arm, said deferentially.

'What were you doing?'

The question was directed at me by the well-dressed man, his voice an educated one, bearing only the slightest trace of a Devon accent, and authoritative enough to suggest that he was used to giving orders and being obeyed

'Who are you?' I retorted angrily. 'Why have you forced your way into this house and hurt my brother?'

'Ah, as I thought, you must be Olivia Courtney, almost as much of a troublemaker as your friend, Lady Tremayne.'

'My God, and you, sir, must be Hugh Graveney, unless I'm very much mistaken.'

'That's as may be, but I've asked you a question you're yet to answer; what were you doing coming up those stairs?'

'I've been visiting the kitchens to speak to our cook about supper, this evening.'

As I told this lie I looked Graveney calmly in the eye as if it was God's truth but he still returned my look with a sceptical shake of the head.

'Is Lady Jane staying with you?' he asked.

'…No, no she's not.'

'So where is she then?'

'I don't know.'

'You're lying. I know she returned from France along with her maid and as Altringham Manor is barred to her she's bound to have come here.'

'She was here, I admit, but then she left. She said it was her intention to return to France.'

'And when was this?'

'Yesterday morning.' Again Graveney looked at me sceptically.

'I allowed her to take one of my horses,' James added.

'And was it you who informed on Thomas Sumner?' I asked Graveney bluntly. It was a question that seemed to catch him off guard as he opened his mouth as if to speak and then closed it again before scowling at me. Then he strode towards the nearest door where he yelled out 'have you found anyone yet?'

'Yes, Master,' came a reply from upstairs. 'There's an old woman in her bedroom and a couple of servants going about their work.'

'Come down here then. I want the kitchen searched. It's below stairs.'

I tensed a little. Hopefully, Jane had already had sufficient time to make her way to the tunnel's end and hide herself in the wood. It was also only too likely that Graveney's men would find the door to the cellar and descend into it. However, they would then need candlelight before there was much likelihood of their discovering the tunnel entrance and making any easy progress along it, while, by itself, its existence proved nothing.

Two men came down the stairs and whilst they proceeded to carry out a search I became more incensed by what was happening.

'You're nothing but a vile criminal, forcing your way into this house,' I said in an accusatory tone to Graveney. 'Why don't you just go and leave us in peace!'

'I came in search of your friend, Lady Jane, but if, as you suggest, she's not here, then you'll do instead.'

'What do you mean by that.'

'I have a ship waiting for us and I mean to take you on board with me. Unfortunately, you're not the beauty your friend is, but the Moors I mean to sell you to will no doubt still find you sufficiently attractive.'

'You can't do this!' I shouted. It was a reaction that brought a sneer to his face.

'Oh, I very much can. There's no one who can stop me.'

'You bastard!' James had risen to his feet and tried to advance on Graveney but didn't get close to him before a sword blocked his path, Becky screamed, and he was shoved back into his seat. Moments later, a young clean-shaven face appeared at the door.

'Master, we've found a cellar, but it's pitch dark down there. We could do with a candle or two.'

'Here, you can take this.' Graveney stepped towards a candelabra, holding three candles, sitting on the table, and then proceeded to light them from the fire burning gently in the grate. I now felt not just tension but a growing sense of panic at the thought of being taken away. I was becoming desperate to escape save that the door remained guarded by the same man who I had met at the top of the stairs. Time then passed with agonising slowness until the youthful face once more appeared

'There's no sign of anyone in the cellar, Master, but we've found the entrance to a tunnel…'

'Have you, by God. Then it wouldn't surprise me if she hasn't used it as a means of escape.'

'We could go after 'er, Master.'

Graveney shook his head. 'I don't think so, we have this Lady instead. And by the way, Lady Olivia,' he added, pointing a finger in my direction, 'I know full well that you've been lying to me. You see, I know you were in Exeter yesterday, no doubt doing everything possible to stir up trouble against me.'

I gave him a defiant stare. 'And do you also know that a warrant has been issued for your arrest on a charge of conspiracy to kidnap Jane's maid?'

Graveney shrugged his shoulders. 'No, but I can't say I'm surprised. It's partly why I've made plans to go abroad. And now it's time we were on our way. Conduct her to my coach.'

'But I am not dressed against the cold, and will you not even allow me to say farewell to my mother?'

'Very well, you may have five minutes to change into something more suitable and say your farewells, but no longer. Time is pressing.'

I put on my thick riding coat and shouted out a desperate farewell to my mother, telling her that she had my undying love. At the same time a fierce altercation broke out between Graveney and James, which resulted in James being hit over the head with the butt of a pistol by one of Graveney's henchmen.

'Damn the man, I've decided we'll take him with us, too,' Graveney declared.

I was in tears as I was frogmarched away from the hall; the grip on my right arm so firm that it hurt. I wanted to scream out in protest at such rough treatment but having become a prisoner, decided that it was pointless to do so. After a short walk we then came in sight of Graveney's sombre, black coach, to which were attached two powerful looking stallions, both with black coats to match the colour of the vehicle they would soon be pulling. There was a coachman, too, already in place, and as I was led forward Graveney himself opened the door to the coach and invited me to step inside.

It was the act of a gentleman, although I felt he was nothing of the kind, rather just a cruel and vengeful individual, intent on utterly ruining my existence for personal gain. As I entered the coach I also couldn't help but gasp at the sight of Mary huddled in a corner with a spotty faced young man sitting next to her, with just the beginnings of a beard and holding a knife. It was clear that she was terrified and she gave me such an anguished look that it brought more tears to her eyes. Graveney, along with one of his henchmen, as well as James, still groggy from the blow to his head, then joined us, and just as Graveney closed the door of the coach, it began to move forward.

Curtains had been pulled across the coach's windows to shut out most of the light and prevent any passerby from catching a glimpse of who might be inside. As if being in such a confined space with our captors wasn't bad enough, unfortunately I soon had a feeling of nausea as the coach began to bounce and lurch along a road which was becoming increasingly rutted as a consequence of autumn rains. The best I could do was bury my mouth and nose in a handkerchief and take deep breaths, helping me to restore a certain sense of equilibrium.

Having been allowed to sit opposite Mary, I also had the freedom to offer her the use of my handkerchief from time to time, but otherwise communication between us was confined to the exchange of a few fearful glances. After a while, I then noticed that she had fallen asleep, so I too closed my eyes in the hope of being able to do the same. However, I was still too much on edge, wondering if there was anything I could possibly do to save myself from this nightmare.

With the coach's curtains continuing to be closed it was hard to judge what progress we were making. Occasionally, Graveney, who was sitting next to the window opposite to me, would draw back the curtain but only fleetingly. I also began to lose much sense of time, but eventually after a journey I judged to have lasted at least two hours, I began to hear the noise of seabirds in increasing numbers and judged that we must be getting close to our destination. Graveney again drew back the curtain slightly and I caught a glimpse of several houses, which I recognised, realising that we had arrived in Topsham.

No more than five minutes later the coach halted and Graveney alighted, immediately closing the coach's door behind him, only to return within a couple of minutes and order that we be taken on board ship.

'Remember, there'll be knives at your backs,' he told us. 'Make any attempt to shout out, or break free, and you'll suffer for it, I promise you.'

Duly intimidated, I was made to leave the coach along with Mary in order to walk the short distance from where it had halted to the gangplank, which took us onboard ship, and thence into a small cabin at its stern. Meanwhile, I assumed James had been taken to a separate cabin. Outside it was now raining steadily and the light beginning to fade.

Should the intention be to set sail before it grew dark then I had to accept that we had no chance of rescue. On the other hand, if for any reason our departure was to be delayed until the morning then there remained at least a possibility of someone coming to our aid. Constables had, after all, been dispatched to arrest Graveney and could even now be searching for him, while Becky and Constance between them would surely do all they could to raise the alarm. Furthermore, Topsham was the most obvious place to look for any ship waiting to set sail.

For her part, Mary was now becoming frantic with fear, shouting out that she could not bear to be taken abroad again, having already been fortunate to survive her previous experience of such treatment. I did all I could to offer her comfort, assuring her that all was not yet lost. At the same time, I could hear voices being raised in anger above us.

'Shush!' I snapped at Mary, who was still close to hysteria. 'I'm trying to listen to what's being said.'

I was sure I could make out Graveney's voice, and caught the words 'but we need to set sail, now.' I couldn't quite make out what was said by way of reply, but I suspected that he was arguing with the ship's captain, who, for whatever reason, was unwilling to comply with his demand.

'Don't give up hope,' I implored Mary. 'I don't believe we're going anywhere tonight. We may yet be saved.'

'Oh, m'lady, I do pray we are!'

32

Jane travels to Exeter

In such pitch darkness, I had to feel my way along the tunnel as if I was a blind woman. My progress was also further impeded by the fact that the tunnel was narrowly constructed and had become damp as well as slippery under foot. As a consequence, my journey of about a hundred yards was tortuously slow. Finally, I emerged into the light, cold and disorientated, as well as fearful that at any moment I might hear the sound of someone coming after me through the tunnel.

I knew I was supposed to be close to the riverbank and only a few strides forward confirmed that. I then hurried along a path in the hope of being able to find somewhere suitable to hide. To my left there were many tall beech trees and increasingly dense foliage, so leaving the path I plunged into this, twice tripping over and also tearing my dress, until I managed to reach a tall tree with a wide girth. Here, I decided to sit down and wait.

Unfortunately, the garments I was wearing were simply too thin to protect me from the elements so I was soon shivering and wrapping my arms around my body. I could see no prospect of falling asleep when I was so uncomfortable and could only pray that it didn't begin to rain or grow even colder. I was alert, too, to every sound and flinched when I heard what must have been some animal scurrying around, but which at first I feared might be human footsteps.

Time dragged by as I tried to make sense of what had brought armed Constables to the door of Fetford Hall. If they had indeed come in search of me, I could not fathom how they had been so quick to get wind of the possibility that they would find me here. After a while, as my discomfort intensified, I decided that in order to try and get a little warmer I needed to stand so began to get to my feet. Then I heard someone approaching and shrank back behind the tree in fear of being discovered.

'Jane, Jane, are you there?'

With a great sense of relief, I recognised that it was Becky's voice calling out to me.

'Yes, thank God you've come. I'm terribly cold.' A few moments later I saw Becky's tear-stained face. 'What's happened?' I asked.

'Those men, saying they'd come in the name of the Lord Protector; it was simply a ruse to gain entry. In truth, it was Graveney and his minions.'

'What! So have they now gone?'

'Yes, but only after kidnapping both Olivia and James. They came for you and when you couldn't be found Graveney said he'd take Olivia instead. It was an act of pure spite, and he said he meant to take her abroad and sell her to the Moors. He spoke of there being a ship waiting for him. Of course, he didn't say where. And then, just before they were about to leave, he decided to take James, too. Again it was out of nothing but spite after he remonstrated with Graveney and was hit over the head for his pains.'

'But Graveney mustn't be allowed to get away with this...'

'But is there's anything we can do to stop him?'

'A warrant's been issued for his arrest, and my best guess would be that his ship's at Topsham, in which case he'll need the tide to be in his favour before he can set sail. I must ride to Altringham Manor and ask Harry to go back to Exeter to alert the Justice to what's happened.'

'But it'll be evening before he can hope to reach the city. What if the tide's in Graveney's favour by then?'

'We can only pray that it won't be. What's more, even if it is, the ship's captain may not want to sail with night coming on.'

Twenty minutes later a horse had been saddled for me and I was ready to depart.

'We pray your efforts will not be in vain,' Constance called out to me just before I rode away. 'I cannot bear to contemplate the possibility that both Olivia and James might be carried off into slavery. God speed.'

'Yes, God speed,' Becky added.

I did not find James's stallion the easiest horse to control, especially riding side-saddle, and feeling so utterly exhausted. I feared that my illness might return again if I was not very careful, and fatiguing myself too much could all too easily have that consequence. Still, it was a short enough journey, and I encouraged myself with the thought that I would be able to see Lucas again far sooner than I would otherwise have expected.

When I reached Harry and Melissa's cottage, I was relieved to be able to dismount before tapping gently on its door. A few moments later Melissa greeted me.

'Why, m'lady, what brings 'e back 'ere so soon?'

I briefly explained. 'I need Harry to ride to Exeter for me and alert the Justice. Is he at home at present?'

'I'm sorry, m'lady, 'e's feeling right poorly and 'as taken to 'is bed.'

'Oh God, no…I…' And then I stopped, realising I was left with but one choice, which was to go myself, even if it was at the risk of my own liberty. With luck I would still be able to enter the city without alerting anyone who would seek to arrest me, and would go straight to Master Overbury's chambers in the expectation that he would be prepared to approach the Justice with my news. I was still concerned that by the time I arrived both he and his clerk would have gone home, but fortunately I had a firm recollection of Overbury having told me he resided in Southernhay Street, so, if necessary, I was prepared to go knocking on doors until I located him.

Unfortunately, the journey to Exeter proved far from easy. Apart from my tiredness, it began to rain, and the stallion remained difficult to control. An ill-fitting riding coat as well as a hat, borrowed from Becky, gave me some protection from the elements but as the rain intensified so did my discomfort. I was naturally anxious, too, to reach Exeter as soon as I could but had to restrain myself. Experience had taught me that maintaining a steady canter was more sustainable over any journey of several miles, while I was also nervous of suffering a fall if I gave the stallion its head.

By the time the city's East Gate came into view it was well after six o'clock and as I rode through it I made a point of keeping my head down and avoiding eye contact with anyone, not that at this time of day there were many people about anyway. I then made my way directly to Master Overbury's chambers, praying that either he or his clerk would still be at their desks on some important matter that required their urgent attention. Having dismounted from the stallion and tethered it, I knocked fiercely on the chamber's front door with little confidence that anyone would respond. Yet, after only a few seconds, a familiar voice called out to me.

'We're closed, I'm afraid. You'll have to call back tomorrow.'

'Master Overbury, it's Lady Tremayne here. Please, I must speak with you. It's most important.'

'Of course. I must say, you've taken a risk coming here.'

'I had no choice. Graveney's been to Fetford Hall with his henchmen and seized both James and Olivia!'

By now Overbury had managed to open the door and gave me the most solicitous of looks before ushering me inside, while at the same time glancing up and down the street in case anyone with prying eyes was watching us. As it happened the street appeared deserted. Hurriedly, I then gave him a further explanation of events, before begging him to seek out the Justice.

'The chances are that any ship waiting for Graveney will be at Topsham,' I added. 'Of course, I can't be certain of that, but it has to be worth looking there first. I just pray that it hasn't already sailed, or be about to do so. Should you be able to speak to the Justice you can also tell him that it's my steward Harry who's brought you news of what's happened. I'd have sent him to you anyway if he hadn't taken to his bed.'

'Very well, I've been working late on an urgent matter, but what's left to attend to can wait until the morning. If you would care to accompany me to my house, it will be an opportunity for me to introduce you to my wife, and I will then proceed to visit the Justice. I ought to find him at home at this hour.'

It came as no surprise to me that Overbury resided in a well-appointed, brick-built residence that looked to be no more than twenty-five years old and was three storeys tall. His wife, Alicia, a handsome woman, who would no doubt have been handsomer still in her youth, exuded natural charm and could not have been more welcoming.

Encouraged to take my ease and enjoy both a glass of claret and some plum pie, I could then do no more than wait as patiently as I could for Overbury's return. I was grateful for the fact that Alicia did not indulge in any idle chatter and after about half an hour he duly returned. One glance at his face also suggested to me that he was the bearer of good news.

'I have spoken to the Justice and he was most alarmed by what I had to tell him. It seems that the Constables who were dispatched to Graveney's country house to arrest him, returned empty handed this afternoon and he has agreed to dispatch them to Topsham as soon as possible. I also suggested to him that they might need the assistance of troops, if Graveney refuses to surrender , and he said he would dispatch a message to the castle's garrison commander requesting this.'

'And you told him that your information came from Harry?'

'Yes, and he did not question that.'

'Thank goodness.'

Alicia then invited me to be their guest for the night, an offer which I was grateful to accept. I wanted the earliest possible news of whether it had proved possible to affect a rescue before it was too late. Indeed, I would have been sorely tempted to accompany the Constables to Topsham, had this not carried with it the prospect of my own arrest. As it was, all I could do was wait and pray.

33
Olivia in jeopardy

Mary and I had now been locked in our small cabin, which looked out to sea, for more than an hour, during which time darkness had fallen. The sound of an argument raging had quickly died away to be replaced by nothing more than the occasional shout and the noise of footsteps coming and going.

In the meantime, the two of us were left totally ignored, without food or water, or even a piss pot, and one narrow bunk bed to share as best we could. As the light faded this left us with no choice but to try and sleep but I at least found this quite impossible as I remained alert to every sound, hoping with an increasing sense of desperation that Constables would soon arrive to rescue us.

The door to our cabin was then suddenly opened and a man appeared with a bald pate, whom I had never seen before, bearing a lamp, followed by a youth, who looked to be no more than fifteen years of age, carrying a tray with two tankards on it, and also some bread. I decided to seize the opportunity to ask them if they knew when the ship would be sailing and the older of the two was prepared to give me an answer.

'It won't be afore midnight, that's for sure. The tide'll be against us until then.'

That response helped to sustain my spirits somewhat. The men then withdrew and I began to lose track of time, until after what was probably about an hour, I heard a bellowing voice calling out from what I was certain must be the quayside. In the still night air I was also able to make out the words.

'In the name of the Lord Protector I order you to let us come on board. I have a warrant for the arrest of one Hugh Graveney on suspicion of kidnapping as well as a warrant giving us authority to carry out a search of this vessel.'

I immediately seized Mary by the arm. 'The Lord be praised, our rescue is at hand,' I cried.

For what seemed to be a long time but was probably no more than a couple of minutes, the demand to be allowed on board was met by nothing more than silence, whereupon the same voice spoke again.

'I warn you, if you don't obey, we'll board you anyway. I'll give you no more than five minutes to make up your minds.'

Moments later, the door of our cabin was thrown open and the man with the bald pate reappeared, this time brandishing a sword, which he waved in our direction.

'Out of 'ere,' he shouted. 'Now!'

Mary shrieked in alarm and I shrunk back, whereupon the man grabbed Mary by the arm and forced her out of the cabin. At the same time another man appeared, stinking of a mixture of sweat, dirt and rum, and also holding a sword, who proceeded to drag me out of the cabin, having seized hold of my hair. When I screamed in pain and began to struggle with him he then hit me hard twice across my left thigh with the flat of his sword before shoving me in the same direction as Mary. By the time both of us reached the deck, Graveney, who was standing by the ship's wheel, was giving his answer to the demand which had been made.

'Make any attempt to come on board this ship and one of the two women we are holding will be instantly put to death. Still persist and the second one will die, too.'

I had wondered why the Constables had not simply boarded the ship in the first place, taking advantage of darkness to achieve a surprise, but as I stood on deck I realised that this had never been an easy option. The ship was large enough to sit several feet above the quayside and as the tide came in was rising even higher in the water. Furthermore, the gangway leading to the ship had also been taken on board in anticipation of an early departure. It was apparent, too, from the activity going on around me that the intention was to seek to affect an escape.

In readiness for this, the ship's sails had been unfurled, but then I noticed that there was barely any wind. This might, for all I knew, be no more than a kind of *lull before the storm* but nonetheless for the present at least I did not see how the ship could go very far at all. All the same, within moments, the ropes that attached the ship to the quay were cut and the very act of doing this was sufficient to cause the ship to drift a few feet away from it.

To my dismay, I couldn't see how the Constables could now realistically do anything to board the ship, even if they were minded to do so in the face of Graveney's grave threat, which I believed he was well capable of carrying out. As and when the wind picked up, I feared he would then be free to make good his escape.

Gradually the ship moved further away from the quayside and then imperceptibly at first the wind began to spring up and the ship's sails began to give it the momentum required to head out towards the open sea. At this point Mary and I were once again taken down to our cabin and I was left feeling close to despair. When Jane and Mary had originally been kidnapped along with Nancy, I thought they had been incredibly fortunate to be able to escape and I could not imagine that such good fortune would also shine upon me. However, after about half an hour, I felt that the ship was no longer moving and this was almost immediately followed by the sound of voices raised in angry cursing.

'God be praised, Mary, I think the ship might have run aground. We're going nowhere!'

The mistake I suspected Graveney had made, for all I knew against the advice of his ship's captain, was to set sail at night when it was simply too dark to be certain of being able to avoid shallow waters. Of course, if the tide was still coming in I imagined it possible that the ship would free itself but as time passed this seemed less likely. Once again the cabin door was then thrust open and the man with the bald pate reappeared.

'You're coming with me,' he snapped, grabbing hold of my arm while at the same time holding a sword to my face. I still tried to struggle with him, but he was too strong for me and dragged me out of the cabin and up onto the deck, where I realised Graveney was about to abandon ship. A boat had been launched and I was ordered to descend into it via a rope ladder that had been thrown over the side of the vessel.

'No, I won't!' I said defiantly, standing my ground,

whereupon the man with the bald pate hit me about the face with such force that I collapsed onto the deck.

'Ye'll do as I say or I'll hit 'e again!'

Reeling from the blow I had just received, I reluctantly complied, and once in the boat, realised that Graveney was already onboard.

'For pity's sake, let us go,' I appealed to him but his response was to simply ignore me. Two more men then joined us, bringing the total present in the boat to ten, of whom all but Graveney and I took up their oars and began to row towards the shore.

As soon as the boat reached the shallows I was made to disembark, which involved me in wading through water up to almost my knees for a few yards. Graveney along with four other men also came ashore, and the remaining men then began to row the boat back towards the ship. I could only assume that this was with the intention of bringing the rest of its crew ashore together with James and Mary. However, Graveney clearly had no intention of waiting for them as he immediately walked off the narrow strip of beach upon which we had landed while I was forced to follow him.

The only light we had came from the moon, which was half-full, but Graveney gave every impression of knowing where he was going, taking a path that led along the banks of the estuary in a southerly direction. By the time we had walked what must have been at least a mile I was struggling to keep up with the fast pace he had set.

Yet the grip around my arm remained unrelenting and forced me to keep going until after about another half-mile we reached the edge of a village where we briefly halted.

Graveney then engaged in urgent conversation with one of his men who proceeded to lead our party down its main street before turning off down a narrow lane until we reached a row of cottages. At the last of these he tapped on the door persistently until a woman's voice finally responded.

'What d'ye want o' me in middle o' night?'

'It's me, ma, it's Jacob.'

The moment the door was opened he stepped inside and the rest of us followed. His mother, who was in her nightdress, was clearly horrified at the sight of four strange men entering her home, whilst I was by now exhausted, and left wondering if there was ever to be an end to this nightmare.

In the confines of a tiny cottage, surrounded by our captors, cold, thirsty, and with only rushes to lie upon, I had slept only fitfully. Now dawn had broken, I was alert to my surroundings, in need of the privy, and feeling stiff as a board. One man was lying right next to the door so I knew there was no question of seeking to escape, while glancing around I could see that Graveney was also awake and that to my discomfort he had his eyes upon me. Immediately, I looked away. I could only guess at what he intended to do next in terms of trying to achieve an escape, but I surmised that his situation must be a quite desperate one, and that his options were very limited indeed.

I was convinced that we had come ashore on the opposite bank of the estuary to where Topsham stood and although that might have made us safer from pursuit, it surely also left us far more isolated. I would have been very surprised indeed if Graveney didn't have a good deal of gold on his person. All the same, he would need to find a better hideaway than our present one, and quickly, if he was to evade the hue and cry, which would surely be raised once it was realised that his ship had gone aground before even clearing the mouth of the river.

Naturally, I wondered, too, what had happened to both Mary and James. For all I knew Graveney could simply have decided that they be left on board ship, or even that they be brought ashore and then allowed to go free. Although I dreaded to even contemplate it, there was even a possibility he had ordered their deaths. Whatever their fate, it was clear that he was determined to keep me prisoner, no doubt hoping that as a last resort he could always bargain my life for his freedom.

My ears were alert to any sounds coming from outside the cottage we were in and at first I heard nothing more than the crowing of a nearby cock. It wasn't long, however, before I thought I could hear the sound of whinnying horses followed by the sound of fists banging on doors and cries of 'open up in the name of the Lord Protector.'

Graveney heard this, too, and was instantly on his feet, sword in hand, kicking at the bodies of two of his men who were still asleep while the other two were already struggling to their feet.

'Wake your mother,' he ordered. 'If it's Constables or soldiers come in search of us, she needs to be at the door to assure them that she's seen nothing. Tell her, too, that she'd better co-operate with us or I'll slit her throat.'

Despite Graveney's threat, I felt a surge of hope. I could not understand how anyone had arrived on the scene so quickly, but the fact of the matter was that they had. What was more I decided that there was one thing that I could do to alert those who had come searching and that was to scream.

The sound of this was surely loud enough to be heard from one end of the village to the other and I followed it by starting to shout 'help' but the word had barely left my mouth before I was seized from behind and a hand placed across my mouth. My reaction to this was to bite with such force that it induced a loud curse followed by a cuff to my head, which was powerful enough to make me scream again As I then collapsed on the ground, holding my head in pain, I was conscious of movement around me and someone going to the cottage's back door in the hope that they might still be able to escape.

'Shit! We're surrounded,' Graveney exclaimed.

Moments later there came the sound of a fist fiercely banging on the front door. 'Open up, open up, in the name of the Lord Protector. You cannot escape. I have twenty armed men under my command.'

'Let us go free or I swear I'll kill Lady Courtney,' Graveney responded.

'I have no authority to let you go free.'

'Then you'd best seek it then.'

'...That I won't do. Kill her if you wish but as God's my witness you'll be signing your own death warrant.'

Such a bold response shook Graveney but he was by now desperate enough to make another threat. 'There's also an old woman in this house. She'll meet the same fate if you don't let us go.'

'No!' This exclamation came from the old woman's own son. 'Ye let 'er be. Don't ye dare lay a finger on 'er.'

'Curse you for a fool,' Graveney responded before dropping his voice to little more than a whisper. 'I say if we make a concerted charge out the back door, we might still succeed in making our escape.'

The oldest looking of Graveney's retainers shook his head. 'Not if there be twenty men out there, Master. We'd be cut down as soon as fart. I say the game's up and no mistake.'

'Fuck you, you'll do as I say!'

'Not anymore, Master, I'm sorry.'

'Then this bitch will die!'

With that, Graveney, who had his sword in his hand took a step towards me and raised the weapon with every intention of thrusting it into my body. Yet, even as I screamed in fear of my life, the retainer he had just argued with locked swords with him and then shoved him backwards.

'Traitor! coward! Are none of you with me!'

All the men present either shook their heads or looked at their boots so with a snarl of fury Graveney darted past them and out the back door of the cottage. After that I was aware of a lot of shouting, and then the sound of several shots being fired followed by a scream of agony. Within moments Graveney's retainers all surrendered and I learnt that Graveney was in his death throes.

34

Jane travels to London

News of the previous night's events reached the Overbury household by around mid-morning, by which time I was in a fever pitch of anxiety. It was Overbury's clerk who arrived to inform me that both James and Mary had been rescued unharmed from Graveney's ship, which had run aground not far from the walls of Powderham Castle, which overlooked the Exe estuary. When he then added that Graveney had not been on board and nor had Olivia my joy had turned to dismay, though he'd added as reassuringly as he could that on foot they could not have got far and that soldiers had been dispatched to scour the near vicinity for any sign of them.

He promised to return as soon as he had anything further of a positive nature to report and I was left with no alternative but to continue to wait as patiently as I could, hoping for the best, but inevitably also contemplating the worst. If cornered, I sensed that Graveney was bound to threaten Olivia's life. Worse, knowing what he'd been capable of in the past I feared he might even carry out this threat, for all that it would do him no good to do so and might well even hasten his own demise.

An hour later the clerk returned along with no less than James and Mary. I was not only delighted to see them both again but also grateful to be able to share with them the concern I felt for Olivia's fate. James, in particular, was understandably worried that his sister remained in the hands of such a ruthless individual as Graveney, whom he called an *evil bastard*.

Again the clerk departed, once again promising to return with further news as soon as it was available. Then finally, to my huge relief, in the late afternoon Overbury himself returned accompanied by no less than Olivia herself.

'Thank the Lord,' I exclaimed as the two of us were able to hug each other warmly. 'I could not have borne it if any harm had come to you,' I added.

'He did try to kill me, you know, but one of his own retainers stopped him. I owe that man my life and you should know that Graveney is dead. He was shot trying to escape and soon bled to death.'

'Good riddance to the man. In his own way he was as evil as that wretch, Turnbull.'

It was now too late in the day for us to hope to reach Fetford Hall in daylight so Overbury insisted on offering us all the hospitality of their house for the night. Further, as we had but one horse, and not a penny between us, he also insisted on providing us with two further mounts from his own stables in order to facilitate our journey in the morning.

'Return them to me as soon as you can, is all I ask.'

I now felt that Overbury had become more than just my lawyer. He was now as well a much valued friend whom I knew I could always turn to for help and advice should the need arise. While I had waited for news of Olivia, James and Mary, I had also fretted over the fate of Thomas, incarcerated in the

High Gaol, only a few streets away, and yet totally out of reach unless I exposed myself to an even greater risk of arrest.

Our marriage to date had certainly been no bed of roses and his tendency to drink to excess had gone someway towards undermining it completely. Yet he was still the father of my child and I continued to feel both physical desire for him and a measure of tenderness, which I was willing to think of as love. Certainly, I did not consider him in any way a bad person, and could sympathise with his frustration at being forced to hide himself away at Altringham Manor for so long.

Now, I faced the prospect of either becoming a widow once more, or, even if he should be shown mercy and escape with only imprisonment, a period of separation, which might well stretch to many years. Meanwhile, Lucas and I would be forced to live on the charity of Olivia's family, or, failing that my brother's. Furthermore, if Thomas were to be transported to the Indies, the chances of my ever seeing him again were also bound to be remote.

That evening Overbury took me to one side and spoke to me in a quiet voice. 'I had some news today that I must impart to you. Thomas Sumner is to stand trial for treason. You will understand the penalty if he's convicted.'

'Dear God, yes. Is there no chance that he would be shown mercy?'

'He might simply be hanged rather than also drawn and quartered. Alternatively, it's just possible that he might be transported to the Indies but I wouldn't bank on it.'

'I see. Well, you've told me no more than I expected. And meanwhile you and your wife have put yourselves at risk by allowing me to remain under your roof . The sooner I'm gone the better.'

'Perhaps so, but tell me frankly, what was your relationship with Thomas Sumner? Did you merely harbour him or was there something more?'

'Why do you ask?'

'Curiosity to an extent, but also because if he put you under duress or perhaps even married you, then I doubt that any charge would be pressed against you. After all, as your husband he would also be your master…'

I looked at him askance, wondering what he suspected. Certainly, he was an astute individual as was to be expected of any competent lawyer. I decided that the time had come to be honest.

'Very well, you should know that we have been man and wife since last year and that I have given birth to his child.'

'It was by contract then?'

'Why yes. Does that make any difference?'

'No, no, provided you have the document to prove it.'

'I have it at Fetford Hall.'

'If I can see it…just to be certain of its validity…then I'd be willing to speak on your behalf to the Justice. I'd say that I'd been approached through an intermediary, show him the document, and ask that the charge against you be withdrawn…'

'And you think he'd agree?'

'I'm confident that he would.'

'And Altringham Manor, I suppose that would still be lost to me?'

'What were the terms of your marriage contract?'

'I reserved nothing to myself, if that's what you're asking. All that was mine became his, at least while he lives.'

'Then you cannot hope to recover it... I'm sorry.'

'At least I have the charity of Olivia's family to rely upon. And then there is my brother, not that we've set eyes upon each other in more than two years, and we were never close. And then to think that Thomas will either be executed, or transported, is hard to bear.'

By now I was close to tears and Overbury was looking decidedly uncomfortable. For once I suspected he was lost for words, but then, ever the gentleman, he pulled out a handkerchief from a pocket and offered it to me.

'Thank you, Master Overbury, you're too kind.'

'There's one more thing I should tell you. I have learnt from the Justice that it was Graveney who exposed the whereabouts of your husband to him.'

'But how did he come to know anything about Thomas?'

'It seems he placed a spy in your midst. I believe you took in a scullery maid...'

'Yes, Elsa, a sweet natured girl from the village.'

'But so Graveney informed the Justice, also with a brother in his employ. She was bribed to put herself forward for a position in your household. I don't imagine that Graveney harboured any particular suspicions against you concerning Thomas. It was simply that once he discovered that you were trying to have him arrested for murder, he thought he should find out as much about you as possible.'

Five days later, having been brought the marriage contract by Harry, Overbury duly paid the Justice a visit. It was probably as well that they were on good terms and that for all his parliamentary sympathies, he was averse to the idea of imprisoning female members of the aristocracy except as an absolute last resort. His willingness to withdraw the warrant for my arrest also only increased when Overbury informed him how much I had suffered at Graveney's hands and all because I had looked to expose him for the evil murderer he surely was.

'I told him that Graveney's downfall was entirely due to your persistence and as Sumner's wife you were doing no more than allowing him to reside in what had become his home.'

My relief at being told the good news was tempered by the knowledge that Thomas was likely to be sentenced to death, but at least I was now free to visit him in prison and bid him farewell from this world, if that was to be his fate. I decided, too, that I should take Lucas with me, but more than that determined on the boldest of plans.

For all that both time and resources were against me, I would ride to London in order to seek to present a petition in person to the Lord Protector himself, begging that my husband's life be spared. The next Assize when he would be brought to trial was due to commence in eighteen days, whilst the journey to London was bound to take six, possibly even seven if the state of the roads, or for that matter the weather, were also against me.

Of course, it would take just as long to return, leaving me with only a few days in London to attempt to present my petition. Horses could also go lame or need shoeing and it was out of the question that I should seek to travel alone, which would only serve to increase the significant expense of such an undertaking, that I could ill afford. James, for one, was scathing of the very idea when I revealed it both to him and the rest of his family over dinner.

'Apart from any other consideration the road to London is notorious for its outlaws. Assuming you were to take Mary as your maid, you would be highly vulnerable. Perhaps with a male companion as well you would be safer but that would only increase the cost of the venture, which might well be to no avail anyway. You might well not be allowed anywhere near the Lord Protector, and even supposing you were able to obtain permission to approach him, I fancy your petition could well fall on deaf ears.'

'All that you say is true, yet I cannot simply do nothing to try and save his life. I'm ready as needs be to throw myself at Cromwell's feet and beg him to show Thomas mercy. If he will not do so then at least it will rest easier with my conscience if I've done everything possible to save his life. You see, I feel guilty that it was my actions that brought him to the sorry state he's in now. Had I not been so stubborn in my pursuit of Graveney, he would never have had cause to spy on me.'

'We must help her, James,' Olivia insisted. 'The maid, Mary, has been through quite enough without taking her all the way to London but I'm willing to stand in for her and you could be our companion, couldn't you?'

'Perhaps but getting to London and back will not come cheap.'

'I have some savings…'

'No, I would not ask that of you, Olivia,' I said firmly. 'If I go to Exeter tomorrow to visit Thomas I'll also pawn my few remaining jewels, not that they're worth all that much.'

'You'll do nothing of the kind, Jane,' James declared. 'If we're all three to travel to London it'll be at my expense, and no one else's.'

'You'll come with us then?'

'Yes, very well, but if we're to do so I suggest, Jane, that you defer any visit to Thomas until we return. If we leave for London from here at first light in the morning we'll make best use of what time we have available to us. Don't forget, either, that a ride to Exeter and back would only tire the horses when they need to be fresh for a journey of a hundred and eighty miles and then back again.

35

Race against time

I was feeling understandably anxious, realising perfectly well that the Lord Protector could be indisposed, elsewhere in the country, or simply unwilling to accept any personal petitions for mercy. In any event, I knew that I would forever be in James and Olivia's debt for accompanying me on the journey we had completed the previous evening, and, although it had been a long and tiring one, there had been no mishaps to speak of.

All things considered we had also made good time, despite the wet conditions, which had given us a thorough soaking on two successive days, and also in places churned up the road to a muddy quagmire, leaving more than one coach we had passed with a broken wheel. At Winchester, too, James's horse had needed re-shoeing, but by then the weather had improved and with it the state of the road, enabling us to make up for lost time.

What had been worst about the journey was having to sleep in a different bed every night and whilst the food provided by the various inns we had halted at had always been wholesome enough, the beds had often been too hard. It left me longing for the comforts of my own bed, not to mention a bath to wash away the grime.

Before our departure from Fetford Hall, I had written out

a short missive appealing to the Protector to spare Thomas's life, which I prayed I would, at the very least, be allowed to hand over to some flunky in the hope that it would be promptly brought to Cromwell's attention. Now as I approached the gates of the Palace accompanied by both Olivia and James, I could see that it was guarded by two pikemen in uniform and realised that without their consent I would be unable to go any further.

'What's your business?' one of them asked me.

'I come to present a petition for mercy to the Lord Protector.'

'And have you any authority on your person that allows you entry?'

'No, I do not.'

'Then I cannot allow you in.'

'Is there no one then I can present the petition to?'

'No more than a hundred yards, just along the street here in the direction of the Abbey, you'll come to a building with a portico over its front door. Ask there and they should be able to assist you.'

Upon our arrival at this place, we were shown into a room which was crowded with people who I imagined had come to the Palace for reasons similar to my own. Here we waited as patiently as we could for upwards of half an hour before finally being called into the presence of a harassed looking individual of middle years with nervous, darting eyes and a reddish complexion. I briefly explained to him the purpose of my attendance; whereupon he frowned at me.

'I can take your letter but I cannot say when it will be brought to the Lord Protector's attention, or when he might then read it. You should also understand he has affairs of state to attend to and that the volume of letters like this which are presented is considerable. If you come back in a week I might have some positive news for you but there can be no guarantees.'

'I cannot possibly wait that long. We need to return to Exeter within three days. Might I not be allowed to present my petition in person?'

'No, that's out of the question, I'm afraid. But look, what you could do is pay a visit to the Lord Protector's daughter, the Lady Elizabeth Claypole. I can tell you where she lives, it isn't far, and if you could gain her sympathy then I believe she'd likely speak to her father on your behalf. It's something she's done before on behalf of others in your position. I hear she's her father's favourite daughter and that he's readily persuaded by her.'

The residence we were directed to was in the Strand, no more than ten minutes walk away. It was far more modest than many of the mansions surrounding it but more modern, too, and in a good state of repair, whereas several of the former had clearly become dilapidated, a sure sign of the times in which we were now living. The maid who then answered my knock informed me that her mistress was not at home, but as my head dropped a little in disappointment, assured me that she was expected to return within the hour.

Taking our ease in a nearby inn, we therefore waited for the time to pass. Observing the street scene, I thought it the most bustling place I had ever been in, not so unlike Exeter, but just on a much greater scale. I was acutely aware of the fact that the Lord Protector's daughter was my last hope and also ruminated on how I would speak to her. As a married woman it was probable that she would have children, so, assuming that to be the case, I was determined to stress that Thomas's execution would leave Lucas without a father.

Once a full hour had passed we then returned to be informed by the same maid they had spoken to before, that the lady of the house was once again in residence.

'And what should I tell her is the purpose of your visit?'

'I am the wife of Thomas Sumner. I ask for only a few minutes of your good lady's time. I have been seeking to present a petition to her father, the Lord Protector, begging for the life of my husband, but I do not know when he will read it and time is slipping by. I am therefore here to humbly ask if she might be willing to intercede for me.'

The maid then showed us into a small receiving room with a fine view out onto the street before withdrawing. Once again we waited for what in the end must have been all of twenty minutes, by which time I was beginning to feel increasingly frustrated.

'I'm sure she'll come soon,' Olivia sought to reassure me, though it was to be another five minutes before she finally reappeared, apologising for the delay and saying that Lady Elizabeth would join us shortly.

'Does she have children?' I made a point of asking.

'Why yes, she has four. The youngest is but a babe-in-arms.'

A few more minutes then elapsed before Lady Elizabeth made her entry. I was immediately struck, not just by her relative plainness, but also her gentle and friendly demeanour as she held out a hand in greeting. Modest in height she was also still young with an unblemished complexion, whilst for all that she was the daughter of the nation's ruler she was simply enough dressed in an off-white, silk gown. Further, her curly, brown hair was unadorned and her necklace no more than a simple, silver cross.

'I understand you wish me to intercede with my father for your husband's life?' she immediately asked.

'I am most grateful to you for giving me your time and yes, I come to humbly beseech you to speak to him and ask that he show my husband mercy.'

I then mentioned that I had been previously widowed before introducing both James and Olivia, whereupon Lady Elizabeth invited us all to be seated before asking me to explain why my husband's life was at stake. I did so as succinctly as I could before explaining that I had given birth only a few months previously to our first child, a son, who would be left without a father if Thomas was executed. I also stressed that time was of the essence as Thomas's trial was due to commence in only ten days.

Lady Elizabeth, meanwhile, heard me out in silence but with a sympathetic expression, which gave me some reason to hope that my appeal was not falling on deaf ears. Once I had finished there was then a pregnant silence of only a few seconds but to me felt far longer.

'Very well, I am willing to speak to my father on your behalf...'

'My Lady, thank you, with all my heart...'

Lady Elizabeth held up a hand. 'I must caution you, though, that by being merciful my father may merely commute your husband's sentence to one of death by hanging rather than...greater mutilation. I will, though, ask that he go further and spare your husband's life , I promise you. He also grows tired of me interceding on behalf of unrepentant renegades and I do not know the full extent of your husband's crimes. My father may not therefore give me an immediate answer, but you are fortunate that I am due to attend upon him tomorrow afternoon about another matter of some importance, and I will ask that he endeavours to do so within two days. That, I think, should still allow you sufficient time to return to Exeter before your husband's trial is due to commence. Return here late tomorrow afternoon and I will have more news for you.'

I felt an overwhelming sense of gratitude that the Lord Protector's daughter should have shown such willingness to help a perfect stranger, married to a renegade, accused of treason. It surely couldn't be because she had any sympathy with his cause. Rather she had a self-evidently gentle nature, and what I suspected could well be a devout Christian conviction, which abhorred violence.

Having three times expressed my grateful thanks, there was nothing left to do but return to the inn where we had spent the previous night in the village of Chelsea, close to the river. The bed that I had slept in there was certainly the most comfortable of any I'd used since we had set out on our journey, but perhaps not surprisingly also the most expensive. Now, buoyed up with hope that Lady Elizabeth might actually persuade her father to spare Thomas's life, I again slept well. Then, the next morning, we decided to spend the day visiting the city of London, which for both myself and Olivia would be a novel experience.

James who had come to London twice before, warned us that we would find it an extraordinarily crowded and noisy place with many noxious odours intermingled with some which were far more pleasant, and so it proved. Of all the sites we saw, I thought London Bridge the most amazing, and could not help but shudder when I looked upon the Tower of London for the first time, remembering as I did so the men and women, including two Queens of England, who had gone to their deaths within its walls. I was reminded only too well of the fate that awaited my husband unless Lady Elizabeth could persuade her father to show mercy.

As the afternoon advanced I grew more anxious to return to the Strand and by five o'clock we were once more outside the door of Lady Elizabeth's residence. Shown into the same room where we had waited the previous day, it was no more than ten minutes before Lady Elizabeth appeared, looking tired, but with the same gentle smile on her face, which I found encouraging.

'I have been able to speak to my father on your behalf and explained your circumstances. I put it to him that it would be cruel if you were to become a widow for a second time in barely three years and your infant son to lose his father. I begged him therefore to consider commuting your husband's likely sentence to one of imprisonment and he told me that he would think on the matter.'

'Forgive me, but did you also explain that I must return to Exeter in less than two days?'

'I told him that your husband's trial was scheduled to commence in nine days and he said that he would reach a decision on the matter in time for any clemency he is minded to grant to be brought to the court's attention before any sentence is passed. He added that it should not take more than five days for this to be sent so long as the autumn rains haven't been too torrential. I cannot press him any further on the matter; you see it might well make him angry if I were to do so. Nor do I expect to see him again for at least another five days so I can only suggest that you return to Exeter without further delay. My prayers will go with you and God willing my father will decide to be merciful towards your husband.'

I tried not to feel too deflated by this news. Lady Elizabeth had, after all, kept her word, there was still reason to hope, and I could ask no more of her. Accordingly, I again expressed my deepest gratitude for her intervention on Thomas's behalf and then left, knowing that our paths were unlikely to ever cross again.

The following day my companions and I began our return journey in depressingly wet conditions. The weather was also turning colder and the days shorter and by the end of the third day our horses were showing signs of fatigue. This brought with it a prospect of our taking as long as a full eight days to reach Exeter, by which time Thomas's trial might well have come to a conclusion. In the face of this I struggled to keep my spirits up.

Still, there was no choice but to press on as best we could without over-taxing our horses. Our discomfort was also compounded by hours of often steady rain even into the fifth day of our journey, at which point I began to develop a cold and feared a return of the illness that had so recently struck me down.

I remained determined to struggle on, however, even though by the seventh day I felt feverish and was not finding it easy to remain upright in the saddle. That night we at least reached Honiton where it was decided that James would head for Fetford Hall in the morning as he had been away from a pregnant Becky quite long enough, and Olivia and I were quite capable of continuing to Exeter without him.

At least it had finally stopped raining and even become a little warmer. The two of us finally reached our destination at around midday, by which time I was not only both ill and exhausted but also fearful that our journey had been in vain and that Thomas would soon be executed.

Leaving our horses at our usual livery stables, we then made our way to the city's courthouse where to my relief we soon came upon Master Overbury. However, his news was grim.

'Your husband's trial commenced this morning and already enough witnesses have given evidence against him to make his conviction certain. The jury'll be sent out this afternoon, and won't need much more than ten minutes to deliver its verdict.'

'And do you know, has there been any news from London? Lady Elizabeth, the Protector's daughter, interceded with her father on my behalf. He said he'd consider the matter and send his grant of clemency here under seal if he was minded to award it.'

'I've no idea, I'm afraid. If any such document's been received the judge will be bound to refer to it when he delivers his verdict.'

I was tense with anxiety, and felt my head spinning to the

point that I might faint. Olivia, recognising this, took hold of my arm and led me to a chair.

'We've had a hard journey to get here and Jane is not well,' she explained to Overbury. 'A hot meal would do us both good, I'm sure.'

'The court's risen until two o'clock so allow me to take you both to dinner.'

Nearly two hours later, fortified by what I had eaten along with two glasses of strong wine, I was in court to see Thomas led into the dock. I was shocked by how tired and bedraggled he looked, his hair long and tussled and his beard equally so. At first he kept his eyes down but then as I willed him to do so he looked up and our eyes met. He managed a smile and raised a hand as did I, whereupon the court was called to order as the judge entered.

As Overbury had predicted the jury were soon sent out to deliver its inevitable verdict and once delivered, the judge sentenced Thomas to be hung, but spared him any mutilation. Was this, I wondered, the full extent of the Lord Protector's mercy. Overwhelmed, I felt tears welling up in my eyes as Thomas was led from the dock, his head held defiantly high and having blown me a kiss. I had done all I could to save him but that it seemed had not been enough and I was utterly devastated.

The execution was due to take place in two days time and before that happened I decided that I had but one priority, which was to ensure that I brought Lucas to see his father. It would mean another round journey of forty miles but that could not be helped and Olivia assured me that she would remain by my side, which was some comfort at least.

As we walked out of the court into the daylight, it was drizzling again, which matched my mood, but as I then looked down the street I saw a uniformed rider approaching on a sturdy dark coated stallion. What struck me, too, was that he was bearing two saddle bags. With a surge of hope I rushed forward and called out to him.

'Have you come from London with post?'

'Aye, madam, I have. It's been a difficult journey and I've been much delayed.'

'And tell me, do you bring with you any letter from the Lord Protector for his honour, the judge.'

'Yes, madam, I have one item for his attention. I have been told to deliver it to him in person.'

'God be praised!' I exclaimed.

'I know nothing of its contents, madam.'

'Nor would I expect you to, but do not let me detain you from your business any further.'

I was convinced that this letter must contain good news and within the hour, thanks to Overbury's continuing assistance, I had learnt that the Lord Protector had decided to commute Thomas's sentence to one of transportation to the Indies. It was not all that I had wished for, but at least his life had been spared and that was sufficient to give me a measure of hope that we would one day be re-united. In the meantime, I would do everything in my power to keep Lucas safe while praying for the hour when England's rightful King would be restored to his throne.

A few days later I was able to show Lucas to his father. It was a bitter-sweet experience, if ever there was one, but some small consolation to us both before our no doubt long separation began.

'I will come back to you, Jane, I swear it,' Thomas assured me and I could only pray that he would.

THE END

About the author

The author is a retired lawyer living near Canterbury, Kent. He's married with two sons and three grandchildren.

Acknowledgements

My sincere thanks to Chris McDonnell for his help in proofreading this book.